MURDER IN DEEP REGRET

ANNE CLEELAND

A DOYLE & ACTON MYSTERY

For Larry Barstow, my faithful beta reader and a past Grand Knight;
and for all others like him.
Colossians 3:23-24

PROLOGUE

The driving rain made it difficult to see clearly, and he wished he'd thought to bring binoculars. Instead, he crouched behind a piling on the adjacent pier, squinting and shielding his eyes with his hands. It appeared that those on board the yacht were making ready to cast off, despite the weather.

Since he wouldn't be able to follow them, there seemed little point in staying. He'd just decided to retreat back into the warmth of his car when his eye was caught by a furtive movement on deck.

Peering intensely into the gloom, he saw a figure—a young woman—dart across the deck, low and stealthy, and then quickly slide off the bow into the water, where she was least likely to be seen by the crewmen. As she disappeared into the waves, he saw that her hands were bound before her.

Lifting an arm over his head against the rain, he leaned around the piling to watch where she emerged, weighing his options. The water was choppy, and he saw her head emerge briefly to take a quick breath, and then go under again. With a wary eye on the crewmen, he left the shelter of the piling and crept closer to the pier's edge so as to better watch the water.

There—her head popped up again for a breath, but she hadn't traveled very far. Too difficult, without the use of her hands, and in such conditions.

With resigned stoicism, he slipped off his shoes and his jacket, and crouched at the pier's end, making a guess at the girl's progress as he dove in. It was possible the guards would not notice she'd escaped for a few more minutes, since they were busy casting off. On the other hand, if they did notice and were armed, he'd be an easy target.

He came up in the waves, treading and watching the area where he thought she'd emerge. Her head appeared at a small distance, and it seemed clear she was losing strength. Quickly, he swam over and felt around in the water for her, seizing her collar and kicking hard to heave her up.

She fought him, of course, and so he said as loudly as he dared near her ear, "Quiet—I will help. Put your arms around my neck."

Gasping, she met his eyes in surprise and then—since she seemed incapable of lifting her arms—he dipped under the water so that she could loop her bound hands around his neck. With the young woman positioned on his back, he spread his arms and swam as quickly as he was able toward the shelter of the pier's support pilings, half-expecting to hear the sound of gunfire as she kicked along with him as best she could.

Their luck held; it seemed the crew was unaware that their passenger had gone missing, and he managed to put another pier between them before he paused, grasping the edge of a dock to catch his breath. "How hard will they search?"

"Hard," she replied.

She'd spoken French, and so he responded in kind. "I would like to get to my car, but that would bring us back toward them. It may be best to continue down the river."

"Yes," she agreed, unable to control her shivering.

"I will free your hands; hold still."

He wriggled his switchblade from his pocket, and then sliced through the heavy tape that was wrapped around her wrists.

"Merci," she whispered.

"De rien," he replied, and then quietly pushed off into the cold water, to navigate his way downriver.

1

―――――

"If you would lift your chin please, Lady Acton."

Dutifully, Detective Sergeant Kathleen Doyle lifted her chin and contemplated the umbrella-like apparatus that diffused the soft gallery light, situated behind the artist's easel. If anyone had told her, back when she was working at the fish-market in Dublin, that someday she would be sitting for a formal portrait she'd have laughed in their face, but life was a crackin' wonderment, and here she was, trying with all her might not to feel as though she'd gone down the rabbit-hole. It was the eighth wonder of the world, truly.

Chief Inspector Acton, Doyle's husband, had managed to cajole Doyle into sitting for the portrait so that it could be hung —along with his—in the august halls of his hereditary estate, which was located a few hours north of London. He held two ancient titles, and—although technically Doyle was only along for the ride—she therefore held two English titles also, even though she'd started life as a working-class Irish girl, sorting the fish and unaware of what fate held in store.

Doyle had met Chief Inspector Acton whilst serving her rookie year as a detective at Scotland Yard, and—almost before she could process what had happened—she found herself married to the man and living in the lap of luxury. In a way, it was a Cinderella story—so long as you overlooked the fact that the handsome prince had something of a dark side, and Cinderella had something of a temper, which was sorely being tested at the moment. There was nothing like devoting your Saturday to portrait-posterity when you'd much rather be noodling around on the rug with the baby and sharing his crackers. The ordeal was soon to be over, though; this was the third of such sessions and then—thank God fastin'–the artist would finish up in-studio.

Javid's brush paused in her graceful hand, and then she turned her head slightly so as to speak to her companion. "Do you see? The reflection in the eye must not be overdone."

"The yellow tone," Munoz agreed. "Yes."

Detective Sergeant Isabel Munoz was an up-and-coming artist in her own right, when she wasn't doing detective work alongside Doyle, and so she'd been allowed to sit in and observe the master at work. The renowned Persian artist was the darling of the upper classes and well-known for her compelling portraiture, so it was a rare opportunity for Munoz to watch and learn.

Doyle didn't think Munoz was one for painting portraits—she tended to paint religious artwork, or landscapes—but she had the sneaking suspicion that Acton had arranged for Munoz's presence so that Doyle would be forced to behave herself—a faint hope, but give the man credit for trying. Doyle was not one to sit still in the first place, and to make it worse, the reserved and elegant artist didn't speak much, but instead studied Doyle with a strange, disconcerting seriousness; as though her subject was an unusual species at the zoo. As a result, Doyle was heartily bored and inclined to seize upon any excuse to interrupt the proceedings.

With careful, delicate strokes the artist plied her brush, and as she did so, remarked, "Only a few minutes more, Lady Acton, I promise."

"I'm sorry, ma'am," Doyle apologized, and forced herself to release a pent-up breath. "The baby will be up from his nap soon." Almost immediately she realized that this wasn't a very good excuse, as they'd a nanny and a butler here at the flat who were at Master Edward's beck and call; next time she should say she needed to pick out a new set of china or something—mental note.

Without turning her head, the artist said to Munoz, "If you have questions, you need only ask, Ms. Munoz."

During these weekend sessions Munoz had been uncharacteristically deferential, which only told Doyle that the artist was indeed a master, and that Munoz was grateful for the opportunity.

The Spanish girl ventured, "I thought it interesting that you'd only sketched-out the shape of the eyes, ma'am, but waited until now, when the face was complete, to fill them in. My instructor believes the eyes come first, so that you don't run into trouble with re-layering the face."

"There are many different techniques," the woman observed, as she continued to make delicate brush-strokes. "You must consider which works best for you." She then paused, and leaned back in her chair, her gaze traveling between Doyle and the portrait, her face expressionless.

There was a soft knock at the door, and then it opened a few inches to reveal Acton. "May I enter?"

"Of course, Lord Acton." The artist raised her thoughtful gaze to Acton, and Doyle had the impression she was studying him also, in anticipation of her next portrait. "We are finished with this session, and I will now complete the project in studio."

"Excellent. May I see?"

With a nod, the artist indicated she had no objection as she picked up a cloth to carefully wipe her brush.

Laying a fond hand on Doyle's shoulder, Acton squeezed past—they'd set up the make-shift studio in the spare utility room—and Munoz promptly rose from her chair to make room for him.

Acton's gaze rested on the portrait for a moment. "Splendid. It is very like."

"An excellent subject," Javid replied graciously. "I can only hope to do justice to her hair." Doyle was blessed with a full head of auburn hair, which oftentimes seemed to have its own inability to sit still.

Doyle watched her husband as he studied the portrait, and was almost surprised by the flare of emotion she caught. Why, he likes it—he likes it very much, she realized. Doyle had an uncanny knack for reading the emotions of the people who surrounded her—fey, the Irish would have called it—and this perceptive ability had served her well in her detective work, but tended to be an annoyance when she was dealing with humankind in any other capacity. For example, in this crowded little room she was uncomfortably aware that Acton was well-pleased, that the artist was well-pleased that Acton was well-pleased, and that Munoz was brimful of secrets, and practically melting from having to suppress them.

Suddenly, a chorus of muffled vibrations from the four silenced mobile phones could be heard. This did not bode well, since an urgent message to all law enforcement personnel usually meant an all-hands-on-deck emergency, and an end to any and all thoughts of a peaceful week-end.

Everyone pulled their phone—including the artist—and there was a profound moment of silence.

"Holy *Mother*," said Doyle aloud.

"Rizzo's dead," Munoz breathed.

Hard on this pronouncement, Reynolds, their butler, appeared in the doorway, his mobile phone in his hand and his attitude one of deep dismay. "Sir—"

But Acton was already on his phone to headquarters. "Acton, here." He listened for a moment, and then said, "Right. I will be straight over."

He then sheathed his phone and said to Doyle, "I must go."

"I will go, also," said Javid, and Doyle was surprised to note that she seemed a bit shaken; faith, the self-contained woman must be a football fan, which just went to show that they tended to show-up where you least expected it. Rizzo was hugely famous; a recent acquisition by the London Kingsmen football team at enormous expense but apparently worth every penny, judging by the way everyone in London seemed to have lost their bearings. Since Doyle herself had little interest in sporting events, she could only watch in wonder as every corner store sold-out on all Rizzo paraphernalia as fast as they could stock it.

"Should I come with?" Doyle asked Acton with an air of hope. She was slated to have a lunch date with another co-worker, Detective Inspector Williams, but she'd like nothing better than to push it off, and a sensational crime would certainly serve as a welcome excuse.

"If you would," was his reply, and he met her eyes for a moment in an unspoken signal. So—he didn't want to brief her in front of the others, which was of interest because—technically—she wasn't allowed to be a subordinate on his investigative team, being as they were married. That Acton would be the Senior Investigating Officer on such a high-profile case was a

given, since he was Scotland Yard's point man for such occasions. Therefore, her husband must have need of her truth-
detecting abilities; as part and parcel of the whole Irish-Doyle-
is-fey package, she usually could sense when someone was or
was not telling the truth.

As an excellent case-in-point, the artist was expressing her
regret to Munoz that they'd not have their usual opportunity to
do a post-session discussion when in fact the artist wasn't sorry
at all, but was instead in a fever to depart this place with all
speed.

"Tell me the *instant* you find out anything," Munoz hissed to
Doyle as they emerged into the main room.

"If I can," Doyle hedged. "Acton doesn't always tell me
things."

As Reynolds passed them their coats, the other girl shook
her head in amazement. "Who'd murder Rizzo?"

"Someone who didn't want to," Doyle replied immediately,
and then was surprised that she'd said the words. She may be
naïve, but she'd worked in homicide long enough to know there
was no such thing as a reluctant murderer.

Any further discussion was curtailed as Javid said her
farewells, and Acton instructed Munoz to liaison with the Public
Relations team to await instructions. Then, Doyle was striding
down the hallway with her husband, hoisting her rucksack and
wishing she'd thought to re-stock her field kit—you never knew
when an assignment would pop up on a week-end, and let this
be a lesson.

Acton called for the lift, and—since he hadn't mentioned it
as yet—she asked, "Where is it we're goin', then?"

"St. Michael's Church." He paused. "The victim appears to
have committed suicide in the sacristy."

Doyle stood with Acton as they contemplated the crime scene before them, which was—truth to tell—not much different than many others they'd contemplated, despite the exalted status of the decedent. The victim lay in the sacristy—a small room located off the church's altar—and it seemed apparent that he'd committed suicide, even though technically, a determinative finding for cause-of-death could only come from the Coroner's office.

Even Doyle recognized Rizzo, being as his face had been plastered on every kiosk in London for several months running. She was somewhat surprised to find that the famous footballer wasn't a larger man, given his stature in the sporting world; instead, he seemed compact and wiry. His skin was olive-toned, which made the lividity marks a bit harder to discern, and he had a luxurious head of very dark hair. He was clad in an expensive track suit, and his neck was adorned with a heavy, gold-linked chain which spilled out onto the floor, a crucifix attached to its end.

St. Michael's Church was undergoing extensive remodeling work, and the victim's body had fallen on the dusty, plastic tarp that had been laid by the workmen to protect the tile floor in this narrow area. The sacristy was in the manner of a glorified storage-room, lined with cupboards where the priest stored his garments and those other items which were necessary for Roman Catholic rituals.

"Such a shame." Officer Shandera was one of the field officers who'd cordoned off the scene, and he regarded the still figure on the floor with true sadness. "A complete tragedy; he may have been the greatest of all time." He paused. "Beat my poor Spurs like a drum, of course, but I can't hold it against him."

Acton, who'd been silently reviewing the scene, said only, "Report, please."

Recalled to his duties, the West Indian man pulled his tablet to check his notes. "The call came in at seven in the morning, sir. A workman came on-site to do plaster-work, and found the victim."

Acton nodded. "Nothing's been moved?"

"No sir. I secured the perimeter, and the workman is sitting in the church with a PC, waiting to make a statement."

"If you would, ask him why he came on-site so early on a Saturday morning."

Oh, thought Doyle; now, there's a good point, and a prime example of why DCI Acton earned his fine salary. The remodeling of St. Michael's Church had been dragging on forever, in part because it was like herding cats to try to get the workers to come in to do their jobs, now that the construction company's owner was presumably dead. D'Angelo, the construction magnate, had been recently lost at sea—whilst sailing his yacht, naturally—and this unfortunate event tended to make the workers a bit wary about getting paid for services performed. That this fellow had come on-site early on a Saturday did seem a bit suspicious, and they taught you at the Crime Academy that you should always take a long look at whoever called-in the crime.

On the other hand, the signs of suicide were evident; the victim had followed the usual form, and the gun that he'd held to his left temple lay on the tarp where it had fallen from his lifeless hand.

"He was left-handed?" she asked, as a matter of form.

Officer Shandera nodded. "He was—rather famously so."

"The Coroner is coming?" asked Acton.

"He is, sir. Dr. Hsu, of course."

This went without saying; such a high-profile death warranted the Coroner himself, and not one of his assistants. Not to mention that Dr. Hsu was well-used to handling a rabid press—although it seemed unlikely he'd be taxed with any particulars, this time. Instead, the press would be striving mightily to figure out why such a man, leading such a life, would have despaired to the point of suicide.

Reminded, Doyle asked, "Didn't Rizzo just sign some amazin' contract?"

"Yes—a record payment, for an athlete," the officer replied. "Maybe it was too much pressure."

Her gaze resting on the still, silent figure, Doyle remarked thoughtfully, "You'd think someone like him would be well-used to pressure."

"Disappointed in love, then?" Shandera suggested. "Love can have a powerful effect on people."

"Can't argue with that." Carefully, Doyle avoided looking at her husband, mainly because she'd witnessed this phenomenon first-hand, in the guise of the complicated man she'd married.

Indeed, the reason Acton had bundled her off to the altar was because—for reasons unknown—he'd become romantically fixated on his red-headed support officer, and this all-consuming devotion tended to reveal itself in some very questionable behavior. A bit nicked, the man was, and his out-sized devotion to his unlikely bride was actually the least alarming of his rather dark inclinations; after their marriage, she'd come to the startling realization that the renowned Chief Inspector Acton was something of a vigilante—often dispatching the villains with ruthless efficiency, if he felt it appropriate, and never missing an opportunity to add to the fortunes of the House of Acton.

Although this realization had shocked her first-year detective soul to the core, Doyle indeed loved her husband, and therefore tried as hard as she knew how to convince him to change his ways–not to mention that murder and mayhem tended to land a body in prison, or worse.

All in all, she was cautiously optimistic; it seemed that Acton was descending less frequently into his black, destructive moods, and that he was—slowly, but surely—coming to trust her. It was no small thing, for someone like him to trust anyone, and as a hopeful sign, it seemed he was no longer going about killing people, willy-nilly. It may be baby steps, but one small victory at a time, as Doyle's mother used to say.

Deep in thought, Acton reviewed the scene before him, and Doyle respected the process and stayed silent as she gazed upon what was left of the man who'd been one of the most famous on the planet. Indeed, for that reason alone Doyle doubted Officer Shandera's lovelorn-suicide theory; presumably, someone like Rizzo had many a fair maiden willing to console him, if he were ever disappointed in love. Therefore, it must be something else–

something else that had driven one of the most admired men in the world to want to depart from it.

Her thoughts were interrupted by Acton, who turned to seek out a pair of forensic gloves from Doyle's rucksack. "Let's have a look, then."

Officer Shandera indicated his tablet. "Shall I record, sir?" The usual protocol was to take a video of the initial examination of the site and the victim, so that any future detectives assigned to the case could draw their own conclusions, based on the raw information.

"Not as yet," Acton replied, as he stepped toward the victim. "Instead, we will await the Coroner."

Why, something's up, Doyle thought in surprise, as she pulled on her own gloves. Acton's wary, for some reason, and he doesn't want to be filmed when he does the initial examination. "Shall I come with?" she asked.

"If you would; I'd like to roll him over."

This seemed a bit unnecessary, and as she carefully stepped behind him toward the decedent, she pointed out, "We don't need to find an ID; faith, even I know who he is."

"Nonetheless," said Acton.

They crouched beside the victim, and at Acton's nod, she helped to carefully roll the body slightly, so as to have a look along the dead man's front.

"Nothin' in his jacket," Doyle observed, pressing the zipper-pockets gently.

With careful fingers, Acton reached into the side-pocket of the victim's track pants, and teased a small mobile phone from within.

"Looks to be a burner," she noted. "Probably standard procedure, for the likes of him." Temporary mobile phones could be purchased pre-paid for a small price, and were often used by those who wished to avoid having law enforcement monitor their movements. In this case, of course, it could be presumed that the world-famous Rizzo was constantly having to change his mobiles to avoid having people trace his whereabouts.

Keeping his hands low, Acton flipped open the phone and scrolled through the record of recent calls.

"Anythin' of interest?" Doyle asked.

"Nothing is marked with a caller ID," he replied, and flipped the mobile closed.

Doyle sighed. "Poor man; forensics will have a field day, findin' out who he has in his list of contacts." She always felt sorry for the decedent, whose life—for the good and for the bad —would now be laid bare for all to see. A necessary evil, but it always seemed so intrusive, to no longer be afforded the dignity of privacy. Of course, in this case the deceased had made his own choices—but still, it seemed so unfair.

Officer Shandera's phone pinged. "The Coroner's arrived, sir," he announced.

"Show him back, if you would, and then please take the workman's statement."

"Yes, sir."

They rose, and carefully stepped away from the decedent so as not to contaminate the scene whilst the Coroner's team came in to set up. Acton greeted Dr. Hsu, and then the two men stood in silence, the solemn little Chinese man taking a long look at the decedent, his face expressionless. "You have noticed?"

"I have," said Acton, and said nothing further.

Noticed what? thought Doyle in surprise.

The Coroner—who owed her husband many a favor—then began to direct his team as one of his assistants began video-taping their actions. He carefully crouched down beside the corpse and began his methodical examination, his movements sure and practiced.

"Should we have Officer Shandera question Father John, too?" Doyle asked. Presumably, the parish priest would be asked to give a statement, although Doyle was almost certain Father John did not know the decedent—mainly because he was a huge football fan, himself, and would not have been able to keep such a thing secret. It was possible, however, that he might have some insight as to why St. Michael's Church had been chosen as a suicide-site; it seemed a strange choice, for someone like Rizzo.

"We will talk to Father John, instead," Acton replied. "Let me instruct the SOCOs, and then I should make a statement to the press."

The Scene of Crime Officers had arrived so as to process the room for forensic evidence, and as they donned their bunny-suits with solemn faces, Doyle could sense their suppressed excitement—it would be worth a pint or two at the pub, to be the ones who'd processed the Rizzo scene, and able to relate any details they could glean.

"Looks to be a suicide," Acton told them. "Please make every effort, however; no doubt there is an insurance interest at stake."

This only made sense; someone like Rizzo probably had a mighty insurance policy covering his health and well-being, and such policies tended to exclude suicide as a triggering event, because otherwise—as an added bonus to doing oneself in— one could leave a fortune to one's heirs at the expense of the insurers.

"Who's goin' to be the Case Management Officer?" Doyle asked.

"DI Williams," her husband replied. "We'll need a careful hand."

She nodded, and then waited quietly as he spoke on the

phone with the Assistant Chief Superintendent, deciding what should be disclosed in the initial press statement.

Something's up, she thought yet again, as she watched the forensics team begin their painstaking work. Acton's wary, for some reason, and he's assigning only his most loyal foot-soldiers to this case—including herself, it seemed. And then there was the interesting fact that he'd signaled to the Coroner that the man should keep whatever-it-was he'd noticed under his hat.

It was a bit alarming—to know that Acton was uneasy about something that he was unwilling to disclose, even to her. The others may not see anything unusual in his behavior, but the others didn't know him as well as his wedded wife, who'd duly noticed that he'd slipped the burner phone into his own pocket, where—presumably—it still rested.

3

A fter Acton delivered a short statement to the press, they stood in the back of the nave to interview Father John, who watched with a troubled expression as the CID personnel filed in and out of the normally quiet church, their voices echoing off the arches overhead.

Doyle had known Father John since the days when she'd first moved to London, and–after she married Acton–they continued to support the church even though technically, they no longer lived in the parish. Indeed, the current renovations were underway thanks to a generous donation from the House of Acton; Doyle wasn't the only one who'd experienced a sudden change of fortune when she'd married in haste.

"You are certain you have not seen him here, before?"

The priest nodded. "Quite certain, Michael. And I'd have known; I've followed his career since his Serie-A days." Father John shook his head sadly. "Poor man. I'll offer up a novena, of course. If only I'd been here—sometimes a despairin' soul needs only a listenin' ear, to change his mind."

"Indeed," said Acton, who was not one to wax regretful. "We will need to see the security feed, please."

"Of course." The priest added, "And the construction people have their own cameras, too. They're very fussy about their equipment, and such."

"Have they taken up work again?" Doyle asked with some trepidation. This was a sore point, with Father John often saying that he'd have never agreed to the renovation project in the first place if he'd known it would take so long.

"Two weeks," the priest retorted with an air of annoyance. "Which is what they told me two weeks ago."

Gently, Doyle pointed out, "It can't be easy for the company, having the CEO go overboard. Mayhap he needs his own novena, Father."

The priest acknowledged this sad fact with a hearty sigh. "Aye, lass—you've the right of it, and I mustn't be impatient. It's a rare hardship for the Church, too; D'Angelo—the owner—was a massive donor, especially to the worldwide charitable relief fund. Which only made sense, I suppose; he did business all over the world, and cultivatin' a good reputation helps to open doors."

Doyle made a wry mouth. "Faith, that's a bit cynical, for the likes of you, Father."

But the priest shook his head, unrepentant. "Just practical, lass; it's the way of the world. Many a church donor may have the motives of a Pharisee, but the money is surely welcomed, just the same."

At this point, Acton glanced up because Detective Inspector Williams had entered the nave's front doors, the murmuring crowd noise briefly audible before the double doors shut closed again. "I must go, Father. I will have an officer accompany you to secure the CCTV feed, and I'm afraid there will be CID personnel here for the rest of the day. Starting tomorrow, I will assign a PC, to help keep the curious out."

"Thank you," the priest replied with weary resignation. "I imagine we're in for a time of it—although it's not much of a hardship, compared to what the poor man's family is sufferin'."

"And his football team," Doyle added. "The Kingsmen will be sufferin', too, after havin' such high hopes."

But Father John only glanced at her from beneath his bushy grey brows. "No comparison lass—'tis the difference 'twixt love and money. Those that love are grievin' for the person, but those who were expectin' a benefit are mainly grievin' for the money."

"Well-said," said Acton.

"It is a mournful blow to the fans, though," the priest acknowledged, as he turned away. "I was so hopin' to see him play."

Inspector Williams stepped up to join them, his expression sober as befitted the occasion. The young detective was a favorite of the powers-that-be, and could look forward to a bright future at Scotland Yard mainly because—aside from being a very clever and dedicated fellow—he often worked off-the-grid with Doyle's wedded husband to mete out a rough brand of vigilante justice. As Williams was a good friend, this left Doyle with the daunting task of trying to hang onto both men's coat-tails so as to prevent a wholesale sidestepping of the justice system—the same justice system that they were supposedly sworn to uphold.

And it didn't help that—due to her reining-in role—both men tended to leave her out of the loop, whenever it came to planning out their questionable doings. It was to be fervently hoped that she'd not been pitchforked into yet another such situation, but—as the pocketed burner phone gave witness—this seemed a faint hope.

Williams nodded. "Good morning, sir; here's a shock."

"Yes. What do the news reports say?"

"They're confirming he's dead, and hinting at suicide— although you can tell that they have to steel themselves to even report it."

Acton nodded thoughtfully. "I will take you back; there are a few points I'd like to discuss."

They turned to head toward the sacristy, and Doyle heard Williams ask in a low tone, "Do you think it could be connected to the gambling scandal, sir?"

Acton tilted his head in acknowledgement. "Perhaps, although he seems an unlikely candidate to be overcome with remorse, or to feel threatened to the point of taking his own life."

Doyle decided she may as well ask. "Rizzo was involved in a gamblin' scandal?"

Acton replied, "Last year. It was kept rather quiet."

She made a derisive sound. "Fancy that; a star player had a gamblin' scandal and they kept it quiet. Knock me over with a feather."

But Williams only shrugged, philosophical. "He's worth a lot of money to a lot of people."

"That shouldn't give him free rein to break the law," Doyle retorted. "Justice shouldn't be pickin' favorites."

Practically, he pointed out, "You can't just slap a pair of cuffs on Rizzo, Kath."

"Mayhap if I had, he'd be alive today," she countered.

"A very good point," said Acton, in a tone that indicted the discussion was at an end.

Officer Shandera lifted the tape to allow them access, and Doyle stood with the two men as they looked over the still figure, lying on the plastic tarp whilst the forensics personnel did their silent work. Musing aloud, she said, "You know, mayhap Shandera was right; mayhap the walls were closin' in, and he felt that he couldn't bear what was comin'.'."

Williams glanced at her and pointed out, "If there were walls closing in on him, Kath, we'd be the ones closing them. But there was no case pending against him."

"Oh—oh, of course; never mind, then." But her scalp was prickling, which was what it did when her intuition was trying to get her to pay attention to something important. What walls were closing in on Rizzo, then, if it wasn't the Met that was after him?

Williams continued, "And anyway, it's not like Rizzo would be worried about it in the first place. He'd just defy anyone to arrest him, and they probably wouldn't dare."

Doyle made a wry mouth. "I suppose that's a good point. It would be easier to arrest the Prince of Wales, and there wouldn't be half the outcry."

Acton had been watching the SOCOs, and he now said to Williams, "I am informed there is secondary security footage, courtesy of the construction company. I would like to take it into custody as quickly as possible, with nothing being said beforehand."

Doyle blinked at the implication behind this directive and—although Williams nodded without comment–she ventured, "And why is that? Do we think it will show somethin' different from the church's footage?"

"I would not be surprised," said Acton.

Trying to hide her astonishment, Doyle's gaze rested on the tableau laid out before them. "So, you don't think this is a suicide."

"No," said Acton. "I do not."

4

As could be expected, this disclosure was met with a moment's silence, and then Acton continued, "With any luck, the killer didn't realize there was a second feed."

Williams ventured, "You think it's a misdirection murder, then? That it's only been staged as a suicide to throw us off?"

"Perhaps," said Acton. "Let's have a look at the victim's electronics, and if you would, have a look into his religious background—whether he's completed the sacraments, and whether he makes any monetary contribution to the church."

The penny dropped, and Doyle realized, "Because someone who's totin' a solid gold crucifix 'round his neck is unlikely to be killin' himself in a church."

"The crucifix may just be for show," Williams pointed out.

"Indeed," Acton agreed. "Let's not mention this particular working-theory until we know a bit more. He was not married?"

"No," Williams replied. "He was rather famously not married. A lot of liaisons, of course."

"It doesn't seem like a scorned-woman's crime," Doyle ventured.

Acton nodded. "No—I would agree, but we should make inquiries, nonetheless." He glanced up a Williams. "Please secure the construction company security feed as a priority."

"Right, sir," said Williams, and he stepped away to confer quietly with Officer Shandera.

Since they were alone for a few minutes, Doyle decided it was past time to rake her wayward husband over the coals. "You know, Michael, you probably shouldn't be pocketin' evidence from a crime scene. Especially evidence that hasn't been bagged-and-tagged."

Her husband did not attempt to disclaim, but only replied, "There is something here that I don't like."

With an exasperated breath, she blew a tendril of hair from her forehead. "That's not supposed to enter into it, my friend. We have to follow the evidence, wherever it may lead."

He was silent, and so she prodded, "Can't you tell me? I'm feelin' mighty uneasy, just now, and I'd rather not have to turn state's evidence against you."

But true to form, Acton did not directly reply to her question, instead asking his own. "Assuming this is a misdirection murder, why did the killer choose St. Michael's as the supposed suicide site? It is not local to the victim—neither to his residence, nor to the football facility."

This was true, as the small church was located in a working-class part of town not often visited by well-heeled worshipers. Although it was not truly a small church, anymore; the current construction was going to expand the facilities substantially.

Thinking it over, Doyle knit her brow. "I suppose if you were the murderer, and wanted to leave the impression that the victim was so despairin' that he did himself in, choosin' a church as the suicide-site would help promote that fiction. And its St. Michael's because RC churches are thin on the ground around here, especially after Holy Trinity Church went under."

But Acton only tilted his head, in the manner of a professor whose student has given the incorrect answer as he waited to hear the correct one.

Doyle took another guess. "This church is under construction–mayhap the killer thought there wouldn't be any security cameras because of it, and also that any tell-tale forensics would be well-hidden under layers of dust."

But Acton had apparently decided that he'd give his favorite student the answer, since she was having trouble getting there on her own. "It is common knowledge that we are closely associated with this church."

Doyle stared at him in surprise. "Well–yes, I suppose that's true." Indeed, as a matter of fact it was no secret that they were financing the expansion which was currently underway. "I'm not sure what you're gettin' at, husband; d'you think the killer is pokin' you in the eye, by stagin' this murder at your church?"

"I am not certain," he replied. "It may be the opposite, in fact. The killer may assume that I will investigate, and is hoping that I will investigate very thoroughly, because I have a personal interest."

Doyle blinked, but before she could follow-up on this extraordinary theory, the Coroner stepped over to confer with Acton, as his team began loading the decedent into a body-bag.

"Time-of-death is three to four a.m."

"Thank you. I will be in touch."

As he moved aside, Doyle decided she may as well ask, "What is it that you noticed, you and the Coroner?"

Her husband replied, "There is a break in the blood splatter pattern. Someone was standing beside him when the shot was fired."

"Oh-*ho*," she breathed. "Now, there's a clue, left out in the wide-open, and I suppose that's another reason you're thinkin' this is not a misdirection murder as much as it might be a revelation murder."

Revelation murders were those motivated by the killer's desire to bring the victims' sins to light, and—in a twist from the usual—revelation murders were often perpetrated by women. A spurned lover—many times the spurned lover of a politician, or other famous man—decided to expose her former paramour to law enforcement's tender mercies by killing him, or by killing her rival. It was yet another illustration of what Father John had just noted; there was nothing more powerful than love when it came to vengeance, or grief, or—or anything, truly.

She paused, because her scalp was prickling again. "You know, Michael, there's a—a *desperation*, here. Someone's desperate."

He glanced at her thoughtfully. "The killer is desperate?" Her husband had a great respect for her intuition—as well he should, since they'd unraveled many a thorny crime based on her instinctive reactions to the facts on the ground. It was also the major reason that they were a formidable team when it came to solving homicides–she was all feelings and impressions whilst he was all logic and hard facts; neither would have been as successful without the other, something that was well-appreciated by both.

She frowned slightly. "I know that doesn't make much sense, if someone's hopin' to inveigle you into takin' a long look."

Acton glanced overhead at the swathed scaffolding, which displayed signs proudly proclaiming the project to be one by D'Angelo Construction. "D'Angelo was involved in questionable activities, and one might say the walls were closing in on him. Conveniently, he was swept overboard, and no corpse has yet been recovered."

"It might be D'Angelo, who's the killer," she agreed. "I suppose he'd be someone who's desperate, if you think he staged his own death. What sort of shady doin's was he involved in?"

"Money-laundering. D'Angelo was an investor in the Kingsmen football team, and money-laundering is prevalent in professional sports because cash can be hand-carried internationally, bypassing reporting requirements." He paused. "Often the players' enormous salaries are a cover for such."

Doyle stared at him in surprise. "You're tellin' me that Rizzo was a *bagman*?"

"Such an arrangement would not be unusual."

She turned to watch the gurney as it wheeled the victim's remains away from the sacristy. "I suppose that would explain why someone like Savoie was an investor in the team."

"Indeed."

Philippe Savoie was a notorious underworld kingpin, currently laying low in his native France. Shrewd and ruthless, he tended to have a finger in many an international-crimes pie, and as a result he was featured on the Watch List, the Interpol Alert List, and every other law enforcement list you would care to name.

It created a bit of a dilemma, because Savoie had once saved the fair Doyle's life, and so she felt beholden to him. Indeed, the two had formed a friendship, of sorts, and at first Doyle had fretted herself to a frazzle, hoping that Acton would never find out—small chance of that, of course—and so it was rather a relief that her husband's reaction to this surprising turn of events was rather benign. In fact, Doyle entertained the uneasy suspicion that Acton had decided to enlist Savoie into some of his own questionable dealings, which seemed a diabolical alliance, and not one the illustrious Chief Inspector should be pursuing. Acton didn't seem to be worried, though; in a strange way, he was very like Rizzo in that he did whatever he wished, and counted on the fact that no one would dare touch him.

Doyle decided she may as well ask the obvious. "D'you think Savoie's the killer?"

"No," he replied immediately, and it was true.

Very much relieved that she wouldn't have to juggle her divided loyalties, Doyle mused, "Then mayhap the killer is another investor, who was in on the shady dealin's? Rizzo had to be eliminated because he was goin' to grass them out, and bring it all down around their heads?"

"A possibility," Acton agreed.

Doyle frowned slightly. "I suppose if the choice is either to kill Rizzo or go to prison, you'd steel yourself."

"Perhaps," Acton said, but he didn't sound convinced.

Doyle decided to test-out this working-theory by stating it aloud. "Rizzo wasn't one to be worried about another illegal-money scandal because he could ride it out, but someone else was worried about goin' to prison, and so he decided to nip the problem in the bud."

They were both silent for a moment, and then Doyle shook her head. "Neither one of us is buyin' that theory."

"No," Acton agreed. "The fact that Rizzo is now dead is even more likely to bring unwanted exposure. There will be a firestorm of speculation, and every stone will be overturned."

This seemed obvious, and Doyle shook her head. "Could the killer be someone like Rizzo, who truly thinks he's untouchable?"

Acton met her eyes. "Yet, you believe he is desperate."

"I do," she conceded. "He bitterly regrets this, Michael."

"Then it may be someone with a motive that is not at all obvious." Acton pulled his mobile. "I will set-up a meeting with the financial crimes unit, to review pending cases that may implicate Kingsmen investors. We will touch base with our informants, also, to see if anyone's caught wind of something."

She glanced up at him. "Are we declarin' it a murder case?"

"Not as yet. If the killer is indeed attempting to manipulate my investigation, his frustration may lead to a mistake on his part. Let's play it quietly, and watch for any unusual reactions."

Nodding, she thought—he doesn't like this, and small blame to him, if he thinks the killer is angling for his attention. However, her husband wasn't one to be angled, and in fact, was a past master of doing some angling, himself. As an excellent case-in-point, he'd managed to avoid telling her why he'd pocketed the burner phone.

The man's an expert at distracting me, she thought in annoyance; he tosses a stick, and I'm like a dog, madly chasing it in the wrong direction.

5

—————

A cton began speaking on the phone to Nazy, his assistant, and as he walked away, Williams returned to stand beside Doyle, watching as the SOCOs continued processing the scene.

She glanced at him. "Did you secure the CCTV feed?"

"Yes. I secured the company's cameras here, and Officer Shandera's going over to D'Angelo's offices unannounced, to take custody of the monitoring software. Hopefully, there will be something on the tape, although whoever staged the cameras didn't do a very good job. They put two in the church basement, where nothing much is going on, and only one in that big room with all the pews."

Doyle smiled at this characterization. "The nave, it's called."

"Whatever. They must have stored equipment in the basement at one time, but there's nothing there, now—just the cameras." He glanced over at Acton, who had scrolled for a number on his mobile and now seemed to be listening more than speaking. "I imagine he wants us to take a look at the feed as soon as we can."

"So much for our lunch plans with Martina," Doyle said, with a show of sad regret. "This wretched Rizzo fellow has a lot to answer for."

Williams smiled slightly. "We'll reschedule, so long as that's all right with you."

"Of course, it is," she assured him, with as much enthusiasm as she could muster.

Handsome and eligible, Williams nevertheless tended to fixate on the wrong women, and Doyle had the strong sense that he was—unfortunately—enmeshed in yet another such relationship. He'd been smitten hard by a witness in a recent case— one who'd originally been charged with jewelry theft, before all charges were subsequently dropped. But even if she wasn't necessarily a cat-burglar, Martina Betancourt was trouble, if Doyle was any judge, and looked to be yet another heartbreak headed Williams' way.

Mentally girding her loins, she reminded herself that she should be supportive, and try to manage a better attitude. Williams was her dearest friend, and he'd helped her out of many a tight corner; she owed him a thousand times over and since this get-together was important to him, it should be important to her, too.

In truth, though, Doyle was not looking forward to the proposed outing; not only did she have the strong sense that Williams was headed for another disappointment in love, she didn't enjoy social occasions in general, where people were constantly shading the truth. It was exhausting, for someone like her.

Williams' phone pinged, and he glanced at it. "Munoz wants to know if we have anything yet."

Doyle made a sound of impatience. "She was gettin' paintin' lessons at my flat this mornin' when we heard the news. Acton's assigned her to liaison with PR."

"I might pull her in on the financial team," Williams replied, as he texted a quick response. "She's good with numbers, and there will be a lot to look though, if we're going to take a hard look at the Kingsmen's finances."

"Good luck to you, tryin' to get her to concentrate on anythin' other than the worthy Inspector Geary," Doyle hinted, with a great deal of meaning.

He smiled slightly. "What's the status now? Has she officially broken it off with Gabriel?" One of their comrades at the CID, Officer Gabriel, had served a stint as Munoz's beau before she'd cast her gaze upon Inspector Geary.

Doyle decided to disclose, "It's worse than that, Thomas; I think our Munoz has up and married Geary."

He turned to her with all the surprise that this disclosure deserved. "*Really*? Where are they?"

"Oh, they haven't gone anywhere, but I do think they've done the deed."

"Just like that?" he asked, incredulous. "I never would have thought Munoz was someone who'd pull that trigger."

"Just like that, Thomas. And mayhap a comparison to a gunfight is not the best one to use."

He smiled. "That remains to be seen—after all, Gabriel's coming back to work next week." This said with some significance, because Officer Gabriel had been unaware that his erstwhile girlfriend was on the cusp of marrying another officer.

With a small sigh, Doyle observed, "I do feel sorry for Gabriel, and I suppose it's a good thing—that he's comin' back to work. He'll need somethin' to take his mind off his troubles; my mother used to say that work is the best cure for sorrow."

"He'll find someone." This, said with the confidence of a man who believed he'd found his own someone.

She cautioned, "Munoz hasn't said anythin', so best keep it quiet. She's got mighty particular relatives, so I imagine there'll be a dust-up about it."

Skeptical, he tilted his head. "I don't think Munoz is someone who's going to be cowed by relatives."

But Doyle insisted, "It's a delicate dance, Thomas; you don't want to alienate everyone, straight out of the gate. Not to mention that all parties involved are as RC as the Pope's hat, so it will be interestin' to find out how they managed it—the Church tends to look askance at hole-in-corner weddin's."

"Like yours," he teased.

She made a wry mouth. "Touché, Thomas. But the exception proves the rule; in the usual situation—that is, where a peer of the realm isn't pullin' the strings—the Church wants the community to be present at the weddin', since the sacrament is supposed to be bigger than just the two people."

With a sudden flare of irritation, her companion retorted, "It's all such nonsense—vows and altars and priests. It's so ridiculously antiquated."

She glanced at him in surprise. "Faith; that's a bit harsh, even for a heretic like you. Look no further than poor Rizzo—it would have been miles better for him if he'd a wife and family to claim his loyalty, and keep him out o' trouble."

But with a set jaw, Williams stood his ground. "It's a two-edged sword, Kath, and you can't pretend that marriage is the cure-all. Minds change, and we've seen our share of miserable people, willing to do anything to get out of it."

Doyle recognized a sore subject when she saw one, and so only offered in a mild tone, "You've the right of that, of course. No argument here."

Her companion paused to put his hands on his hips. "Sorry. No offense meant."

She touched his arm. "None taken, my friend. I know you get the willies when you're in a church, and can't be held responsible for any blasphemy you may happen to spout."

But he wouldn't be teased, and instead lifted his chin so as to contemplate the ceiling. "It's Martina. I get the sense that she is very religious-minded."

Thoroughly amused, Doyle lifted her brows. "Oh-*ho*; now, how's that for irony? Best brush up on your Bible, and I must say that it will be all sorts of gratifyin' to see you raisin' up your hands and witnessin' along with all the evangelicals at the prison ministry."

With some surprise, he glanced at her. "Martina's RC, Kath."

"Oh—oh, is she? I didn't know. It's not as though we have a secret signal, or somethin'."

Tentatively, he suggested, "Do you think we can reschedule for brunch tomorrow? Depending on how this case unfolds, of course, but it sounds like Acton wants to keep the murder-aspect of the investigation quiet, for now."

"Love to," Doyle said brightly. "Truly lookin' forward to it."

"Thanks. She seems quite keen to get to know you; I think she's a fan."

This, because Doyle was semi-famous, having once defied death by jumping off a bridge into the Thames to save Munoz, her fellow detective. The last thing Doyle wanted, of course, was to be semi-famous, but between jumping from the bridge and marrying the reclusive Chief Inspector Acton, her goose was well and thoroughly cooked in that department and let this be a lesson that God had a mighty strange sense of humor.

"Brunch it is, then. Shall I speak of your many virtues to her?"

He smiled. "If you would."

And—since he'd repented of his sharp words—she ventured, "How's your health, by-the-by? Can I ask without your snappin' my head off?"

He studied the floor. "Much better. The problem seems to have resolved itself."

This was a relief in more ways than one; Williams was a diabetic and had recently suffered from an insulin-adjustment problem under best-be-forgotten circumstances. He hated to talk about his health, and Doyle always had the uneasy suspicion that he didn't take care of himself as he should, instead choosing to ignore such an embarrassing weakness.

His call completed, Acton returned to them. "We will reconvene with a team at headquarters."

"Yes, sir," said Williams.

"Me, too?" asked Doyle, rather hopefully.

"If you would," Acton said. "We'll need every hand."

She interpreted this to mean that he was willing to skirt the protocols in order to have her present, and she could only agree with his strategy; if someone was trying to manipulate Acton's investigation, then best ferret-out whoever-it-was as soon as possible—no doubt the manipulator held the key to the case.

6

After giving a brief run-down to the press, Acton was now driving Doyle back to headquarters, and she'd decided she'd allowed him to distract her long enough. "What are you goin' to do about the burner phone?" She paused for a moment, and then added, "Sir."

"What burner phone?" he asked in a mild tone.

"Not jokin', husband."

He reached for her hand and replied in a thoughtful manner, "I am trying to decide the best way forward."

She eyed him. "Because—whilst you think this may be a revelation murder, and someone is tryin' to lead you down a path—you're not sure it's on the up-and-up. You think the revelation murder may actually be a misdirection play, in and of itself."

He raised his brows. "Exactly. That is impressive, Kathleen."

She quirked her mouth, as she turned to watch through the windscreen. "I know you like the back o' my hand, my friend, which is both a blessin' and a curse. What's on the burner phone that makes you so uneasy?"

"One of the top numbers is connected to Philippe Savoie."

She decided not to ask why he'd recognize a phone number connected to Savoie, and instead resolved to stay on-topic. "So; you think it may be a frame-up? Someone's tryin' to frame Savoie for Rizzo's murder? Or mayhap this revelation murder *is* on the up-and-up, and Savoie was knee-deep in the money-launderin' rig and is about to suffer for his sins. It truly wouldn't be much of a surprise, Michael, and it would explain why someone like Savoie got himself involved with the Kingsmen in the first place."

"Unfortunately, there are more than a few unsavory characters who have become involved in the Kingsmen football club."

His tone was mild as he continued thoughtful, which was how he always seemed when he was in the process of deciding how to start arranging matters more to his liking. She pronounced in a firm tone, "If it's not some sort of unholy frame-up, and Savoie is truly goin' about murderin' famous athletes, then we've got to put him away, Michael. Let the chips fall where they may."

But Acton gave her one of his patented non-responses. "Recall that the murder site is a church we are known to frequent, and then consider that the potential suspect—whose phone number comes up immediately–is someone known to be an acquaintance of ours."

She frowned, thinking this over. "Yes, it does seem a bit—a bit heavy-handed, I suppose. But whether it's heavy-handed or not, it could still be a revelation murder, Michael. The killer may want to expose Savoie's dark doin's to you, and if that's the case you have to play it straight."

"If Savoie goes to prison, we'd get Emile," he reminded her, half-joking.

This was unfortunately true; Savoie had a young son, and in a moment of weakness Doyle had agreed to stand-in as the boy's guardian in the event anything happened to Savoie. Indeed, Emile had already lived with them for a few months under best-be-forgotten circumstances whilst Savoie was doing a short stint in Wexton Prison.

"We'll manage," she said firmly. "We're expandin' the flat, after all—we'll just stow him downstairs."

As he made no comment, she emphasized, "I mean it, Michael; if Savoie's behind this, don't let him get away with it on account of me." This, because past events had shown that Acton went all aristocratic when it came to what he considered "debts of honor," and for Acton there could be no debt more honorable than Savoie's having saved the fair Doyle's life.

Again, he made no immediate response—he knew she'd catch him in a lie—and so she decided she may as well say it. "I'm worried that you're plannin' on manipulatin' the evidence, husband, and you mustn't; especially in a high-profile case like this one, where all eyes will be upon you."

But his answer surprised her. "I have the opposite reaction, actually. I believe it is important to immediately counter the killer's attempts to manipulate the evidence."

"Oh." She knit her brow, thinking this over. "We don't know *why* he's doin' it, though."

"No," he agreed. "But if we can frustrate him, we may discover more."

Shrewdly, she observed, "And you're not one who likes bein' manipulated."

"I cannot disagree. Therefore, I would like to first discover why the killer has gone to the trouble."

Doyle suddenly realized she may be overlooking the obvious. "D'you think someone knows about your dealin's with Savoie, Michael, and they're tryin' to expose you, in some way?"

"Perhaps," he conceded. "Although this seems an indirect route to take, if that is indeed the killer's aim."

She was forced to agree. "Aye; if he's only tryin' to twist your tail, no point in killin' poor Rizzo."

Somewhat relieved by this realization, she turned to gaze out the windscreen again. "All in all, this killer doesn't seem very clever. He left the suspicious blood spatter pattern, and he didn't realize there was a second security feed at the church—although I'm not sure how much good it will do us. Williams says the construction company cameras didn't seem to be placed very well."

She could feel Acton's sudden surge of interest, as he glanced her way. "Tell me."

Surprised, she tried to remember. "Williams said there were two cameras in the empty basement, but only one in the nave, where most of the construction was."

"Hold a moment."

Acton pressed his mobile call-up, and Williams' voice could be heard on the speaker. "Sir?"

"See to it that the church basement is secured, with no one in or out. Try to keep it quiet."

"Yes, sir."

Both men rang off, and Doyle waited a beat before asking, "I give up, husband; what's in the basement?"

"It is empty, now," Acton replied. "But D'Angelo Construction would not have placed operational cameras in the basement by mistake."

"Never say the church basement was bein' used for illegal

doin's," Doyle lamented. "Poor Father John; *none* o' this is goin' to impress the new bishop."

With a raised brow, he suggested, "We may have to manipulate the evidence."

"Not funny," she retorted.

7
_____

A cton's team had scrambled to meet in a conference room at headquarters, and Doyle took her place at the lesser-important end of the table whilst Acton spoke to the Assistant DCS, a competent Indian woman who listened solemnly as he gave his report.

The others on the team filed in, everyone outwardly serious as they suppressed varying degrees of excitement, depending upon how much money they'd sunk into Kingsmen tickets. It was a high-profile case, and so the room was crowded with bright-eyed personnel hoping for an interesting assignment; this kind of case was a resumé-enhancer, no matter how tangential the person's role.

Not to mention it was as scandalous as all-get-out, Doyle added fairly. This investigation was shaping up to be an epic cautionary tale, given the victim's fortune, his love-life, and his previous brushes with the law. It's that "hubris" thing again, she realized, and then paused to decide if she'd the right word. Yes, that was it; _hubris_—when you think you are untouchable, and then fate decides to serve you a turn so as to remind you what's-what. Rizzo was a pattern-card for hubris. So was Acton, for that matter—both thinking they were untouchable, and not for an instant considering the possibility that it could all come crashing down around their heads.

Her scalp began to prickle, but before she could determine why this was, Nazy—Acton's young assistant—approached him to politely interrupt his discussion. "Pardon me, sir, but I have Sir Vikili on the phone, and he would like to speak with you. I am afraid he insists."

This was not entirely unexpected; Sir Vikili was the high-level criminal defense solicitor who shrewdly represented any and all defendants who were wealthy enough to afford him–Rizzo himself serving as an excellent example of such. The solicitor was no doubt concerned on behalf of the other high-level blacklegs he tended to represent, depending on what unsavory information might be unearthed in connection with Rizzo's death.

"Please tell Sir Vikili he no longer has a client," Acton replied, "and then wish him a good day."

Dutifully, Nazy turned to relay this message, but Doyle knew her emotions were mixed, because the young Persian girl harbored a mighty crush on the handsome and wealthy solicitor, and was loathe to deliver such a resounding snub.

It was just as well, though; Doyle hadn't had the heart to tell Nazy that Williams was of the opinion that Sir Vikili didn't pay much attention to females because such was not his preference. Not to mention that it was not as though someone like Sir Vikili would be interested in someone like Nazy in the first place–may as well let the girl have her air-dreams. And Nazy's glass was half-full, anyways, because she also harbored a massive crush on the worthy DI Williams, who was here in the flesh, and less likely to be involved in shady underworld doings.

The meeting commenced, and apparently Acton had made his decision about how to play this particular homicide, because straight-out-of-the-gate he announced, "There are several troubling evidentiary aspects which may indicate the victim was murdered."

As could be expected, there was a rustling of surprise in the room, and after a pause, Acton continued, "Therefore, I would like to focus on two potential groups of suspects; Kingsmen backers who may be involved in illegal gambling or money-laundering, and those persons who were involved in his personal life."

"Which would include half the women in Europe," a female DS joked.

Acton smiled slightly in acknowledgment. "Nevertheless."

"Time-of-death?" asked Williams.

"Between three and four in the morning. It appears the victim came of his own accord, and it is not clear why he'd come to this particular church at such an hour."

"Not a body-dump, then?" asked the female DS, who'd apparently decided she'd best scale back on the joking, being as Acton wasn't the joking-about sort.

"No—the evidence suggests the homicide occurred at the church, and we will move forward on that assumption unless otherwise indicated. DI Williams is the CMO, and DS Syed will act as Evidence Officer."

"Yes sir," Williams said. "DS Munoz is our point-contact with the PR office?"

"All PR releases must be first run through me," Acton replied, "as we'd like to keep our working-theory quiet for as long as possible." He paused. "I imagine I needn't warn you to refrain from discussing this case with anyone outside the team."

Everyone nodded, and then Williams asked, "For purposes of personnel allocation, sir, which of the two groups of suspects has priority?"

"Both groups are of equal priority."

Williams nodded, and then began dividing-up assignments as Acton resumed his discussion with the Assistant DCS, no doubt deciding on when to coordinate the next press conference —the public liked to be kept informed, even if the update was only to the effect that nothing further had been learned.

Williams tasked one team with reviewing pertinent CCTV tapes on the adjacent streets, and another one was asked to track down known acquaintances, sweethearts and family—although it wasn't clear if any of Rizzo's relatives were currently residing in London.

When he came to Doyle, he said, "Would you accompany me to the Kingsmen offices as a support officer, DS Doyle? We have arranged to meet with the team's Chairman, as well as the Manager and his staff in an hour."

"Yes, sir." This was of interest; Acton must want her to listen-in to the initial questioning and see what there was to see. There was no doubt in her mind that Acton would be doing the questioning, but he was sending her under Williams' auspices so as to avoid any appearance of the officers-who-are-married impropriety. Not that it mattered; unlikely that the Assistant DCS was going to tell the bridge-jumper she had to stand down because her even-more-famous husband was handling the case.

With a nod, Williams indicated Doyle was to accompany him to the unmarked-vehicle parking garage, and as they exited down the hallway he remarked, "It's interesting that Acton is so keen to pursue the personal aspect. It doesn't seem like a crime of passion to me—much more likely it's a misdirection murder."

Doyle didn't want to tell Williams that Acton was pursuing the personal angle due to her own impressions at the scene—that the killer was desperate, and regretful—and so instead, she offered, "Well, there's the amateur nature of the murder to think about; the killer doesn't seem very professional, what with not knowin' about the extra cameras, and leavin' a clue in the blood spatter. Mayhap it *was* personal."

But Williams continued skeptical. "An ex-lover wouldn't kill him, I don't think. It wouldn't be in her self-interest."

She glanced at him. "It wouldn't?"

"A man like Rizzo pays women to go away, if his interest lands elsewhere. With the money he's got, he probably had an entire team dedicated to it. A woman would be a fool to kill the golden goose."

But Doyle frowned as they waited for the lift. "I don't know, Thomas; if there's ever a choice 'twixt love and money, for most people love outweighs everythin' else by a mile. Love is a motivator like no other." As she was married to Exhibit A in this regard, she knew of which she spoke.

As they entered into the lift, he conceded, "Well, I suppose that's a fair point, but this doesn't look like a jealous woman's crime, Kath—it's too well-staged. She'd have to plot to murder Rizzo and make it look like a suicide; with someone this famous, that's a plan that would take a strong set of nerves."

"It would," Doyle agreed. "But that's what's happened, after all."

As they made their way toward the parking structure, she decided she may as well tell him, "Acton seems to think the killer staged the scene so as to leave bread crumbs for us. He thinks it may be a frame-up, or the killer is leavin' a message, for some reason."

Williams lifted his gaze to the fluorescent lights hanging from the garage's cement ceiling and tested this theory out loud. "The killer's afraid there'd be repercussions if he grassed to the police, and so he set up this 'suicide' so that a spotlight could be shone on the whole situation without its implicating him personally."

"A revelation murder," Doyle agreed. "I think that's what Acton's thinkin'."

But after considering this, her companion could only shake his head. "That's a far-fetched working-theory, Kath, mainly because there's plenty you could do short of killing Rizzo. An anonymous tip, for example."

"Yes. It doesn't make much sense, does it? He regretted killin' the man, but he felt he'd no choice."

Opening the car door for her, he cocked a skeptical brow. "We have a regretful killer?"

She sighed. "I think we do. I don't know why, but there it is."

"Then maybe it's a personal crime, after all." Williams mused, as he turned into the mid-day traffic, and headed toward the Kingsmen facility. Williams was familiar with Doyle's perceptive abilities, having had his own experiences with them.

"Nothin' adds up," she declared. "A rare tangle-patch, it is."

"I hope the investigation doesn't interfere with our brunch, tomorrow," he replied, and it was the truth.

And there's a prime example of love being a motivator like no other, she thought, and smiled to herself.

8

They were assembled in a theatre-seating type film room at the Kingsmen facility, where a semi-circle of tiered seats faced a dais with a screen behind it. Those present included the Chairman and Vice-Chairman of the team, the Manager and his coaching staff, and law enforcement personnel. Acton was seated up front at a table on the dais, along with the Chairman and Williams.

Doyle was relegated to taking notes from the first row, which was the task Acton tended to assign when he wanted her to listen-in and spot any untruths that were being told—she'd signal him surreptitiously, and so she needed to sit somewhere within his line of sight.

She'd noted that Sir Vikili, the team's solicitor, had taken a seat unobtrusively toward the back. She wasn't fooled, however; although his appearance was understated and refined, Doyle knew that he'd the soul of a street-fighter, and anyone involved in criminal prosecution would be automatically wary when he was present. He was here, no doubt, to make certain Acton didn't have an easy time of it, and small blame to him, if the murder was indeed connected to the money-laundering rig; there would be a lot of important people having trouble sleeping tonight.

As could be expected, the general mood of the attendees was one of shock and dismay, as the team's personnel came to grips with the terrible realization that their golden goose had departed this mortal coil before having the chance to deliver-up on the aforesaid gold.

Acton began the meeting by expressing his deep sorrow at this unfortunate turn of events, and he explained that an investigation was pending. "If anyone has any information that could bear on Rizzo's death—however trivial-seeming—we would greatly appreciate it."

"Bollocks," declared the man who'd been introduced to Doyle as the team's Manager. Upon shaking hands, he'd eyed her up and down as a matter of form, which she took in good part because she'd the impression he wasn't even aware that he did so. Apparently, he was a rather famous fellow, and equally famous for his uncertain temper. "Utter bollocks," he repeated.

Acton addressed him. "You'd no idea the decedent was despondent?"

"None," the Manager declared, leaning back in his chair. "He wasn't a moper; he always gave as good as he got."

Acton's tone was mild. "You've had words with him, then?"

"Every time we spoke," the Manager proclaimed without shame.

The tension in the room was broken-up as everyone began to chuckle, and Acton had to smile, himself.

The Manager elaborated, "Of *course* I had words with Rizzo —good God, I'd blister him up one side and down the other, because that's the best way to handle a prima donna who thinks he knows best. You have to establish some sort of authority, or he'll do whatever he likes, and bollocks to everyone else."

One of the Assistants piped up to say, "He wouldn't be scared by the likes of you, sir; he survived Maldonado, in Italy," and everyone chuckled again.

But this general lightening-of-spirits was interrupted when Sir Vikili spoke up from the back of the room. "Is this an interrogation, Chief Inspector?"

Doyle shifted in her chair at the pointed question. Because it was a group conversation, Acton hadn't read anyone the caution—meaning that it wasn't a formal interrogation that could put anyone's rights in jeopardy. Of course, if anyone present said something incriminating—even under these informal circumstances—such a slip couldn't be blamed on law enforcement, who would then profess profound surprise that such a thing had occurred, and promptly take the incriminating-statement person into custody. It was a time-honored ruse by the police, to go on a fishing expedition disguised as friendly conversation.

"No, this is not a formal interrogation," Acton replied. "Instead, we are searching for leads that may be helpful in our investigation."

Enlisting help was yet another time-honored ruse; for whatever reason, people were always dying to help the police, even when they'd be much better off buttoning their lips and walking away.

Sir Vikili, who was no stranger to these time-honored ruses, continued in a smooth tone, "Because—while I represent the Kingsmen as a team—these men may not be aware that I do not represent them as individuals."

"Thank you," said Acton. "That is indeed an important point."

Two heavyweights, sluggin' it out, thought Doyle; all polite, and such.

Acton made a show of considering the notes on his tablet. "Was there anything in Rizzo's personal life that would cause him to take such an action?"

There's my influence again, Doyle thought. Ordinarily, Acton would think this murder was connected to the money-laundering rig, but he's got a fey wife who's wringing her hands about a distraught killer, so he's casting about. I hope I'm not leading the poor man astray.

"Rizzo made a run at MacGregor's girl," one Assistant offered. "That actress—what's-'er-name."

Acton took a note. "MacGregor is a team mate?"

There was a general murmuring of shocked disclaimer, and the Manager explained, "Oh, no; your team mates' women are strictly off-limits. It's an unwritten rule–there's no faster way to ruin the chemistry in a clubhouse. Instead, MacGregor is the darling of Sunderland, and Rizzo was just pulling on his tail."

Everyone chuckled again, as apparently this attempt to steal a rival's girlfriend was to be greatly admired; presumably, football players had their own time-honored ruses.

Again, Sir Vikili's voice interrupted the general merriment. "Is there a question of foul play in the Rizzo case, Chief Inspector?"

But Acton was not discomfited by the question, and instead offered, "I'm afraid every death is considered suspicious until the Coroner can definitively rule it a suicide or an accident. Such a rule ensures that the police are diligent."

There was a small silence, and Doyle could sense a general wariness descend on those assembled as this information sunk in. They're not so very surprised, she thought; no doubt there'd been rumors of dirty dealings, even if the wrongdoing itself hadn't filtered down to these people, who were more interested in winning games than in skimming money.

Again, Acton made a show of reviewing his notes. "There was the unlawful gambling issue last year. And—perhaps, not as a coincidence—one of the investors who'd made it possible for Rizzo's transfer to the Kingsmen met an untimely death—Antonio D'Angelo, of D'Angelo Construction."

The Chairman raised his brows. "Is D'Angelo dead? I thought they weren't sure."

"Thank you—he is missing, and presumed dead," Acton corrected. "Is it possible these two incidents are related?"

In the silence, the Manager was seen to shake his head. "Killing themselves over the gambling scandal? That doesn't seem likely—and there was only light coverage in the news anyway, because no one wanted to put the kibosh on the Rizzo transfer."

"And no one's shocked to hear that there's illegal gambling, in the first place," another man offered in a dry tone. "Definitely not worth killing yourself over."

From the back, Sir Vikili said, "I believe that matter has been completely resolved, Chief Inspector, with the UEFA meting-out an appropriate punishment. I hope you will not malign this team by stirring up the dead ashes again."

Acton raised his head to address the solicitor. "Nonetheless, I would like to follow up with the team's Chief Financial Officer, if I may. I note that he is not present."

Now, there's a punch thrown, thought Doyle.

"He is out-of-town," Sir Vikili countered. "I will make him available as soon as may be."

"My office, first thing Monday," said Acton in an even tone, and closed his tablet.

9

T he meeting had adjourned, and Doyle was walking
with Acton and Williams out to the parking lot as the
three detectives exchanged their impressions.

Doyle offered, "I don't think anyone there knew very much,
Michael. They're all thoroughly miserable about Rizzo, but no
one seems personally invested, or guilty."

"That confirms my impression," Acton agreed.

"Sir Vikili seemed a little defensive," Williams offered. "And
he must have warned the CFO to make himself scarce."

But Doyle had to disagree. "I don't think Sir Vikili's the
defensive type, Thomas—nerves of steel, that one has. Instead, I
thought he was just doin' the usual jawin' at Acton, so as to play
his part. It's a lot like that Rizzo-and-MacGregor thing; he's
playin' his role and rattlin' his sword because that's his job."

Williams had to smile at this comparison. "If it's like Rizzo
and MacGregor, I hope Sir Vikili doesn't try to make a run at
you, Kath. Although I suppose there's little chance of that, since
you are female."

She teased, "Best watch yourself, Thomas; mayhap he'll make a run at you, instead."

Acton asked, "Did you think the Manager was trying to lead the conversation away from the gambling scandal?"

Doyle knit her brow, thinking this over. "No—instead he sincerely doesn't think it was a'tall connected to Rizzo's death. When he said that no one was goin' to pursue the gamblin' charges so as to throw a spanner into the Rizzo trade, that was truly his opinion." She glanced at him. "And anyways, I thought we were thinkin' it was the money-launderin' rig that got him killed, not the gamblin' scandal. The gamblin' scandal was last year's news."

"Unlawful gambling is another form of money-laundering, Kath," Williams explained. "It's probably all tied together."

"Oh," she said in surprise. "Well, if it's all on-goin', and with so much at stake, I suppose we're back to thinkin' there was an investor who was worried about what Rizzo was willin' to tell law enforcement."

"The investors do seem to be the most likely suspects," Williams agreed.

"Perhaps," said Acton. "Although the investors stood to lose substantially with Rizzo's death, also."

They walked a few paces in silence, and then Williams concluded, "Someone must have chosen to save his own skin by killing Rizzo. The killer's priority must have been staying out of prison, even though it meant a huge loss of revenue."

"A likely theory," Acton agreed, and Doyle duly noted that this was not exactly her husband's true opinion. But small blame to him; death-by-investor didn't seem a logical theory to her either, given that the killer was trying to point a big shiny arrow at Savoie, who was, after all, an investor. She said no more on this subject, however, since she didn't think Acton had told

Williams about the attempt to frame Savoie; he was keeping it very close to his vest, and no doubt wouldn't have told even her, save that his sharp-eyed wife had seen him pocket the burner phone.

"Let's check into MacGregor and the girlfriend," Acton suggested.

"It didn't look like a crime of passion," Williams observed doubtfully. "And very unlikely they were having such an argument in a church sacristy in the middle of the night."

"No," Acton agreed. "But there does seem to be a personal element to this homicide. I cannot think of any rational interest that would be served by dispatching someone like Rizzo, and then staging it as a suicide."

They'd paused at Acton's Range Rover, and Williams said, "I'll put together a case management report by tomorrow morning, sir."

"Don't you dare cancel our brunch," Doyle teased in a hearty tone.

He smiled. "Not to worry; I'll get it done in time."

Of course, he will, she thought with a twinge of regret; the man's a prime example of that whole love-is-a-great-and-mighty-motivator phenomenon.

She made to climb into the car, but Acton stayed her with a hand, and bent his head for a moment. "I have an assignment for both of you that I would like to keep off-the-record, for now. I'd like you to visit St. Michael's Church, and meet Mathis there. Not tomorrow—there will be too much of a crowd, but please go Monday morning, under the guise of attending the morning service. I'd like you to conduct a forensic search of the basement, with no one the wiser. Look for prints, in particular."

Doyle nodded, trying to mask her uneasiness that yet again,

her husband was acting off-the-books on this high-profile case. "Right, then; shall I give Father John the head's up?"

"Only if you think it necessary."

Williams nodded, and then made to leave. "I'll pick you up Monday morning, Kath. Although I'll be seeing you tomorrow, first."

"Can't wait," she replied cheerfully.

Acton started up the car, and as soon as they were underway, Doyle offered, "I can't help but wonder if I'm leadin' you astray, with all my the-killer's-motive-is personal, Michael. It truly doesn't make a lot of sense—Rizzo's hardly been in London long enough to make a dent on anyone's personal feelin's."

"On the contrary, I think your theory may have merit," he replied. "This rather clumsy attempt to frame Savoie has all the earmarks of someone acting irrationally."

"We're not tellin' Williams, about the Savoie-framin'?" she ventured.

"Not as yet," he replied. "I would like to know a bit more."

As he drove them through the guard-gate, Doyle offered, "Well, the killer may be actin' irrationally, but not so irrationally that he didn't set it up very carefully, Michael. And you yourself said that it looks as though he's castin' a lure at you, hopin' you'll be drawn-in."

He ducked his chin in agreement. "It does seem a contradiction; the killer's actions seem well planned-out, but at the same time, there is an element of panic in them–even though it is unclear what caused that panic. Law enforcement was not yet closing in."

Doyle made a wry mouth. "Not to mention there was truly no reason to panic; even the DCS himself would think twice about arrestin' Rizzo, just before he started playin' for the Kingsmen. Faith, the man could probably murder someone in Trafalgar Square and get away with it."

"Indeed," he agreed. "Rizzo was essentially above the law."

"Too famous for his own good," she concurred. "So, what was it you were thinkin', husband, when you mentioned D'Angelo to them? D'you think whoever killed D'Angelo killed Rizzo, too?"

"Perhaps," he suggested. "Both men were wealthy and high-profile, both men were believed to be involved in the money-laundering scheme, and both men are now dead."

"Somethin' triggered a fallin' out, amongst thieves? Some blackleg is in a desperate panic, and annihilatin' everyone else?"

"Perhaps," he said again. "I will need more information."

She eyed him. "Am I truly lookin' for D'Angelo's prints in the church basement? Talk about a sleeveless task—like findin' a needle in a haystack."

Thoughtfully, Acton replied, "I am not certain what you will find, if anything. But the placement of the cameras indicates that the basement was housing something valuable that is no longer there, and it is unlikely that it was used for the storage of construction equipment, due to the narrow staircase. We will see if you can find any trace of whatever it was."

Doubtfully, Doyle reminded him, "Father John did say that D'Angelo was a massive donor to the Church's world-wide relief fund. That doesn't seem in keepin' with someone who's hip-deep in murky doin's."

But her husband pointed out, "It may have been a cover for cultivating other participants in the money-laundering rig."

She nodded, as this was indeed a good point. "Or mayhap he was hedgin' his bets, and hopin' to buy his way into heaven."

He smiled slightly. "I am not certain that is the way it works."

Making a face, she observed, "I suppose it all depends on

how big the fortune, and how serious the sin. There's probably a big chart somewhere, with a slidin' scale for measuring one against the other."

"No doubt."

After she watched out the windscreen for a few moments, she reminded him, "You know, Michael, if I'm rootin' around at the church first thing Monday morning, you'll not have me there when you interview the Kingsmen's Chief Financial Officer."

"All the better to keep the search under wraps," he explained. "I think that should be the priority."

Doyle could understand his thinking, but on the other hand, one would think that Acton would be very interested in having a truth-detector listen-in to whatever the CFO had to say for himself. Before she could follow-up, however, he glanced over at her with a small smile. "Shall I come rescue you from your brunch tomorrow? I don't have the impression you are looking forward."

She grimaced slightly. "I appreciate the offer, Michael, but I'm not such a baby that I can't have stupid brunch with stupid Williams and the young woman he admires. I should be happy he's finally found someone, and shame on me, for grousin' on about it."

"Text me if you need me," he offered.

"Best not," she teased; "Can't let Martina get distracted by your *beaux yeux,* or else we'll wind up in a Rizzo-and-MacGregor situation, with poor Williams takin' a swing at you."

"Bad for team chemistry," he agreed.

10

That night, Doyle had one of her dreams.

She had them, on occasion, and they seemed to be part-and-parcel of her perceptive abilities; she'd entertain a visiting ghost in her dreams—sometimes more than one ghost—and the visit always seemed to serve as some sort of warning. Not that the dreams were ominous, or frightening like a scary-ghost-story, though; instead, they were compelling, and commanded her full attention whilst she tried to puzzle out what she was supposed to be understanding. Experience had shown that the message delivered was important, even though it was never expressed in very clear terms.

Oftentimes, she would be warned about some plot being knitted together by her renegade husband; a ghost would give her a head's-up with respect to his misdeeds, and as a result of the ghostly warning she would manage to thwart whatever he had planned. It didn't seem to be a coincidence, that she was the only person on earth Acton was willing to listen to, and at the same time she was the person who was receiving these warnings. She'd be dim indeed, if she didn't come away with the conclusion that she was tasked with saving the man from himself.

The dream-visitors were always someone unexpected, and the ghost who stood before her was no exception. Doyle observed a middle-aged man, rather pale and stout in the best English tradition, and holding a cap between his hands. "Hallo, ma'am," he said, leaning slightly forward. "I hope I didn't startle you."

"That's all right," said Doyle, who'd been plenty startled, and by many a ghost. "I don't believe we've met."

"Once," he explained, with an apologetic tilt of his head. "I tipped my hat to you, in passing."

"Oh—right," said Doyle, who hadn't a clue. "Of course."

In an eager voice, he continued, "I have to say that it's a pleasure to speak with you, ma'am. I'm a big fan—had your newspaper article on my fridge, right next to Rizzo's; the one where he was hoisting the cup for the Champions League."

Doyle had to smile. "Me, right next to Rizzo; now, there's a high compliment."

Shrugging one shoulder slightly, the ghost fingered his cap. "I used to play, once upon a time. You wouldn't know it, to look at me now, but in my day I was a terror in the backfield." After a small pause, he offered his tentative smile. "I never played offense, and so it's a bit strange that I'm to play the decoy, this time around."

"Well, good on you," said Doyle, who wasn't certain what was meant.

With a faraway look, the ghost continued, "I followed Rizzo's career from the start–everyone who followed football knew he was something special. A complete end-to-ender—the youngest player to one hundred caps. A shoe-in for the Hall of Fame, and no one could believe our luck when they said he was coming over to the Kingsmen. A champion like no other; the biggest thing to happen to England since the Class of '92."

The ghost paused to consider this in pleased wonderment, and seemed disinclined to offer any further insights, but Doyle was well-aware he wouldn't be standing before her without good reason, and so she ventured, "Could you remind me where it was, that we met?"

His attention drawn back to her, the ghost said politely, "Why, yes, ma'am—it was at the church, and I was mixing up a new coat of primer for the arches along the ceiling. It's a tricky business, with plaster; you have to have a good primer coat or the paint will get patchy and pool up."

Doyle nodded. "You're a painter, then?"

"Yes ma'am. Like m'father before me, and his before him." He paused, and ducked his head a bit. "I've no son of my own, though. Not like you, with your brace of boys. No, I never married—just kept myself to myself."

There was a small silence, whilst Doyle tried to decide what she should ask. In these dreams, it was always difficult for her to put her thoughts in order; instead, she struggled with an almost overwhelming sense of impressions and abstract emotions— nothing seemed straightforward, and she always wished she knew how to better understand whatever-it-was she was supposed to be understanding.

It didn't help, of course, that she hadn't the first clue why one of the painters from the St. Michael's renovation work was now a ghost. Small wonder the construction was behind schedule, if everyone was dyin', left and right.

Her jumbled thoughts were interrupted when the ghost continued, "I liked working there, I must say—I'd never been inside a church, before. I'd come in early, when no one else was about, so's that I could work, and listen to the silence. Such a lovely silence, it was—not empty, by any means."

Doyle smiled. "I know exactly what you mean."

"I'd walk about and have a look at the statues—the ones in the nooks, on the walls." He leaned toward her, and confided, "They were all so plain; could have used a touch of paint, so as to add a bit of dash."

Doyle decided she may as well ask, "So, what happened to you?"

He shrugged slightly. "I saw something I wasn't supposed to see."

This was of interest, and—making the logical leap—she ventured, "Rizzo?"

The ghost regarded her in surprise. "Oh, no—never got the chance to see Rizzo in the flesh. I so wanted to, of course—in fact, that's why I took on the church job, to make a bit of extra money, on the side." He sighed, and shook his head. "The ticket prices were through the roof, but it would have been well worth it—to be able to say that I'd seen the great Rizzo play." He let out a resigned breath. "Ah well—not to be. I was never one for boats."

"I'm sorry," she offered.

The ghost met her eyes and nodded earnestly. "It was a professional foul, you know—Rizzo's death."

"What's that?" asked Doyle.

But the painter had moved on, and joked, "At least we have something in common, now; me and Rizzo."

"Not funny," Doyle scolded. "No one deserves to be murdered."

"Oh, no," he agreed. "She doesn't, certainly."

Startled, Doyle stared at him. "Who is 'she'?"

But she was suddenly awake, and staring at the darkened wall of her bedroom, her husband's warm body lying next to her own.

11

The next morning Doyle overslept, and then had to hurry to prepare for the brunch date, leaving her little time to ponder about the puzzle presented by her dream. It was going to take some pondering, since it was not at all clear what was needed, except that it appeared some female was in danger, and it must be someone in Doyle's orbit or the ghost wouldn't have bothered.

She'd have to think about it after she'd managed the brunch —one crisis at a time—and so she firmly resisted the urge to delve into the CID database, trying to find out who her ghost was, and what it was that he'd witnessed. Besides, she'd awakened with the strong sense that she shouldn't tip-off Acton about anything the fellow had said, which was another thing that didn't bode well for her peace of mind–sometime during the night she'd come to the uneasy conclusion that her husband was carefully hiding something from her, what with trying to protect Savoie's phone number, and the strange fact that he didn't want her to listen-in to his coming conversation with the Kingsmen CFO.

Don't think about it—not yet, she commanded herself; one crackin' crisis at a time, Doyle.

Williams and Martina swung by to pick her up, and Williams informed Doyle that they were to dine at Candide's, which was Doyle's favorite restaurant and apparently chosen in a calculated attempt to soften her up—not that she needed softening up, she mentally assured herself; she'd respect Williams' choice and place no further burdens on the poor boyo, who'd always been so loyal to the fair Doyle through thick and thin. Love was something that couldn't be controlled, after all, as Doyle herself had learned one fine day at a rather messy Somers Town double-homicide.

Because the restaurant was a local favorite for Sunday brunch, Williams dropped them on the pavement out front so that they could be put in the queue whilst he parked the car. This was to the good, as Doyle had a few questions she was hoping to ask her companion without having a spoilsport like Williams trying to head her off.

The two young women stood together near the restaurant's entrance, smiling at each other in the way people do when they are expected to be amenable for the sake of a third party, and Doyle decided that Martina was rather handsome, although not necessarily beautiful; much of her beauty came from the sense of poise she portrayed—she was a *presence,* was Martina, even though she was fairly small, and truly not very imposing at all.

Before Doyle could wind-up to ask her first question, however, she was to discover that Martina had her own seize-the-opportunity questions. "It is so nice to have this get-together, Lady Acton. Will your husband be joining us?"

Doyle was a bit surprised that Martina seemed unaware that

Williams was contriving to make them friends, and so replied, "Please—call me Kathleen. And I think Thomas set this up so that the two of us could become better acquainted."

"Why, that would be wonderful," Martina smiled, and it was not exactly true.

Doyle ventured, "Are any topics forbidden? I ask because I'm not certain Williams knows about your time at Trestles." For a brief period, Martina had hidden out at Acton's estate, posing as a maid.

"Whatever you wish," her companion replied easily, as though it didn't matter to her at all.

"Is Martina your true name?" Doyle figured she may as well ask—the young woman had used several different aliases in connection with a previous case.

"I do like it best."

It was a strange conversation, and Doyle's forthright nature hovered on the edge of telling the girl that she'd hate to see Williams duped; at first blush, Martina certainly wasn't behaving like someone who was trying to get on the good side of her beau's best friend.

On the other hand, mayhap she didn't consider Williams her beau in the first place; he was keen, but he'd mentioned that she was not as keen, so it was probably best that the fair Doyle keep her lip buttoned at the risk of putting a foot in it, and then having to deal with mopey-Williams for months on end. Been there, done that.

As she made a determined effort to move on to more innocuous topics, Doyle nonetheless felt a stab of sympathy for Williams, because she'd the sense—she'd the sense that Martina was rather *amused* by the situation, if that was the right word, and that sense did not bode well for the Detective Inspector's hopes-and-dreams.

It was therefore with mixed emotions that Doyle greeted that self-same DI when he joined them, apologizing for having to take a work-call in the meantime.

"No matter, I imagine everyone's busy, what with the Rizzo news," Martina said. "Such a terrible shame."

"Were you a fan?" asked Doyle.

"I followed his career," the young woman replied, and for some reason, Doyle's antenna quivered.

Williams disclosed, "Martina is more of an art enthusiast than a sports enthusiast."

Doyle smiled brightly. "Are you? Well, that's grand; what sort of art?"

"I enjoy modern art—especially abstract art. It's hugely collectible, nowadays." Again, Doyle had the sense that the girl was amused, for some reason.

"Oh," said Doyle, who cast about for something to offer on this alien topic. "I know Acton has some famous Gainsbrook, hangin' at his estate."

"Gainsborough, Kath," Williams corrected.

"I knew what she meant," Martina chided him gently.

Worried that Williams had not shown to advantage in this exchange, Doyle hastily assured her, "Oh; I don't take offense, Martina, truly. Thomas steers me right all the time, and its more needful than not—he knows miles more than me about lots of things." She then thought she'd throw in, as an added bonus, "After all, he's the youngest Inspector at the CID since Wensley, and that's truly sayin' somethin'."

"Enough, Kath," Williams joked in embarrassment.

"Whist," Doyle retorted in mock-reprimand, "I'll sing your praises if I wish."

He smiled upon his companion. "Well, I definitely don't know as much as Martina, when it comes to art."

With a playful gleam, Martina disclosed, "But he's learning; I take him with me when I go to the Modern Art Museum."

Williams acknowledged, "I have to say that I was never very interested before, but Martina is very knowledgeable."

Now, there's a man in love, thought Doyle, hiding a smile. Acton would say exactly the same thing, if it were me leading him around some hideously boring art museum.

Williams added, "Speaking of such, Kath is in the process of having her own portrait painted."

"Are you?" the other girl asked with interest.

Doyle made a face. "Yes—thankfully, we're almost finished. The artist's name is Javid—have you heard of her?"

"I have," the other girl said. "She is well-known for her insightful likenesses."

"Well, I don't know if it's insightful or not, but Acton seems to like it, so far, and that's a very high bar."

Doyle had the impression the girl's interest suddenly sharpened. "Oh? Is Lord Acton very discerning, when it comes to art?"

"I suppose," Doyle equivocated, because she wasn't sure what the word meant.

"He married you," Williams pointed out in a teasing tone. That's pretty discerning."

"Plucked me out of the hedgerow," Doyle agreed.

Martina laughed. "How *did* you meet your husband, Kathleen?"

Again, Doyle had the fleeting impression that beneath her casual manner, the girl's interest was razor-sharp. "He was my commanding officer, of all things. There's nothin' like takin' down the villains to inspire a romance."

Martina was silent, and Doyle had the sudden sense that the words had hit home, for some reason. Unfortunately, she also had the sense that the young woman was not thinking of

Williams with fond nostalgia, but instead was thinking of someone else.

With some dismay, she contemplated what seemed to be the inevitable heartache coming Williams' way—he deserved better, poor man–and wasn't it just a *flippin'* shame that you couldn't package-up love however you wished, and fall in love with someone who loved you back.

"A lot of people meet their spouse at work," Williams observed. "I think that's very common."

"Very common," Doyle agreed. "So, ours is not exactly an epic love story, I suppose." Hearing the lie in her own voice, she ducked her head to hide a smile, and pretended to study the menu.

12

_____

Casting about for a topic, Doyle asked, "Where do you hail from, Martina?"

"Castile," the girl replied easily, and it was true.

The name rang a distant bell, and Doyle strained to remember. "Oh—oh, I think that was where Father Ambrose went to seminary. One of our local priests," she added, in explanation.

"Yes, I've met him," Martina said. "A fine priest."

"I never actually knew him," Doyle admitted. "But he was friendly with our own pastor, Father John." Best not mention that Father John had been made uneasy by Father Ambrose's willingness to bend the priest-rules. Doyle added, in case the girl didn't know, "Father Ambrose was killed, unfortunately. Rather recently."

"That is a shame," Martina replied, and Doyle had the strong sense that she was already aware of this sad fact. For a startled moment, she wondered if Martina was a murderer, which was an alarming thought, when one considered that Williams seemed to believe she could do no wrong. But it was not so very far-fetched, after all; the girl had played some sort of role in a shadowy vengeance group from a previous case—although the role that she'd played was unclear. She was brimful of secrets, was Martina, and Doyle had the strong sense that there was more to her than met the eye.

Thinking to explore these rather disquieting thoughts, Doyle ventured in a hearty tone, "It all just goes to show that God works in mysterious ways. It can't have been much fun—bein' wrongfully held in Detention as you were–but on the other hand, you wouldn't have met our Thomas, else."

"Very true," Martina agreed readily, and smiled sweetly at her companion.

"It was fate," Williams happily agreed.

With her own smile, Doyle replied, "Well, it didn't hurt that fate got a bit of a push, I think. Didn't Sir Vikili represent you? Small wonder you were released without further ado—he's considered top-o'-the-trees, around here, and the bane of every-one's existence."

"Yes," Martina agreed. "A very clever and competent man."

Interesting, thought Doyle. She knows I'm fishing, and she's not going to offer me even the tiniest little nibble.

"I immediately went to check-out your record," Williams teased his companion. "You seemed a little too comfortable, hanging out in Detention."

She laughed. "My record is as clean as the driven snow, Thomas."

He laughed in return. "Exactly."

With a gleam, Doyle informed him, "Whist, Thomas; Martina felt snug-as-a-stoat in Detention because bein' held in Detention is a lot like a bein' locked up for a church retreat. You learn stoic endurance, which serves you well in all future hardships."

"Truer words were never spoken," the girl laughed. "Where did you attend school, Kathleen?"

"St. Brigid's, in Dublin. We held a retreat every year and I don't know who dreaded it more, the nuns or the girls."

"Oh yes; St. Brigid's. It is one of your charities, I believe."

A small alarm sounded in Doyle's head, but she replied easily, "Yes. I'm that lucky I've a husband who indulges me—faith, I wouldn't be surprised if he was fonder of the wretched school than I am."

"And I suppose the same could be said for St. Michael's, here in town."

"Acton's been very generous," was all Doyle would reply because again, a small alarm sounded—this time a bit louder. Williams' light-o'-love seemed a little too up-to-speed, when it came to the charitable doings of the House of Acton.

Almost as though she could sense Doyle's uneasiness, Martina easily turned the subject to the abject misery of the ongoing transportation strike, and the remainder of the meal passed uneventfully as they spoke of other innocuous topics.

Williams and Martina dropped Doyle at her building, and as the doorman hurried forward to assist her from the car, Williams reminded her, "See you first thing tomorrow, Kath."

"Bright and early, my friend." With her best social smile, Doyle leaned down to say to Martina, "This was lovely; we must get-together more often."

"I'd love to," Martina replied, and it was not exactly true.

Don't know where that's going, Doyle thought as she smiled her thanks at the doorman; but I'll bet my teeth it's not going where Williams wants it to go.

Upon her arrival in the lobby, the Concierge signaled that he'd a message for her, and handed her a folded note which read

"Code 5" in Acton's spidery handwriting—the police code meaning that an undercover operation was going forward.

With an inward smile, she gravely thanked the man, and then took the lift to the floor below theirs, which was to serve as a second level to their living quarters once construction was completed. Never one to let the grass grow under his feet, Acton had set up the new master suite almost immediately, so that they could steal away from the various babies, nannies and butlers and have a bit of alone-time on those days when the workers weren't working.

He was waiting at the entry door, and immediately swung her up as he pulled her in, kissing her with pent-up anticipation.

"Faith, I've been waylaid," she murmured against his mouth, as she twined her arms around his neck.

"Now, there's a pun." With a firm sense of purpose, he carried her toward the new bedroom.

Blissfully happy, she bestowed lingering kisses on his neck. "Where are Edward, Mary and Reynolds?"

"Not here." After setting her down on her feet, he began to unbutton her blouse with practiced fingers.

As she returned the favor, she teased, "You aren't goin' to ask me how my brunch was?"

"No." He bent to nuzzle her neck as he pushed her blouse to the floor. Impatient, the man was.

She lifted her chin to grant him greater access. "Is Rizzo still dead?"

"Unfortunately."

"Want me to stop talkin', husband?"

"You may suit yourself."

"I'd rather unsuit you," she rejoined, and in a jumble of cast-off clothes, they fell onto the bed for a heated round of after-noon sex, which wasn't as preferable as night-time-so-can-drift-off-to-sleep-sex, but needs must when the devil drives, and Acton was a driven man when it came to having his way with the fair Doyle.

Afterward, they lay together on the luxurious new bed, and Doyle resisted the temptation to glance at the time; she missed baby Edward—what with football stars inconveniently dying, and best friends wanting to set-up friendships with their sweethearts. However, the care and feeding of husbands was certainly a priority, and so she possessed her soul in patience and lay in Acton's arms, idly pulling on his chest hairs whilst he lay in drowsy contentment.

"Tell me of your brunch," he said.

"You're just bein' polite," she accused.

"Nonetheless."

She lifted her gaze to the windows and sighed. "Well, to the good, I had some of Candide's excellent coffee, which was much appreciated because it was tough sleddin', and I was needful of fortification."

He pulled her toward him in the crook of his arm, so that he could kiss her forehead. "That is a shame."

"The upshot is this: Williams is serious, but she's not."

Idly, Acton ran his hand along her arm and offered, "She was willing to have brunch with you. Surely, that is a hopeful sign."

Doyle frowned slightly. "Yes—well, it was all a bit strange, if you ask me. She was probin' a bit about you, of all things. I know we were just kiddin' about a Rizzo-and-MacGregor situation, but I hope she's not another one hopin' to make a run at your handsome self. There've been so many I've lost track.'"

She could sense his surprise. "I've not spoken more than a few words to her, but I never caught that sense."

"A rare bird, then," she teased.

Thoughtfully, he propped an elbow under his head. "What did she ask?"

"Well, she thought you might be joinin' us for brunch, which seemed a bit odd, since that would have undermined Williams' well-laid plans for settin' it up in the first place. She wanted to know how we met—you and me—and she knew about St. Brigid's—about how you were helpin' to fund them. St. Michael's too—but that's not much of a secret, hereabouts."

He considered these revelations for a long moment. "I would ask," he said slowly, "that you be careful about what you say to her."

This was alarming, and Doyle lifted her head to look at him. "Bein' discreet is not my strong suit, husband."

"Nevertheless."

"What is it you're thinkin'?"

He tilted his head, slightly, and she felt his chest rise and fall as he considered his answer. "I am not certain, as yet. But we know she was connected to the vengeance group from the Council-murders case, so perhaps she is only feigning a romantic interest in Williams."

Doyle considered the impressions she'd gained from the meal. "It's not that she doesn't likes him—she does, but she's definitely not as smitten as he is." She shifted her head to meet his eyes in apology. "I know you're pig-sick of me worryin' about stupid Williams, Michael, but I can't seem to help it."

"Nonsense; you are a good friend."

She made a wry mouth. "A good friend would leave him to make his own mistakes, I suppose. I'll say no more."

He was silent for a moment, and then asked, "What else did you observe about Martina?"

"She wasn't lyin' about anythin', if that's what you mean."

He nodded. "Any other impressions?"

Doyle sighed. "Well, she's not tryin' to floozy him into bed, that much seems clear, and it only adds to my general impression that the relationship is takin' the fast road to failure. Faith, she' wasn't tryin' to be sexy a'tall—she wore only a touch of make-up, and her nails were unvarnished. No jewelry a'tall— except for a little pendent necklace in some geometric design. It looked a bit like a Celtic cross, except there was a long loop." Thinking it over, she added, "All in all, it was a bit odd; she seemed—she seemed secretly *amused*, or somethin'."

This caught his interest, and he tilted his head to her. "Why so?"

Doyle frowned at the ceiling. "About the situation, I think— the three of us bein' there together, and Williams tryin' so hard to make a good impression. It started when I asked if she was a Rizzo-fan." After a pause, she decided to tell him, "I thought for one horrible moment that mayhap she was Rizzo's killer, but then I decided I was jumpin' at shadows."

"Yes—you believe the killer is a man. A desperate man."

She nodded. "I still do. Our Martina doesn't fill the bill."

He was silent for a moment, and then squeezed her in his arm, as she lay against his side. "I am sorry you were uncomfortable."

"I was, a wee bit," she admitted.

"If there is another such occasion, I will accompany you."

She smiled as she nuzzled the side of his chest. "You just want to observe her for yourself, husband. I'm wise to your wily ways."

He didn't disclaim. "That, and I would not like to see Williams misled, either."

She teased, "Exactly right; who'd help you out with all your skullduggery, if Williams was left weepin' by the wayside?"

He smiled but made no comment, because Acton didn't like

to talk about his skullduggery, mainly because he knew she'd only give him a scolding and he was hoping for another round of sex—she knew the signs.

Tentatively, she ventured, "You know, Michael, mayhap you *could* take him aside, and give him some advice. I truly can't be unsupportin'—is that a word?"

"It is now," he replied.

"Well, I can't, but you'd have no such qualms. You could look all disapprovin' and try to steer him aright. It's not like you're without influence."

Slowly, he offered, "I am not certain such a course would be appreciated."

With a sigh, she acknowledged, "I suppose not; no one wants to hear that they're makin' a cake of themselves."

He nodded. "It may be best to allow matters to play out, instead."

She lifted her head to stare at him in mock-surprise. "Who are you, and what have you done with my husband?"

He pulled her atop him, so that her hair spilled around his chest. "It is true, though. Any attempt to intervene may only make matters worse."

Doyle had to acknowledge the wisdom of this, and lowered her head to kiss him thoroughly. "Sorry—I wasn't goin' to talk any more about it, and now I'm ruinin' your well-thought-out Code Five." She began to nuzzle him. I'm ready for round two, Code Three."

"Code Two," he corrected.

"Whatever," she murmured into his throat.

13

That night, the ghost of the painter came for a return visit to Doyle's dreams, and she viewed his appearance with a guilty start.

"Oh—oh, faith, I'm so sorry," she apologized. "I was all caught up in Williams, and I forgot to find out what's happened to you."

Again, his manner was cheerfully deferential, as he held his cap in his hands. "Please don't worry, ma'am—I know you're busy."

"There is a female in danger," Doyle said, striving to remember, and wishing she weren't such a knocker—how could she have forgot? Of course, this particular ghost wasn't very compelling, but shame on her for not giving him her full attention.

"There is," the ghost agreed. "And so he's pulled a professional foul, because he didn't have the numbers. And now he's going to get gutted, because I'm the decoy."

"Oh," said Doyle.

"Outmanned," the ghost declared. "Clattered to pieces."

Tentatively, Doyle asked, "Who's outmanned? Is it Acton, that we're talkin' about?"

"Oh, no," the ghost said, surprised by the very idea. "Now, there's one who's always on the front foot—a real bone-rattler."

"I'm afraid I'm not sure what it is that you're sayin'," Doyle confessed, but found she was speaking into empty space as she awoke with a start, her heart pounding.

Carefully, she shifted her weight and listened for a moment, to make sure that she hadn't awakened her husband. What did it all mean? Who was in danger? Martina? This would be rather surprising to Doyle, because she'd the impression that Martina was well-able to take care of herself. Lizzy Mathis? Stupid Munoz? Someone Doyle hadn't heard of, as yet?

She rolled to lay on her back and rub her face in frustration. The football-talk might be bewildering, but it seemed as though the ghost was saying that Rizzo's killer was desperate because he was outmanned—that much seemed clear. It couldn't be Acton —Acton was never outmanned, and even on those rare occasions when he was, he always found a way to turn the tables so as to make his enemies pay. So—who was outmanned? Williams, perhaps?

She thought this over, and then decided she'd be very surprised if it was Williams, because she'd bet her teeth that this ghost was connected in some way to Rizzo's murder—the painter had seen something at the church that he wasn't supposed to, he'd said, and then he must have been murdered for it. Besides, Williams was too busy mooning after Martina to be desperately murdering famous football players—or at least, as far as she knew, she amended fairly; had to keep an open mind, after all.

But she must be on the wrong track, thinking the killer was

Williams or Acton or anyone she knew—that made no sense
a'tall, for heaven's sake. Besides, the ghost had almost made it
sound as though it was Acton who was doing the outmanning,
which made much more sense, because this meant that the
ghost was trying to get her to put a stop to whatever scheme her
husband was putting forward, and this aim was a common
ghostly theme when it came to the ghostly ghosts in her life.

Somewhat heartened by this conclusion, she thought it over
for a moment, and concluded—rather easily—that Acton's
scheme must be connected to the money-laundering rig. After
all, he'd skimmed money from other criminal enterprises in the
past, and could easily be doing the same here, because for some
reason Acton was unable to resist helping himself to ill-gotten
goods. Indeed, that would explain why he seemed to be stepping
so carefully on this case, and why he didn't want her listening-in
to the Kingsmen CFO.

But how these various events came together—and how they
were somehow tied-in to an unremarkable painter's murder–was
a complete mystery, and she wished she had a capperman's clue
as to why this fellow was visiting her dreams.

I'm that flummoxed, she decided. But one thing's for certain,
I've got to find out who this painter is, and what's happened to
him. I'll work on it tomorrow, and shame on me for not making
it a priority.

With this resolution, she turned toward the warmth of her
husband and drifted back into sleep.

The next morning dawned with Doyle rising early, in sleepy
preparation for her clandestine visit to the St. Michael's basement. Nursing her coffee like a pilgrim at the font, she helped
feed Edward his breakfast, and then waited until Acton was in
the shower before addressing their butler.

"Reynolds, you know a lot about football, right?"

"Some, madam. I played a bit, when I was a schoolboy."

Doyle decided not to be sidetracked by the utterly fantastic idea of Reynolds as a schoolboy, and instead continued, "What's a 'decoy'?"

Reynolds paused in refilling her coffee cup, and drew himself up to consider the question. "I believe the term is used when there is a player who is far-and-away the main scoring threat. The offense uses another player as a decoy, in an attempt to fool the opposing team's defense into concentrating on the decoy, and this allows the true scorer to operate with as little impediment as possible."

"Oh," said Doyle doubtfully.

Observing this reaction, Reynolds further explained, "It prevents a double-team, madam. It is a calculated feint."

"Oh," said Doyle.

"Rather like a misdirection play," the servant offered doggedly.

"*Oh*—I see," said Doyle, as the light dawned. "Now we're speakin' English." She paused, frowning as she mulled this over. "I wonder what he meant, when he said he was the decoy?"

"Who, madam?"

But Doyle did not respond because she'd just entertained an alarming thought. "D'you know who's top o' the trees, when it comes to misdirection plays? Acton is, that's who. He's got decoys comin' out of his ears."

Understandably confused, the servant ventured, "Oh? Did Lord Acton play football, madam?"

"Everyone did, save me," she replied crossly. "I was too busy workin' at the stupid fish market."

"Yes, madam; I am careful never to serve fish," the butler soothed.

But Doyle hadn't much time, and was back to the main topic. "Is it dangerous, to be the decoy?"

Reynolds knit his brow at the unexpected question. "I suppose it is no more dangerous than any other position, madam. There is always the risk of injury."

Frowning in concentration, Doyle tried to remember what the ghost had said. "Does the decoy 'get gutted'?"

"No madam; the decoy ensures that other team's defense gets gutted, so to speak."

Doyle began to mop up after baby Edward, taking a towel to his little fingers. "What's a 'brace', then?"

Reynolds seemed a bit confused. "If we are speaking of football, madam, a 'brace' is the number two. When a player has scored two goals, he is said to have scored a brace."

"Oh," she said, and paused to knit her brow as she gazed out the window.

The servant hovered by the breakfast table. "I can procure a pamphlet if you'd like, madam. One with a simple explanation of the rules and strategy."

Doyle's reverie was broken, as she looked upon him in amusement. "Now, why would I be needin' a pamphlet, Reynolds, when I have you here to tell me anythin' that I could possibly wish to know?"

"I stand ready to answer any questions you may have," the servant agreed. "But it may be helpful to have a pamphlet, if you'd like to study the rules."

"I would, indeed," she promised solemnly. "I would study it like it was the holy writ."

With the air of someone who knows he is being teased, Reynolds offered with a tinge of disapproval, "More coffee, madam?"

Doyle checked the time, and—with a stoic air—rose to make her way toward the door. "No, thanks. Wish me luck; I'm off to church, and I hope I'm not about to get gutted, myself."

"Stay on frame, madam," the servant advised.

14

The driving service dropped Doyle off at St. Michael's, ostensibly to attend the early morning service, but in short order she met-up with Williams and Lizzy Mathis inside the vestibule. After they had a quiet word with the PC on cordon-duty, the three then slipped away to the basement, to see what there was to see.

On their descent down the narrow stairway, Williams took the opportunity to ask Doyle, "What did you think about Martina?"

Doyle, who was well-aware that she was to be debriefed on the subject, said with all sincerity, "She's lovely, Thomas. Truly."

He nodded, as they turned at the landing. "I think it went well. Thanks so much for going; I get the sense she's holding me at arm's length."

"She does seem a bit guarded," Doyle admitted. "And small blame to her, considerin' she met us when she was bein' held in Detention on a false charge. She'll soften." Privately, Doyle wasn't so sure; it seemed to her that the young woman was a little too practiced at turning aside questions.

Thus reminded, she ventured in a low voice, "Are you *sure* she's not a cat-burglar, Thomas? Because that would put a serious dent in any commitment-hopes."

But he wasn't offended by the question, and replied, "I'm not that dumb, Kath. Not only did I check her record, I did a deep dive into everything I could find. It all seems straightforward."

Doyle frowned slightly as they stepped down the last step into the basement. "I will say that she doesn't seem very Spanish, to me. Not like our Munoz."

"No—she said her parents were missionaries."

Doyle blinked. "Oh? Hard to imagine RC missionaries in Spain—it's not as though the Spanish need much convincin'."

"It was some sort of outreach group—she was a little vague about it."

Doyle quirked her mouth. "And you didn't press, because you get the willies whenever the subject of religion rears its ugly head."

"I should have an open mind," he acknowledged. "I can tell that it's important to her."

Doyle teased, "Have I mentioned that love is a strange and mighty thing, Thomas? I'm tempted to point out that you've never given me the slightest hint of open-mindedness, when it comes to the forbidden church-subject."

"Point taken," he conceded. "I suppose this is not the time to ask for crib notes?"

"Ask *Martina* for crib notes," she chided in mock-exasperation. "Honestly, Thomas; do I have to think of everythin'?"

Mathis had been quiet during their conversation, but apparently had decided she was tired of hearing about Williams' sweetheart, being as she'd been hopeful of holding that position, herself. "What's the protocol—are we trying to keep a clean site?"

Even though they'd not brought bunny suits or paper footies, there were certain procedures to be followed if the detectives wanted to be careful not to risk further contamination.

Williams shook his head. "No—there's no point. In fact, it's almost a perfect cover for a crime, because construction people have been in and out over months at a time, and it would be impossible to process this room in the first place."

"An easy way to cover their tracks, if they're up to somethin'," Doyle agreed. "And anyways, I think Acton wants to find out what's been happenin' here, more than anythin' else."

"Are we recording?" Mathis asked.

"No," said Williams. "In fact, Acton wants to keep everything off electronics. If you have any questions about that, you'll have to take it up with him."

"I wouldn't question the Chief Inspector's orders," Mathis replied in an even tone.

Williams tilted his head. "Sorry. I didn't mean to imply that you would."

"No need to apologize, DI Williams; I don't question your orders, either."

Faith, thought Doyle with a tinge of exasperation; I hope they don't come to blows, these two. But all this talk of recording reminded Doyle of a niggling loose end. "What did the construction company's CCTV show?"

"Nothing," he replied, and cast her a significant glance. "They'd been wiped. The church's feed, too—everything was clean."

"There's another red flag," Doyle duly noted. "All signs point to murder."

Williams signaled that Doyle was to take the left side of the room whilst he took the right, and then they started on the outer perimeter, moving slowly and looking for anything unusual whilst Mathis waited in the doorway. It all appeared very straightforward, though; the basement—chilly, due to the thick stone walls—dated from the construction of the church over two hundred years ago, and it certainly looked the part. The floorboards were solid oak, and had been worn down by countless passing feet to the point that the knots in the wood protruded higher than the surface of the floor itself.

Clean but ancient cupboards lined Doyle's wall, and she dutifully opened each to look inside at the various church accoutrements that had been relegated to the little-used basement.

Williams paused to watch her for a moment. "Anything?"

"Not unless you are interested in chipped candle stands, and such." She moved to the next cupboard. "Father John mentioned that the construction people found a hidey-hole in the floorboards, with some old papers hidden within. He was worried he'd have to call-in the Heritage people and shut down construction, and so I think he decided to keep mum about it."

His hands on his hips, Williams surveyed the floor with interest. "Where is this hidey-hole?"

"I can ask him, if we can't find it. Under the floorboards, he said."

"Is that a smudge of paint?" Lizzy asked, from her position at the doorway. "Where?" asked Williams, glancing back at her.

The other girl indicated what appeared to be a tiny daub of orange-brown paint, on the edge of a cupboard's lower frame. "It looks recent to me."

"It does seem out of place," Doyle agreed, bending slightly to peer at it. "I can't imagine they were doin' any paintin', down here."

"They may have been storing their paint here," Williams pointed out. "Let's take a sample."

Carefully, Lizzy stepped forward and donned her magnifying glasses, which contained a focused, bright light. After observing the small discoloration for a moment, she gently scraped a sample with a delicate razor blade instrument. "Interesting," she said.

"What's interesting?" asked Williams, in the tone of someone trying to check his impatience.

Mathis frowned slightly, as she examined the sample on her blade. "It looks fresh, but it's not house-paint—more like a specialized epoxy."

"They may have been touching-up the idols, or something," Williams suggested.

"Or the divinin' stones," Doyle added. "Which are used when we paint our faces blue, under the full moon."

Williams smiled. "All right—sorry I didn't use the correct term, Kath."

"The statuary does seem a likely use," Mathis said to Williams, so as to make him feel better.

"Let's just keep looking," he replied shortly, not willing to cede the girl an inch. "We have only an hour."

At the conclusion of the survey, they'd found little of interest, and so the two detectives began tapping on the floorboards, looking for the hidden cavity.

"Here," said Williams, crouching down. "You can see that this plank's not fixed down, like the others."

Doyle stepped over to join him as he looked around for something to use as a lever.

"You can use my blade," Mathis offered.

But Williams was reluctant. "It's thick wood—I wouldn't want to break it. We'll need a screwdriver, or something."

"I didn't see any tools," Doyle offered, "but there's a candle-snuffer in the cupboard—let me fetch it."

Mathis and Doyle stood and watched Williams as he worked the metal device under an edge of the wood, and then popped-up the plank from its place. He then set the wood aside to expose a dark cavity that dropped down approximately eighteen inches. As they leaned over the hiding place, Mathis clicked on her light so that they could better see within.

"No documents," said Doyle. "Father John must have put them elsewhere."

"It looks water-tight," Williams observed.

"Yes," Mathis agreed. "An old tin box, perhaps."

"There's something at the bottom." Williams reached down to grasp a small crumpled paper bag.

"Someone left their lunch, fifty years ago," Doyle joked.

"Let's see." Williams shook the bag to empty out the contents, and an ornate necklace spilled out onto the floor, the stones glowing bright blue in the gleam of Mathis' bright, focused light.

15

There was a moment of profound silence, and then Doyle said, "Now we know why the construction company was wantin' cameras in here."

Carefully balancing the glittering cache in the palm of his hand, Williams slid it back into the bag. "Yes. They must have been smuggling jewelry."

Doyle raised her brows in amazement. "Seems an odd business plan—to be restorin' churches and fencin' stolen goods, on the side."

But Williams lifted his gaze to her. "Remember this was D'Angelo's company, Kath, and we know D'Angelo was involved in some shady dealings before he disappeared—money laundering, for one. Jewelry's an easy way to transport value because it raises no alarms—not like packets of cash does. It's easier to transport, too—easily hidden."

"It seems a large risk, for such a small return," Mathis offered.

Doyle could only agree. "If they're money-launderin', this

paltry little necklace is hardly worth the rigmarole. More like they accidentally left it behind, during the last transfer."

They were silent for a moment, and then Williams nodded in agreement. "Yes—I imagine this was a collection point, and it had to be emptied quickly. Someone must have missed this bag, at the bottom."

"Should we try to process the cavity?" asked Mathis. "Although we're running out of time. I can stay behind, if necessary."

Williams checked the time. "Let's dust the cavity for prints and bag the jewelry; Acton can decide how this goes from here. We'll reconvene at my office, traveling separately."

"Do I go?" asked Mathis.

"We'll let you know, if we need you," Williams said firmly. "I don't want to raise any alarms, so wait for word, and keep radio silence."

"I know the protocol for this assignment, DI Williams," the girl replied, her cheeks a bit pink. "You weren't being clear about whether I should stay or go."

"Sorry," he said rather abruptly, in the tone that men use when they really aren't sorry at all.

Doyle decided she may as well point out, "Acton trusts Lizzy, Thomas."

"I wasn't insulted," the girl immediately defended Williams. "I just needed to know where to go."

Love is a shameful, shameful, thing, thought Doyle. "Right then; we've cleared it all up."

But they hadn't, actually, and so Mathis ventured, "I'm going back to my lab, then?"

"Yes," said Williams in a clipped tone. "As I said, to wait for word."

But Doyle decided to interrupt the bickering, because she

knew her husband better than the others, and held a sudden thought. "Do we take the evidence and secure the site, or do we just leave everythin' be? Once the Rizzo-frenzy has settled down, someone's goin' to come in to fetch this forgotten bag, one would think, and mayhap Acton wants to set a trap."

This gave Williams pause, but then he decided, "I think we take it with us. I'd like to call Acton for instruction, but we're not supposed to use our electronics."

"I've a secure line to him," Doyle offered. "I can call him on my private mobile."

Williams considered this, and then nodded. "All right; but be careful what you say."

With a nod, Doyle rang up Acton on their private line and as always, he answered promptly.

"Kathleen."

In a breezy tone, she began, "Cheers, Michael; Williams is wonderin' if we could meet-up after church—are you puttin' out Rizzo-fires, or can you meet for coffee?"

But her husband only asked in a serious tone, "Who is with you?"

"Mathis and Williams." She paused. "We're in the basement."

"What did you find?"

Lowering her voice, she replied, "A fancy necklace, hidden 'neath the floorboards. It looks to be a money-launderin' operation, and we'll be needin' some direction because we're not sure whether we should leave everythin' be or take it into evidence." Belatedly, she added, "Sir."

There was a small pause. "Please put Mathis on."

Doyle raised her brows and passed the mobile to Mathis. "He'd like to speak with you, Mathis."

The two detectives stood by whilst Mathis listened, making no response until she calmly handed the phone over to Williams. "You're to arrest me for jewelry theft, DI Williams," she said.

16

D oyle stared at the girl in abject astonishment as Williams held Doyle's mobile to his ear, struggling to hide his surprise. "Sir?"

Whilst Williams listened, Mathis pulled the jewelry bag from his distracted hand, and then clumsily dropped it on the floor. "Oh," said the girl in consternation, and bent to retrieve the necklace—taking longer than it should have, and with her back to them so that her actions were obscured.

She's wiping it clean of prints, Doyle realized; and she'd doing it on Acton's orders which does not bode well for the fair Doyle's peace-of-mind, going forward.

"Yes, sir," said Williams, and rang off. Slowly, he handed the mobile back to Doyle. "I'm to bring you in, Mathis."

"Should I wear cuffs?" the other girl asked in a practical tone.

"Not just as mornin' Mass is gettin' out," Doyle pleaded. "Mother a' mercy, poor Father John is goin' to take up swearin'."

"No—Acton wants us away from the church, and he doesn't want you in the lab, either. Go home, instead, and I'll come by in an hour or so—he wants to have a theft report filed, first, so that all normal procedures are followed."

There was an awkward silence, whilst the other girl carefully tucked the jewelry bag into her kit.

"I'm that sorry, Lizzy," Doyle offered. "I'll smuggle you in a cake, with a file within."

With her dry smile, Mathis replied, "Thank you, Lady Acton. I'll be off, now." With no further ado, the young woman turned to march up the steps.

Into the silence, Doyle ventured, "Well, here's a twist."

Thomas glanced at the time. "We'd best go up."

But Doyle stayed him with a hand to his elbow, and felt obligated to mention, "There's a troublin' angle to all this, Thomas, and I'd not be much of a friend if I didn't point it out."

"I know," he said, and studied the floor for a moment. "I know—thanks."

Doyle nodded. By an extraordinary coincidence, Martina Betancourt had been accused of jewelry theft, until she'd been let go for lack of evidence. Williams was nobody's fool, of course, and had no doubt drawn his own troubling conclusions.

Doyle continued softly, "It looks as though Acton is turnin' the tables, Thomas— sendin' our own version of Martina to take a turn in Detention, under a false charge. I think he's sendin' some sort of message, in spades, and it certainly looks as though that message is directed straight toward Martina."

"Yes," he agreed, rather heavily.

But—thinking on this—Doyle paused in confusion. "On the other hand, it seems unlikely that it's Martina who's smugglin' the jewelry here, Thomas. She'd be too noticeable, goin' in and out of a construction site."

"Sir Vikili was her solicitor," he reminded her. "That's a red flag, too."

She squeezed his arm. "Whist, that may not mean anythin'—other than she's got plenty of money to spend on her defense. Everyone knows he's the best, after all."

"I wish I knew what Acton was thinking." He glanced at her. "Can you ask him?"

It was a measure of his concern that he'd even make such a suggestion—Williams was normally very careful to avoid pitching the fair Doyle into a divided loyalties situation—but Doyle sympathized with the poor man's distress, and offered, "I'll try, but I'm not sure even Acton knows exactly what's goin' on—or at least, that's the sense I have. And surely, if Acton *did* think that Martina was an out-and-out villain he'd have warned you off, and in no uncertain terms. He's not one to worry about wounded feelin's, after all."

Williams' brow lightened considerably. "Yes—yes, of course. You're right; if he really thought she was a player, he'd have given me the head's up already."

Doyle ventured, "Has Martina ever said anythin' about anythin'?"

He blew out a breath, and admitted, "She asked me once if I'd ever run into Savoie, when his son was staying with you."

She stared at him in dismay. "Oh. I can't say that bodes well either, Thomas."

"I know. I asked her how she knew Savoie, and she said she'd a run-in with him, once. She didn't seem to be a fan."

Thinking this over, Doyle shook her head. "I suppose the jury's still out, then. And besides, if she's thick-as-thieves with Savoie, she wouldn't be askin' you about him."

Distracted, he ran his hands through his hair. "I can't believe that she's dishonest, Kath. I'm not like you, but I've developed a sense for people, too."

"Of course you have," she soothed. "Any good detective has

that sense, or they wouldn't survive. Let's wait and see what Acton's got on tap—it's got to be a corker, if our Mathis is to be locked-up."

"Mathis is loyal to the bone, I'll give her that," he conceded with a half-smile, as they moved toward the steps.

Silently, Doyle added; more than some I could name.

17

On pins and needles, Doyle was nevertheless forced to wait before she could winkle-out any information from her husband, because he was still conducting his interview with the Kingsmen's Chief Financial Officer. Therefore, she fetched two cartons of soup from the canteen and then hung around Acton's office door, awaiting her opportunity and trying not to distract Nazy from her work.

"Sir Vikili is in there, too," the assistant whispered with suppressed excitement. "He is *so* handsome."

"That he is," Doyle agreed. Then, because she thought the rather naïve girl might need a bit of a warning, she added, "Odd, that he never seems to be datin' anyone."

"He is dedicated to his work," Nazy explained with a serious expression. "That is what Marjan in Personnel says. She is jealous, that I see him more often than she does."

"He's somethin'," Doyle agreed diplomatically, as she was not necessarily a big fan of guileful defense solicitors. Although she probably should be a fan; Sir Vikili was a lot like Acton, in many ways, and it was only fair that the defendants had someone to act as a counter-weight, so as to keep the system honest.

For some reason, her scalp began to prickle, but before she could puzzle out why this would be, Acton buzzed Nazy to let her know that the meeting had adjourned.

As though she hadn't been lying in wait, Doyle smoothed her hair and picked up her soup cartons whilst Nazy prepared the parking validations, and then the door opened to reveal Acton as he bade farewell to the two other men. One would think such an interview would make for a very uncomfortable hour for the witness—if Acton's theory about the money-laundering rig was correct—but the bespectacled CFO seemed only relieved that the meeting was over.

Acton's playing his cards close to his vest, Doyle decided with a pang of misgiving; which unfortunately only confirms my theory that he's hip-deep in pulling off his own scheme, here, and making hay whilst the money-laundering sun shines.

Sir Vikili was on edge, and hiding his wariness behind a polite, noncommittal expression—it was hard to successfully second-guess Acton, of course, and good luck to the solicitor, who was tasked with that chore on a daily basis.

"DS Doyle," the man nodded, in his restrained way. "Ms. Chaudhry."

Nazy turned a bit pink at being thus recognized, as she handed the men their validations and Acton shook their hands.

Acton offered, "I will be in touch, of course."

"Certainly," said Sir Vikili, and then he walked away with his client.

When they were out of earshot, Nazy said to Acton in a low voice, "I have heard from the gentleman, sir."

"Excellent," said Acton, as he ushered Doyle into his office, and closed the door after them.

"Who's 'the gentleman'?" Doyle asked. "Unless I'm not allowed to know."

"What's this, soup?" Acton lifted one of the cartons, understandably surprised because the fair Doyle had always felt that soup was a sorry excuse for a decent meal.

"It's just my cover story, Michael; I know you're busy, but I'm dyin' to touch base with you."

Carefully, he set the carton on his desk. "No excuse needed; you may touch base with me whenever you wish, Kathleen."

"I'd be happy to touch your base," she teased a bit wickedly, "but one thing always leads to another, and then Nazy might overhear."

He smiled as he carefully pried-off the cardboard lid and considered the contents of the carton. "You shock me, DS Doyle."

Reading him aright, she offered, "You don't have to eat it, Michael—truly. It was just somethin' close to hand. And don't think I haven't noticed that you didn't answer my question."

"The 'gentleman' Nazy referenced is a Kingsmen accountant who would like to speak with me. He has declined representation of counsel, and would rather no one else knew of it."

Doyle raised her brows. "Now, there's a crackin' lead, with bells on."

He glanced up at her. "Perhaps I could persuade you to sit in on the interview."

Shrewdly, she concluded, "Because you're not so sure this isn't yet another misdirection play like the burner phone, meant to lead you astray."

He tilted his head in acknowledgment, as he took a tentative taste with a plastic spoon. "I am not responding to Rizzo's murder as was hoped, and so I would not be surprised if I was to be prodded."

Doyle ventured, "Should we shove this 'gentleman' fellow into Detention with Mathis? Can't be too careful, nowadays, and it does seem as though Detention has lately served as a home for wayward witnesses."

After setting the carton aside, he leaned back in his chair. "Mathis has been released on her own recognizance. The matter will be kept quiet, being as my mother is the claimant, and I have hinted that my mother may be mistaken. She is elderly, after all, and prone to paranoia."

"Good one," said Doyle with approval. "Although they may instead think you're havin' an affair with Lizzy, and busily handin' over your mother's jewelry as a token of your affections."

"Even more reason they'd keep it quiet," he replied practically.

Reminded of why she was here in the first place, Doyle ventured, "Well, don't think I can't see that you're pullin' Martina Betancourt's tail, what with this Lizzy-business, and anyone who thinks you don't have a sense of humor is sadly mistaken."

He did not disclaim, but replied in a mild tone, "It seemed the best course. Someone is leaving bread crumbs for me, and I am not one who likes to be led."

"This I know, my friend—believe me. But the killer is that determined, it seems—between the jewelry, and the burner phone, and the blood spatter pattern, and the clean CCTV tape." Then, because there was nothin' for it, Doyle felt compelled to confess, "Martina's been askin' Williams about Savoie, which seems a bit disquietin', if you think Rizzo's murder involves some elaborate scheme to frame Savoie."

Thoughtfully, Acton gazed out the window. "Has she indeed?"

As he offered her no insights, Doyle left William's troubles aside for a moment to take up her thankless law-enforcement mantle yet again. "I can't be easy about all of this, Michael. I know that you're sendin' some sort of message, by throwin' poor Mathis in the nick, but you shouldn't be muckin' about in the evidence, even if it's only in response to someone else's muckin' about in the evidence."

"Yes. I completely understand, Kathleen."

This was—naturally—an equivocal answer if she'd ever heard one, and small blame to him; keeping his mitts out of the evidence would be a heretical thought for the likes of him. Doyle decided that she may as well ask, "You think our Martina's a player in the money-launderin' rig—is that what this merry chase is all about? If that's the case, poor Williams is goin' to melt down."

But her husband's answer surprised her, as he continued gazing out the window. "I am not certain, as yet, what is at play here."

This was true, and Doyle raised her brows in surprise. "But you must think Martina's in the thick of the money-launderin'— you *must*. Why else turn the tables with Lizzy Mathis?"

Thoughtfully, he drew a hand along the edge of his desk. "To the contrary, I do not actually believe Martina is involved. There has been no indication of such, and I have been following this particular operation for some time. I do find it interesting, however, that she has arrived on the scene for these events." He paused. "I also find it interesting that it is no easy thing to trace her background."

Doyle offered, "She's from Spain, or at least that's what she told Williams. Told him her parents were missionaries."

He glanced at her with some interest. "But you don't believe it?"

She sighed. "I'm skeptical with no particular reason to be, Michael. Pay me no mind."

But he nodded. "You've every right to be skeptical, Kathleen. After all, she had some involvement in the Council-murders case, although her exact role was not clear."

Doyle ventured, "We could always bring her in for some follow-up questionin' on that case, and hear what she has to say." She added, "For Williams' sake, it's best we know straight-away whether she's a blackleg or not."

But he only tilted his head. "On what premise can we bring her in? The Council-murders have been resolved. I think it best to await further events."

She eyed him, as she considered this advice. "You've a bushel more patience than I have, my friend."

"Perhaps." He offered nothing more.

Doyle had the sudden impression that her husband was—gently—trying to remind her that with all her Williams-worrying she was getting her priorities wrong, which was a rich, rich irony, and much appreciated.

Smiling slightly, she acknowledged, "I know, I know—I can't try to spare Williams' stupid feelin's at the risk of jeopardizin' this case. Besides, if Martina's one of the blacklegs, best let Williams take his lumps, and let this be a lesson."

"Agreed," he replied in a mild tone.

Doyle caught a nuance in his words that made her lift her head and look at him narrowly. "What is it? Never say you know somethin' that Williams doesn't?"

"Not about Martina," he assured her.

Doyle wasn't certain that this reply answered her question, exactly, but she let it go, and continued, "Well, he's smitten, poor boyo—she's an art critic, or somethin', and he lets her drag him to the art museums, and such. It's the eighth wonder of the world."

Slowly, Acton observed, "It is not clear how she earns her

living. She seems to have access to a great deal of money, and receives payment from a blind account, every few months."

Doyle stared at him for a moment, because this revelation did not seem to line-up with Acton's sense that Martina was not, in fact, a blackleg. "But—but you don't think this blind account is connected to the Kingsmen or the money-launderin'?"

"No, I don't. I can find no connection between Martina Betancourt and the money-laundering rig. It is almost a shame; if I could, all would be easily explained."

But his words had raised a new and different concern, and Doyle decided there was no time like the present to speak her mind. "It makes me uneasy, Michael—that you know so much about this money-launderin' rig, but at the same time, you say that law enforcement is not closin' in. It sounds a bit as though you're monitorin' it all on your own."

Reacting to her tone, he leaned across his desk to take her hand in his. "Please don't worry, Kathleen."

Small chance of that, but she'd learned from experience that if she came down too hard on his tendency to skim funds from criminal enterprises, he'd only take measures to make it even less likely that she'd ever find out. Instead, she had to be content with the fact that she'd raised her concern, and hopefully he'd think twice before poking his finger in this money-laundering pie; lucky for her, she was worth more to him than all the illicit currency in the world, and thank God fastin'.

Since they'd wandered off-topic, she returned to the main point. "Well, if you do find out that Martina's a bad 'un—and it's hard to imagine this is all a massive coincidence—you'd best tell Williams straightaway, Michael. He may be smitten, but he's no fool, and you can tell he's a bit fashed about it already."

"I will see to Williams, Kathleen; again, please don't worry."

She thought she caught a nuance in his tone, which was

rather a relief; Acton knew the stakes here, and he would look out for Williams, if for no other reason than he knew that Williams was dear to her. She should take a page from his book and trust him to sort it all out—a man had been murdered, after all, and those who'd arranged for it should not escape justice, let the chips fall where they may.

Reminded, she turned her thoughts back to the homicide case which was supposed to be her priority, and shame on her, for letting a personal friendship muddy her waters. "So; Rizzo's was a misdirection murder, because someone's tryin' to frame-up our innocent Savoie. Tell me, husband—is there any chance that Savoie is truly the villain, here?"

"Unlikely."

"Because?" she prodded.

Choosing his words carefully, Acton replied, "Savoie is unlikely to conduct an illegal operation where I have jurisdiction."

The penny dropped, and suddenly Doyle understood exactly why Acton knew straightaway that Savoie was being framed. Although Acton never referred to it, she knew that he'd formed-up several illicit enterprises—gun-smuggling amongst them—by teaming up with the notorious Frenchman. Presumably, the last thing Savoie would do would be to rock that particular boat and commit any major crimes where Acton would be forced to roll him up; it's not every day that you have the opportunity to team up with a DCI on an illegal enterprise, after all, and a criminal must step carefully lest he lose such a valuable connection.

Nazy buzzed in. "I am sorry to interrupt, sir, but the Detective Chief Superintendent and the Assistant Detective Chief Superintendent are here."

"Holy Mother," Doyle said, hurriedly retrieving the soup

cartons. "I'll remove all evidence that we were dilly-dallyin', here."

"No matter; they wish to strategize how to handle PR on the Rizzo case, and how best to move forward."

"Do they know that Rizzo was probably involved in the money-launderin'?" She may as well ask; Acton was not one to keep the chain-of-command in the loop, if it didn't suit his purposes.

"They do. Hence, the strategy session."

She leaned to kiss him. "Well, hence, I will see you later."

He rose and put a hand to her back as they moved toward the door. "I confess I would like to see your portrait finished."

Doyle blinked, as this seemed to be an unlooked-for change of topic. "I haven't heard from Javid," she admitted. "She was that upset about Rizzo's death—mayhap she's still lyin' on her bed and weepin' into one of his jerseys."

He paused before opening the door. "Perhaps we will hold a dinner party to unveil your portrait. Having such a deadline would inspire her to complete the task."

Doyle blinked yet again. "A *dinner party*? A dinner party at our flat?"

"Indeed."

She stared at him in abject surprise. "We don't have people *over*, Michael. Faith, I'm that worried about your mental state, to even suggest such a thing."

"A small gathering," he soothed. "The Javids, along with McGonigal and Mathis, perhaps."

Doyle raised her brows as she suddenly saw the method to his madness. Timothy McGonigal was Acton's oldest friend from university days—a good-natured surgeon who'd recently suffered a disappointment in love. "Now, there's a good thought, Michael; mayhap we could try to match-up Lizzy Mathis with

Tim. He's so nice, he wouldn't care that she's a bit prickly, and he needs someone well-grounded, after the last one."

Smoothly, Acton continued, "Perhaps Savoie could join us, since he is lately in town. And then Williams and Martina Betancourt, so as to round out the numbers."

Staring at him in astonishment, she breathed, "Holy *Mother*, husband—what is it you're up to? You're not hostin' a dinner party, you're rippin' open the seventh seal, and the devil take the hindmost."

He tilted his head in disclaimer. "Surely not. A small gathering of friends."

Nervously, she asked, "Is Savoie wanted for anythin'?"

"Not at present," he soothed.

Katy bar the door, Doyle thought in grave alarm; and then pinned on a smile as he opened the door to greet the waiting brass.

18

—————

The next day Doyle spent the morning at home, which was the part-time arrangement they'd worked out when she'd come back to work after Edward. After she'd lunched with her son, Reynolds called for the driving service, and as she was being ferried into work Acton pinged her on the phone.

"Ho, husband," she answered. "Have you had a chance to come up for air? I can always bring you more soup."

"I am scheduled to meet with the gentleman, and if you would join me, we will see if his tale is helpful."

"The accountant-fellow," Doyle remembered. "Are you leavin' now? Want me to meet you?"

"I thought I'd meet you here, and we could walk, instead."

There was a silence, as Doyle quirked her mouth. Her husband had apparently decided that she needed to exercise more, since Doyle was not one to see the benefit in going to all the trouble. "Fine, then. Have it your way."

"Too late," he teased.

But she would not be drawn, and only replied, "I'll be there in ten."

She rang off, and duly noted that Acton didn't seem to think this informant was going to turn up helpful—particularly since he'd kept the man waiting an extra day. In truth, an unsolicited informant was a mixed blessing, because most times they'd an axe to grind, or were looking to be paid for tips to the police, and so law enforcement always tended to take whatever they had to say with a grain of salt. This one, of course, was a supposed Kingsmen accountant, and so perhaps he was a bit more likely to be on the up-and-up. On the other hand, Acton was already wary, due to the clumsy clues being dropped to catch his attention, hence the decision to have his helpful wife listen-in.

Acton stood on the pavement out front of headquarters, speaking with the PC who was stationed there, and as Doyle emerged from the limousine, he lifted her rucksack to give it to the officer, and then steered her down the pavement. "How does Edward?"

"Edward is excellent—never finer. Although more teeth are comin' in, so he's constantly knee-deep in drool. I should just keep a mop and bucket at the ready, or wear one of those under-water-diver suits—make sure to take off your tie, before you come in."

"I imagine I will be too late to see him again, tonight," he said in apology. "After this week, I should return to a more normal schedule."

"Whist; I know you've your hands full." She glanced up at him. "Anythin' new?"

"Not as yet," he advised.

"Hence this informant, insistin' on himself." She'd decided

that she very much liked using the word "hence." If I've a fancy portrait, she thought fairly, certainly I'm justified in using the occasional fancy word.

"Yes. We shall see."

"Where're we goin', then?" She noted they were walking toward the St James's station, and cautioned, "Tell me we're not ridin' the tube somewhere." Doyle didn't like riding the subway due to the cross-currents of emotion she always experienced in such a crowded space, and Acton was not one to take public transportation under any circumstances.

"No; instead, it was suggested we wait to be contacted near the RAF Memorial on the Embankment."

Doyle lifted her brows. "He's a nervous Nelly, then, to want to meet where it will be open, and crowded. Mayhap he truly has something worthwhile to say."

"We shall see," was all Acton would offer.

They walked in silence for a time—one of the hallmarks of their relationship was the fact that neither felt the need to fill the silence—until Acton offered, "I've made contact with Javid's husband, who manages her commissions. Not only did he accept our invitation for the showing, he also assured me my own portrait will be completed in short order."

"You bribed him," she guessed.

"I did offer an expedition fee," he admitted. "Her work is very much in demand."

Doyle blew out a breath. "So, we're truly havin' a dinner party; faith, I'd half-decided that I hadn't heard you aright."

"We'll be among friends," he soothed. "And the portrait is very well-done."

"You've got some scheme in mind that will turn my hair grey," she countered. "Don't think I'm fooled for one minute, husband."

He made no response, and so she prompted, "Is it your plan to ask a few pointed questions of the fair Martina?"

"I would never make Williams uncomfortable in such a way," he protested with a hint of reproach. "Not at a social gathering; it would be impolite."

The words were true, and she conceded, "I suppose we've got to make the best of it; he's a grown man, and fit to make his own choices, after all."

"One would hope," he agreed.

They came to the Embankment walkway next to the Thames, the area rife with tourists since the weather was holding fine. As they loitered near the Memorial, Doyle asked in a low voice, "Do we know what it is we're lookin' for?"

"We do not," he replied, but seemed very much unconcerned, and Doyle had the sudden and rather unwelcome thought that her husband already knew all there was to know about the Kingsmen's murky finances.

She ventured, "You think this is only another misdirection play, to try and frame-up Savoie?"

He took a quick, keen survey of the immediate area. "I do, but I cannot neglect the possibility that the witness will offer something worthwhile."

"You never know," she agreed, and lifted an idle hand to trace one of the figures on the Memorial. Acton's grandfather had been a part of the RAF's heroic defense, and she was moved to say, "Imagine, having to risk your life again and again, because so many other lives were on the line. It makes someone like Rizzo seem like a paltry excuse, and not so very heroic, in comparison. Especially if he was usin' his fame for evil deeds."

Acton tilted his head in mild disagreement. "Not a valid comparison, perhaps. We will never know how Rizzo would have behaved in wartime."

But Doyle only insisted, "I don't know Michael—a champion should behave like a champion, even if no one knows about it, save God." She lowered her hand. "It's that *hubris* thing, again, remember? Rizzo thought he was untouchable, and so he was slated for a nasty reckonin'."

"IT DOES SEEM akin to a Greek tragedy," he agreed. And—although her husband was merely indulging her—Doyle's scalp started prickling, because Acton suffered from a touch of *hubris*, himself. Faith, when you thought about it, the comparison to Rizzo cut a bit too close to the bone—

They were interrupted by the man who sold boat-tour tickets for Westminster Pier, who approached with all the boldness of someone who hawked tickets for a living. "Oi," he called out. "You're Mike Sinclair?"

Doyle blinked, but Acton simply said, "I am."

"Thought so. A bloke gave me this to give to you." He handed over a large envelope.

Causally, Acton glanced up to take a survey of the area. "How long ago?"

"'Bout half-hour. Gave me a tenner."

Acton thanked the man, and then tucked the envelope under his arm. "Shall we return?"

"Well, there's a disappointment," Doyle observed, placing a hand in the crook of his elbow. "It does look as though this 'gentleman' fellow was just a straw-man to feed you information."

"Documents with no witness foundation," Acton added. "Therefore, inadmissible in court."

She eyed him sidelong. What are the odds there's somethin' in them that incriminates Savoie?"

Acton considered the trees that branched overhead. "I imagine that was the entire point of the exercise."

"Hence," she agreed.

19

This is exactly why you don't have people over, Doyle thought, as she pinned on a smile and tried to look pleased. She never did very well in social groups and, since Acton was well-aware of this fact, she could only surmise that he felt this dinner party was more important, for some reason, than his poor wife's peace of mind.

Dressed in her best black cocktail dress—which also happened to be the only one she owned—Doyle stood self-consciously beside her completed portrait as Javid graciously accepted compliments. The woman wore a rose-colored silk hijab for the occasion, and you'd never guess that beneath that serene exterior beat the heart of a Rizzo-fanatic.

She hasn't quite recovered from his tragic death, Doyle decided, because—although she hid it well—the artist seemed wracked, and profoundly unhappy. Of course, if Doyle were married to Mr. Javid she'd probably be feeling much the same way—Javid's husband had proved to be brusque and rather unfriendly, tending to avoid conversation and treating his wife with an autocratic indifference that bordered on contempt.

Reynolds doesn't like him, Doyle decided; I can tell by the angle of his bow. It's subtle, but it's a snub—a butler-snub, which can't be very obvious by necessity.

"Shall we move into the living room?" Acton asked when the viewing had concluded.

"Yes—please," Doyle seconded, and wondered what it was that her husband had planned. That he had some sort of plan seemed evident; the wretched man didn't want to throw a dinner party any more than she did.

His hand on her back, her husband brought his head down close to hers. "All right?" he murmured.

"I am perfectly fine," she assured him in a stout tone, pronouncing it "foine" so as to tease him. "Not to worry." Then, because he hadn't mentioned it, she asked, "Am I to listen-in to anyone in particular?"

"No," he said, and it was true. "Instead I am trying to sort out a few things."

"Savoie's not here," she noted, eying him.

"He will be," was her husband's mild reply, and then his attention was drawn away by Mr. Javid, whom Doyle didn't wish to speak to, and so she drifted over to the sofa grouping where Williams and Martina Betancourt were politely conversing with Timothy McGonigal.

Happy to rest her poor high-heeled feet, Doyle sat down to join them as she signaled to Reynolds for coffee. She had to signal twice, because Reynolds did not think it appropriate to serve coffee during cocktail hour, but Doyle was in need of fortification and she didn't drink alcohol—although it was possible she may rethink this resolution, after another hour or so.

Although Lizzy Mathis had been invited as a dinner guest, she was currently working in the kitchen so as to lend Reynolds a hand. Reynolds did not mind this intrusion, because—although Mathis was a fine cook in her own right—she was perfectly willing to obey all instruction by the exacting butler, which was much appreciated; it wouldn't do to have more than one king in the kitchen.

Thoughtfully, Doyle lifted her gaze to watch Mathis, as she steadied the oven rack with a towel whilst Reynolds lifted-in the tray containing the Cornish game hens. Mayhap if this Timothy-matchmaking business didn't work out, she could set-up Mathis with Reynolds. He'd be very loyal, one would think, and she could do worse.

Her attention came back to the conversation at hand, because Martina was making an effort to draw out Timothy McGonigal, her voice warm and interested. "I believe you belong to *The Curing League*, Dr. McGonigal."

"Why, yes—yes," the doctor answered, a bit flustered. He said to Williams in explanation, "A charitable medical group; we provide free surgery to those in need who cannot afford it."

She's done her homework; you've got to give her that, thought Doyle, a bit surprised. Mayhap she's trying to curry favor with Williams' friends, which would be an encouraging sign for the romance.

"Such well-respected work—helping those who most need help," Martina added, and Doyle was surprised to realize that—beneath her sincere approval—the girl was being insincere.

"It's nothing, really," McGonigal protested, embarrassed. "I am happy to help where I may."

Oh, thought Doyle—that's interesting; he seems a bit grave, and truly doesn't want to talk about it.

"Is the *League* affiliated with any particular hospital?" Williams asked politely.

"No, we're not affiliated—not at present, anyway. In the past, we operated a free clinic through Holy Trinity Church—before it was shut down, of course—and so now we have to request operating room time at various medical clinics throughout the city. But we're hoping to set up another home clinic soon—perhaps through St. Michael's."

Interesting, thought Doyle, sipping on her coffee and averting her eyes; he's troubled about it, for some reason.

"Kath used to volunteer at Holy Trinity Clinic," Williams offered.

"A short-lived stint," Doyle admitted. "I was all thumbs."

"Oh—I would love to volunteer for the *League*," Martina offered.

"Why, that would be much appreciated, Ms. Betancourt," McGonigal replied. "We could always use an extra hand."

"Does that mean I'll have to volunteer, too?" Williams joked.

"Of course, it does," Martina teased him with a smile. "Although the patients may not want a police officer in their midst. You'd have to play it down."

At this juncture, latecomer Philippe Savoie approached the group, and paused in a casual manner directly behind Martina's chair so as to light up a cigarette. Timothy McGonigal had met Savoie on previous occasions, but was thankfully unaware that the Frenchman was an enduring feature on various law enforcement Watch Lists, and so with a smile, the doctor offered, "Hallo again, Mr. Savoie; we were speaking of Kathleen's volunteer work at Holy Trinity Clinic."

"Ah, yes," Savoie said, and drew on his cigarette. "It was there I made the meeting with Madame Acton."

This, in a veiled reference to the fateful day that Doyle had first met Savoie, when he'd saved her from an attacker.

Surprised, McGonigal asked, "You were a volunteer, sir?"

Amused, Savoie inclined his head. "*Bien sûr.*"

"Well, good for you," McGonigal said, very pleased. "I'm sorry I didn't recognize you, but I didn't always get to meet all the volunteers."

Doyle decided it was past time to change the subject, since she didn't like the way that Savoie was hovering behind Martina, with that young woman having made no acknowledgment of his presence. She'd the uneasy feeling that Acton was keenly interested in putting Savoie in the same room as Williams' sweetheart, and presumably there was no love lost between the two. Doyle could only hope that whatever-it-was, it wouldn't lead to an out-and-out donnybrook since Williams had already been shown to have a hair-trigger for fisticuffs, when it came to Savoie.

Doyle's uneasiness was even further compounded by the fact that—despite Martina's continuing friendly-toward-McGonigal conversation—Doyle was well-aware that the other girl was suddenly on high alert.

Quickly, Doyle offered, "Well, the St. Michael's construction project is at a standstill, I'm afraid, so I don't know how fast any new clinic is goin' to rise up." Best not mention that as an added complication, the construction company seemed more interested in fencing stolen goods than putting hammer to nail. "Father John is that fashed about how long it's takin'."

"And of course, there was Rizzo's death," McGonigal shook his head sadly. "Poor man; you'd think he'd have so much to live for."

"You must be careful not to pick at that wound," Martina said lightly. "I believe Mr. Savoie is an investor."

"This is true," Savoie said, and drew on his cigarette with supreme indifference.

Martina continued, "Indeed, we should spare a thought for

the poor investors; there'll be a fortune lost in merchandizing alone."

"I did buy a jersey for Edward," McGonigal confessed.

"Did you? Well, he'll be none the wiser," Doyle assured him. "He'll love it."

Martina had apparently decided it would be bad form to continue throwing veiled darts Savoie's way, and instead she addressed Doyle. "Will Edward make an appearance tonight, Kathleen?"

This, of course, was to be ardently avoided, since her son was a rolling ball of destruction and sticky fingers. Doyle hedged, "I wasn't plannin' on it. He's downstairs, and he'll be put to bed soon."

Martina smiled. "That is a shame; Thomas tells me he's a very engaging little boy."

"Williams is very good with children," Doyle offered, seeing an opening and taking it. "He's got a quiverful of younger cousins who think he's the cock's comb."

"Well, there's a good sign," Martina teased with a coy glance at Williams, and Mathis could be heard to drop a pan in the kitchen.

"We took your Emile to the zoo, once, Philippe," Doyle offered, hoping to diffuse this awkward situation, with Savoie standing behind Martina, and neither one apparently willing to move an inch, or address the other. "It was a close-run thing; between Emile and Thomas' cousins, we were lucky no one climbed into the tiger cage."

"Ah, yes?" Savoie said, and negligently blew out a puff of smoke that curled around the seated girl's head.

"Here," said Williams in a constrained tone. "Let me find you an ash-tray, Mr. Savoie."

But Martina only smiled. "Not on my account, Thomas.

Dunhills, I think; it takes me back—it was the brand of ciga-rettes my father smoked."

Doyle could only admire yet another dart thrown at Savoie, and thought in reluctant admiration that the young woman never seemed cowed, no matter the situation. I should take a leaf, she thought, because even though it's my stupid dinner party, I'm cowed to pieces.

Williams was apparently also in the not-cowed category, as he said to Savoie, "Perhaps you could move into the kitchen, Mr. Savoie?" The question seemed a little too pointed for good manners.

"You must call me Philippe," Savoie demurred. "We have much in common."

There was a tense moment of silence.

"Dinner is served," Reynolds announced.

20

T hey sat down to dinner, with Reynolds in his element as he began to serve-out the bisque, starting at the table's head.

Savoie was seated next to Doyle, with Mathis on his other side, and Doyle noted with some surprise that Mathis was a bit tense, beneath her calm and efficient façade. Mayhap she didn't appreciate being set-up with Timothy McGonigal, and small blame to her; Doyle could appreciate the girl's not wanting to be the subject of such an obviously contrived situation. On the other hand, she was loyal to the House of Acton, and so probably felt she'd little choice, if Acton was pushing her in McGonigal's direction. It didn't help matters that Mathis' gaze kept straying to Williams, who didn't appear aware that anyone other than Martina existed.

Timothy McGonigal would make a nice husband, Doyle thought stoutly. Not to my taste, of course, but as my mother used to say, there's a lid for every pot. And besides, not everyone's cut out for that sort of overwhelming, nothing-else-matters love affair; having a practical arrangement with mutual respect is certainly nothing to complain about. Carefully, she avoided thinking about how truly awful it would be if she and Acton had a practical arrangement instead of a torrid, sneaking-away-to-have-sex sort of arrangement. *Love is a crackin' wonderment,* she thought, and not for the first time; *I am lucky beyond all reckoning.*

She looked over to her husband and found his gaze resting upon her. *He's worried that I'm hating this,* she thought, and smiled her reassurance. *I* am *hating this, of course, but that's neither here nor there; he's got something up his sleeve, and whatever it is, it's more important than humoring his foolish wife. Therefore, I'd best stop being such a baby, and start paying a bit more attention.*

But—try as she might—she couldn't see what Acton's aim was. It seemed to her that everyone in attendance was masking their uneasiness—except for McGonigal, who was speaking to the artist and her husband with deep respect. Javid herself was not happy to be here—even though she was the guest of honor, and seated at Acton's right. Beneath her quiet graciousness, she seemed a bit bleak, and distracted.

She's rather like Rizzo, Doyle thought in sympathy; *by all accounts she should be on top of the world, but instead she's steeped in misery, no doubt in large part because she's been burdened with such a husband.*

Reynolds appeared at her shoulder so as to ladle out the bisque, and Savoie took this opportunity to address the servant in a low voice. "Monsieur," he said as he discreetly placed an envelope on the table. "I must speak of my many thanks for your help to my son, when he stayed here."

Stiffly, Reynolds inclined his head not quite as far as he usually did. "I have no need of additional payment, I assure you, Mr. Savoie. Master Emile is a delightful young man, and I quite enjoyed our time together."

Doyle hurriedly changed the subject lest Reynolds be struck by lightning for such an out-and-out untruth. "Emile's grown so much, Philippe. It's amazin'—isn't it, Lizzy?" Lizzy Mathis had also pitched-in with the taking-care of Emile, much to her credit.

"Indeed, he has," Mathis agreed politely. "I think he favors you, Mr. Savoie."

Savoie bowed his head in pleased acknowledgment, despite the fact he didn't share a single molecule of common ancestry with his son. "*Merci*, Mademoiselle Mathis. I have yet to thank you for *les secours;* you are *l'héroïne*, I think."

Her cheeks slightly pink, Mathis demurred, "It was a group effort, certainly."

Since Reynolds had moved on to serve Mathis, Doyle took the opportunity to admonish Savoie in an undertone, "Don't be bribin' the servants, Philippe; now Reynolds is goin' to be all offended, and I'll have to jolly him up."

But Savoie was unrepentant, and his gaze rested on the butler. "It is the rare man, who does not appreciate his reward."

"Well, Reynolds is indeed a rare man, so don't you dare insult him." Crossly, she added, "And for heaven's sake, don't flirt with Mathis; faith, that's all we need." After reflection, she added, "And she's not bribable, either, if that's what you're about."

"You have such suspicions," Savoie chided, amused. "*Très malheureusement.*"

"You're a wily one, and no mistakin'," Doyle retorted, unrepentant. "And so's Acton, for that matter." She decided she may as well ask, "Why on earth would he bring you here? What's he about?"

In a Gallic gesture, the Frenchman shrugged slightly. "There are many secrets, at this table."

With mixed emotions, she eyed him, having come to this same ominous conclusion herself. "What sort of secrets?"

Again, he shrugged. "I do not know if I should say."

In a low voice, she prodded, "Does Acton know about these secrets?"

He tilted his head in mild rebuke, to remind her that he wasn't about to grass on her husband, which she took in good part, and therefore abandoned her interrogation. Instead, she took a covert glance down the table as she lifted her spoon. "He must be movin' the chess pieces in place, which is why he's assembled such an unholy assortment of people. I wish I knew what he was up to—it makes me very uneasy."

"I have the secrets, too," her companion confessed, almost apologetically.

"Yes—you had a previous run-in with Martina, apparently." Doyle hesitated, and then added in an undertone, "If you know anythin' to her detriment, you should try to stop antagonizin' Williams for half-a-minute and tell him what it is that you know. Williams is—well, Williams is a friend, and I'd hate to see him hurt."

"Me, I know nothing to her detriment," her companion replied, and it was true.

Rather surprised, Doyle observed, "Well, she definitely doesn't want to speak with you."

"*Non*," he agreed, and smiled his thin smile.

Probing, Doyle asked, "Is she afraid of you, for some reason?"

"*Non.*" His gaze rested on the other girl for a moment, where she was deep in conversation with Javid's husband, who looked as though he wished he were anywhere but at this particular dinner-party. "She fears no one, that one. She holds the sword."

"What sword is that?" Suspicious, she added, "I hope that's not an off-color remark, Philippe."

He cocked his head. "What is this 'off-color'?"

Oh-oh, Doyle thought; serves me right. "Saucy," she suggested.

He raised his brows in confusion.

Nothin' for it. She leaned in to whisper. "Sexual. A sexual remark."

"Ah—I see." Greatly amused, he shook his head. "No—she is not the sexual."

This, strangely enough, was true—or at least Savoie thought it to be true, and it seemed an odd thing to say, since Martina was clearly here as Williams' date, not to mention she'd some sort of history with Savoie, himself.

But Doyle was to receive no further insights, as—with a show of resolution—Savoie laid down his soup spoon. "*Bien,*" he said. "Because you ask me, I will help your friend."

Oh-oh, thought Doyle, who harbored a bad feeling about this, but before she could restrain him, Savoie breached all decorum and leaned to address Martina, down the table. "We meet again, Madame."

At this unlooked-for interruption, a small silence settled over the guests, and Martina turned away from her conversation with Mr. Javid. With a polite smile, she offered, "Yes, Mr. Savoie. It is good to see you again."

Interestingly enough, the girl's generic greeting was not exactly true, but it was not exactly false, either, which did not mesh with the cold shoulder she'd offered Savoie all evening.

Before Doyle could puzzle this out, however, Savoie lifted his wine glass in Martina's direction.

"Tell me, Madame; have you heard news of your husband?"

21

T here was a small, shocked silence.

"I have not, Mr. Savoie," Martina answered calmly. Then, to Williams, "Unfortunately, my husband is missing, and is presumed dead."

"I see," Williams replied, trying to keep an even tone. It could not have been more obvious that Williams had not been apprised of this significant little fact.

Rescue came from an unexpected source, as Mathis rebuked Savoie, "Not dinner table conversation, perhaps, Mr. Savoie."

"*Pardon*," Savoie said, and lowered his head to address his soup.

McGonigal stepped into the breach by turning to Javid and asking about her training in Paris, and the other guests hurriedly followed suit, with the exception of Savoie and Williams, who were as silent as the others were artificially chatty.

Holy *Mother*, thought Doyle, who was thoroughly distracted even though Mathis was doggedly trying to have a conversation with her, speaking across Savoie as he ate his soup. Poor Williams—what a *massive* blow, and shame on Martina, for leading him down the garden path. Although—although in her defense, it would depend on how long the husband had been missing—mayhap it had been years. And it's not as though she'd been making a dead run at Williams, in the first place. Still and all, it seemed a bit shocking, that the girl wouldn't mention her marital status whilst Williams was clearly intent on courting her.

Savoie interrupted Doyle's thoughts by turning to her and asking in too loud a tone, "Have you yet learned to swim, Madame Acton?"

"No," said Doyle shortly, wondering why on earth he'd bring up such a subject.

Leaning back in his chair, Savoie regarded her in mild disbelief. "You must learn to swim. You may need to make the jump again, sometime."

"Faith, I hope not." In as hearty a tone as she could manage, Doyle continued, "Once was enough."

As could be imagined, the other guests regarded Savoie with varying degrees of disapproval–save Martina, who had lowered her face.

"I'll second that—it wouldn't hurt to learn to swim," McGonigal offered, laboring to smooth over the awkwardness. "Safety first, Kathleen."

"I suppose you've the right of it," Doyle conceded, deciding that it wanted only this—that everyone would start talking about the *stupid* bridge-jumping incident. Mother a' mercy, but she should have just left Munoz to drown and deemed it a deed well-done.

"Technically, you managed it quite well even without knowing," Mathis pointed out fairly.

"More like dumb luck," Doyle admitted. "It's true; I should learn for Edward's sake."

Savoie nodded sagely, and it suddenly occurred to Doyle that Martina—Martina was *amused*, again, which was why she now held a hand across her mouth and kept her gaze lowered. A very strange sense of humor, that one had, if she thought the stupid bridge-jumping incident was something to snigger at.

With the attitude of someone attempting to make amends, Savoie addressed Williams in a conciliatory tone. "And you? You made the jump too, yes?"

In a clipped tone, Williams replied, "I did."

"Came to my rescue," Doyle agreed, trying to catch Williams' eye with a smile. "Saved me and Munoz, both. Faith, what a night that was—"

"It was daytime," Williams corrected.

"Dusk, more accurately," said Mathis.

"It's truly not important," Doyle offered hastily. "What's important is that it was much appreciated."

"*Eh bien*," Savoie agreed. "*Très héroïque.* Madame Acton owes you the thanks, yes?"

It was a strange thing to say, and the words seemed to linger in the air.

"Faith, I owe Thomas a massive debt, and so does Munoz," Doyle joked. "He'll never pay for lunch again."

With a chuckle, Savoie bowed his head. "*Exactement.*"

Apparently, Williams didn't appreciate the thread of amusement in Savoie's tone, and it seemed that he'd imbibed too much wine to overlook it. "I'll thank you to mind your own business," he replied tersely. "No one owes anybody anything—I was happy to be able to help."

"*Much* appreciated," Doyle offered brightly.

"*Très héroïque,*" Savoie repeated in an ironic tone, and smiled into his wine glass.

Mathis leaned in to admonish in a low tone, "You mustn't provoke Mr. Williams, Mr. Savoie."

With an air of suppressed belligerence, Williams ground out, "He's not provoking me; he's lucky no one's arrested him yet."

Again, a small, shocked silence fell across the table, and Doyle hurriedly explained to everyone, "Not that Mr. Savoie is *currently* wanted—not for any major crimes, leastways."

Savoie raised a brow as though he was inclined to disagree with this assessment, but was too polite to do so.

In a mild tone, Acton—who'd been a silent observer, up till now—addressed Williams. "That's enough."

Struggling to control himself, Williams fixed his gaze on the table. "I beg your pardon, sir."

Martina laid a hand on his arm. "Perhaps we should go—"

"No," said Williams, as he abruptly pulled his arm away. "I'm fine."

The remainder of the meal passed in the awkward manner that one would expect, with the other guests making a mighty attempt to pretend as though nothing was amiss, and everyone declining after-dinner drinks so as to clear out with all speed.

It was no surprise whatsoever that the fair Martina sought to be the first to depart—Williams had not even looked her way, after the revelation about the woman's erstwhile husband.

"It is probably best that I leave," she said in a quiet aside to Doyle. "Please accept my sincerest apologies, Kathleen."

Doyle mustered up a polite face, and offered, "Whist, Martina—the least said, the soonest mended. I'm sorry Savoie put you on the spot like he did."

If she was hoping for a revelation or two, she was not to receive any hint of such. The other girl only suggested in a low tone, "Thomas may need to lie down for a bit."

"Two minds with the same thought," Doyle assured her. "I'll see to him, never fear."

Martina left, and it did seem as though Acton's mild scolding had been effective, since Williams sat in quiet conversation with McGonigal, and didn't deign to even look up when Savoie left immediately after Martina did—which was much appreciated, and the first thing the Frenchman had done all night that showed a modicum of social awareness.

The Javids then rose to leave, and whilst Acton was occupied saying his farewells, Doyle pulled Reynolds aside. "Should we put Williams in the downstairs bedroom and keep an eye on him? He's a diabetic, remember, and in no shape to drive. I can ask Timothy to give him a once-over, just to make sure—he's had such a blow, poor man."

Reynolds nodded, and then went over to address Williams in a kindly tone. "If you would come this way, Inspector Williams. A shower may be in order, perhaps."

"Don't be ridiculous," said Williams, who pulled his arm away from Reynolds' grasp and then had to steady himself with a hand on the back of a chair. "I'm quite all right—I'll be off."

"We've a fancy new suite, downstairs," Doyle teased him gently. "Come down and check it out."

"No. I'm leaving." He then bent his head for a moment. "Sorry, Kath."

"I'm the one who's sorry," she replied, and touched his arm. "At least let me call the drivin' service for you."

"I'll see him home, Lady Acton," Mathis volunteered. "Just give me his coat, and we'll be off."

"I'm *perfectly* able to drive," Williams declared, eying her askance.

"We'll see," soothed Mathis, and steered him out the door.

22

W hilst Reynolds was clearing away the remains of the wreckage, Doyle pulled Acton into their bedroom so as to conduct a post-mortem out of the servant's hearing. "*Holy* Mother of God, Michael—I would have appreciated a warnin'."

But Acton only seemed mildly amused. "Acquit me of having any foreknowledge, Kathleen."

She stared at him in surprise. "You didn't know Martina was married?"

"I did not."

Doyle made a derisive sound. "That's doin' it too brown, husband; there must be a reason you brought this wretched mish-mash together, waitin' to see what's goin' to happen like some sort of upside-down morality play. Spill."

But his response surprised her yet again, as he leaned back against the desk and crossed his arms. "I was as surprised as anyone." He paused. "With the exception of Savoie, of course."

Lifting her brows, she regarded him in confusion. "Did you

at least find out whatever-it-was that you were hopin' to find out?"

"Not as yet."

Crossly, Doyle observed, "Well, there's a first, and now we've the battle-scars to show for it. Are you sayin' that Savoie's never told you he's got some sort of history with Martina?"

"He has not."

Doyle considered this rather alarming piece of information. "Faith—that's crackin' strange—and I had the impression he was teasin' her, or somethin', with his bridge-jumpin' talk. It's all we need, for Savoie to be in league with her against you."

She intended the remark as a joke, but she saw that her husband considered the suggestion seriously, because—after all —Acton didn't trust anyone, save his fair bride.

After a moment, he shook his head slightly. "Unlikely."

But Doyle's mind had already leapt to another unwelcome thought, and she ventured, "Could Martina be the one who's framin' Savoie? Is that why they're crossin' swords?"

Judging by his lack of reaction, it seemed clear that her husband had already considered this aspect, because of course he had—he was Acton, after all, and was highly motivated to discover who was trying to send the Frenchman to prison, since that road could also lead to Acton's sharing a cell with him.

He took a slow breath. "I do not know, but I am skeptical. Martina seems to have no culpability when it comes to the money-laundering rig, and so it is unclear why she would be involved in Rizzo's death, or in the attempt to cast blame elsewhere."

Knitting her brow, Doyle had to agree with this reasoning. "Right. Well, that's a relief, I suppose—Williams is in love with a bigamist, but not necessarily a murderer."

He tilted his head in mild disagreement. "Not a bigamist; at least not as yet."

But Doyle was not willing to give the mysterious young woman any benefit of the doubt. "She's a two-timer, then. Three-timer, if she's got a history with Savoie, although I suppose it's not at all clear how they know each other."

"No, it is not."

Doyle eyed him. "Seems a bit alarmin' that he hasn't told you, Michael."

But her husband didn't seem as worried about this fact as his wife was. "Not necessarily; recall that Savoie operates under his own code of honor—indeed, you have experienced its effects, yourself."

This, of course, was undeniable. Savoie had saved the fair Doyle's life with no incentive to do so, and then had refrained from exposing their connection for no other reason than he knew she'd be in trouble for it.

Slowly, she ventured, "So; you think he's coverin' for Martina, for some reason?"

Thoughtfully, he gazed out the window at the streetlights below. "I don't know. But I would be very much surprised if Savoie would choose her interests over mine, so I can only assume that he's keeping her secrets out of a sense of chivalry, or something similar."

She cocked a skeptical brow. "Not what one would expect from the likes of him, Michael."

But her husband only tilted his head. "Again, look no further than his dealings with you."

She had to acknowledge the truth of this. "I suppose that's true. And don't forget Emile—Savoie took in someone else's loose-end child without a hint of hesitation."

Acton nodded. "That, too."

"He's RC," she mused. "That might be the reason. Deep down in the dark recesses somewhere, he's RC, and has an RC's dread of being held accountable."

"Dread?" Acton teased. "That seems a bit strong."

"Oh, they try to dress it up with nice words, Michael, but we all know that we're bein' threatened with hellfire, starin' us straight in the face. Mark me."

He smiled and came over to clasp her fondly about the waist, pulling her against him to kiss her, but she suddenly pulled away. "Oh—oh, there was somethin' I wanted to tell you—what was it?" Doyle shut her eyes for a moment, willing herself to remember. "With all the other fuss, there's somethin' I'm forgettin'—I should have made a note on the napkin, although Reynolds would've looked all askance, like he does when I pick up the wrong fork."

"Was it something Savoie said?" he prompted. "Or Mathis?"

She lifted her head. "Oh—oh, now I remember, Michael. Javid is unhappy. More than unhappy, actually; she's sunk in misery, poor thing."

Acton ducked his chin, thinking about this, because he had great respect for Doyle's perceptive abilities. "Javid's reaction to Rizzo's death did seem excessive, but I could find no connection."

Doyle ventured, "Has she done his portrait? Mayhap she feels connected, after somethin' like that." She paused, and duly noted that her scalp was prickling. "I think her paintings mean a lot to her."

"I will look into it."

Fairly, Doyle pointed out, "She may be miserable because her husband's a horror-show."

Acton nodded. "I think he very much resents the fact is wife is so talented. During our conversation, he never mentioned her work at all."

Doyle made a face. "Shame on him; he should be her champion, instead of jealous of her."

"Indeed. On the other hand, he was also very interested in any information he could glean about Rizzo's death."

This was surprising, but—as Doyle had witnessed firsthand —football fans turned up where you least expected them. "Mayhap that's what keeps their marriage together, then—their love of football. You and I should take up some sort of hobby, so as to save ours."

"I believe we already have one." This said with some significance.

"Sex doesn't count, Michael," she declared in mild exasperation. "Mayhap we should take up birdwatchin', or such. Somethin' peaceful and quiet, where there's not a lot of people about."

With some remorse, he pulled her to him, so as to rest his mouth against the top of her head. "I am sorry this was such an uncomfortable evening for you."

"Whist; mine was nothin' compared to poor Williams'. And there's somethin' else—somethin' else I needed to tell you." She brought her palms to her eyes for a moment, thinking. "Somethin' about what Savoie said."

"About the missing husband?"

"No—well, yes, in a way." Remembering, Doyle slowly brought her hands down. "It was a remark he made about Martina. She's datin' Williams, she has a missin' husband, and she has some sort of past with Savoie, but Savoie made a remark about her not bein'—not bein' *sexual*, or somethin', and it was true."

Understandably, Doyle's husband was very much surprised. "You were speaking of sexual matters with Savoie?"

"No—no, Michael, for *heaven's* sake. I said somethin', and he misinterpreted it—it's like the blind leadin' the blind, when the two of us are talkin'—and so I had to explain what I meant, and then he made the remark." She frowned, remembering. "When he said it, I wondered, for a moment, if she was a nun; but that makes no sense, in light of the trail of broken hearts she's left in her wake."

Thinking this over, Acton offered slowly, "I am reluctant to ask Savoie absent something more concrete. They may have had an affair, which would explain why he is willing to keep her secrets."

"No, that's not it," she said immediately, and then wondered why she was so certain. "But he does admire her, in his way. He admires brave women."

"Brave?" he repeated.

"Yes," she confirmed thoughtfully. "Brave. In fact, that's what started the whole misinterpretation-of-a-remark business; he said Martina wasn't afraid of anythin' because she 'holds the sword'. I asked him what he meant, but he never gave me an answer; instead he was on to the next thing, which was to ruin poor Williams' night."

Straightening up, Acton gazed out the window, considering this. "She holds the sword? The sword of Damocles, perhaps?"

She eyed him. "As if I'd have a *clue* what that means, Michael."

"It is a Greek myth—the sword is suspended overhead by a thread, in a metaphor for impending doom. If she holds the sword, that would mean she has the means to ruin her target."

Doubtfully, she ventured, "I don't think Savoie is a Greek-myth sort of person, Michael. That's more like somethin' you would say."

"Fair enough. Do you have any idea what he meant?"

"No—although her necklace—remember? She wears a necklace that looks like a fanciful Celtic cross? I suppose you could say that it looks a bit like a sword."

He cocked his head, thinking. "I did not notice."

"Well, I think it's the only jewelry she wears, but it was covered-up by her neckline, tonight."

He turned to open his desk drawer. "Could you draw it for me?"

She made a face. "I'm not much of an artist, Michael."

"Just close enough to do an image search," he coaxed. "It may be important."

Frowning, she applied pencil to paper and sketched the pendant as best she could remember. "There—it was somethin' like that."

He studied it for a moment. "Nothing with which I am familiar."

"I may not have it right, Michael," she warned.

"Let's run an image search." He sat at the desk, and opened his laptop to suit action to word. After a moment, it seemed that he had a hit, because suddenly he leaned forward, his brows drawn together.

"What?" she asked, sensing his deep surprise.

"The Order of Santiago," he replied thoughtfully. "An ancient Roman Catholic Order out of Spain."

Astonished, Doyle exclaimed, "Holy *Mother*; that *can't* be a coincidence, Michael. Then she *is* a nun?"

Acton leaned back in his chair. "It is of interest that neither her connection to this Order nor her marriage shows up in a background search."

Doyle could only agree; anyone with the ability to alter the information that law enforcement could find on-line meant two things; first, that they had a very sophisticated knowledge of technology, and second, that they were no doubt hiding something from the aforementioned law enforcement.

Doyle ventured, "If she's in a Holy Order but she's scrubbed her background, could she be in intelligence, somewhere? A spy-nun? Is there such a thing?"

He glanced at her. "You would know better than I."

Doyle shook her head, slightly. "Then I vote 'no'—hard to imagine a nun who would go about bearin' false witness, left and right." She paused, thinking this over. "And besides, when she spoke of her husband, it was true—she had a husband, and he is indeed missin'."

Thoughtfully, Acton looked out the window at the night sky. "I think it may be time to pay a follow-up visit to Father John. A routine matter, to give him an update on the Rizzo suicide."

This was unexpected; Acton was not one to follow-up on routine matters, being as he had better things to do. Suspiciously, Doyle asked, "Are you goin' on a fishin' expedition, to see if he knows anythin' about the fair Martina?"

"No; instead, I would very much like to touch on Father Ambrose's background."

Doyle stared at him in dawning comprehension. "Father Ambrose, who got himself murdered."

He bowed his head. "The very same."

The connection hadn't occurred to her, but she could see where her husband's mind was going; Father Ambrose was the elderly priest who'd studied in Spain, and had been involved, to some extent, in the vengeance-murders they'd recently investigated—the same vengeance-murders where Martina was also somehow involved. It did seem to be an amazing coincidence, and Acton rather famously didn't believe in coincidences.

With some trepidation, Doyle ventured, "So; the plan is to hoodwink a priest into betrayin' another priest's confession? Have you forgot what I just told you about the hellfire, husband?"

"All hellfire will be kept to a minimum," he assured her.

23

Once again, Doyle and Acton were seated in Father John's office at St. Michael's. Acton had given the priest a brief update on the investigation surrounding Rizzo's death, and the priest now confided, "I'll be that happy when this whole ballyhoo has died down; we've had a healthy crowd of visitors comin' in—they want to see where he died, of course—and I have to explain that the sacristy is off-limits to the public."

The priest shook his head in wonder. "A lot of people leavin' flowers, and notes—and footballs, of all things. I didn't know what to do with them, at first, but now I donate them to the local children's hospital. I set-up a continuin' novena for the repose of his soul—nine days was not enough, apparently. It's an odd thing, to be sure, but you see it, sometimes; people decide some-one's a saint, despite all evidence to the contrary."

"Well, he was the youngest player in the Champion's League to get a hundred caps," Doyle noted. "Love takes many a form, and is a mighty force."

"I don't know as this truly counts as 'love', lass," the priest offered doubtfully. "These grievin' people never truly knew the man, after all."

But Doyle held firm to her point. "Everyone loves the blessed saints, Father, despite not knowin' 'em. And a ton of people love me, due to the whole bridge-jumpin' incident." She paused, and with an air of wisdom, added, "Hence."

With a nod, Father John conceded this point. "I suppose that's true, lass. Love takes on many shapes and guises—we see it in my business, and no doubt you see it in yours, too."

"Indeed." Since Acton was not one to wax philosophical, he pulled-up the image of the Cross of Santiago on his mobile phone with no further ado. "Are you familiar with this symbol, Father?"

"Ambrose," Father John said immediately, and then leaned back in his chair to say with some firmness, "I can't break the seal of the confessional, Michael."

"There you go," said Doyle to Acton, in an I-told-you-so tone.

"Of course not," Acton soothed. "But if you could tell me what you know about his Order, it would be very helpful with respect to a pending case."

Father John ran a hand over his face as he considered what to say. "They're out of Spain; an old and respected Order. It was founded by St. James—the Spanish call him 'Santiago', and that's where the name comes from."

The penny dropped, and Doyle said "Isn't Spain where the pilgrims go, to walk the 'Way of St. James'?"

The priest nodded. "Indeed, lass. There's a route for pilgrims that's been there since medieval times—it attracts many of the devout, every year."

"The Order is well-funded?" asked Acton, who was clearly intent on keeping his companions on-topic.

Father John raised his brows at the question. "I've no idea." He thought about it for a moment. "Ambrose spoke of the cathedral in Salamanca, where he went to seminary—he said it was a beautiful place, with a fine collection of priceless artwork."

"No priceless artwork anywhere at St. Brigid's," Doyle wryly noted.

"Nor here, either," Father John agreed with a small smile. He then explained, "There's a difference of opinion, amongst the religious Orders—and it's been there since it all got started. Some of the devout believe that religious artwork constitutes a 'graven image' and so runs afoul of the Commandments. Others believe that the art is only another means to glorify God."

But Acton was not as interested in religious points of contention as he was in major crimes. "In law enforcement, we often see fine art used in lieu of currency, for money-laundering operations."

Father John stared at him in surprise. "Is that so? You'll not be tellin' me that the Order of Santiago is doin' *money-launderin*'?"

Acton met his gaze. "Is it possible?"

The priest hurriedly disclaimed, "Oh, no—no, I'd be very much surprised. Instead, they've the reputation of bein' very much on the side of the angels. Faith, in the old days, the Order of Santiago was one of the military wings servin' the Vatican, like the Crusaders were. That's why they've a sword, in their symbol."

Doubtfully, Doyle ventured, "If they're swingin' a sword about, that doesn't much sound like the side of the angels, Father."

Shrugging, the priest countered, "I suppose it's all a matter of perspective, child. Throughout history, plenty of Catholics were on-board with smitin' the enemies of the Church. And our very own St. Michael is famous for swingin' a mighty sword."

"Indeed, he is," Doyle agreed, and carefully did not look at her husband.

The elderly priest gazed off into the corner of the room for a moment, and then shook his head. "I'll not believe Ambrose was involved in somethin' like money-launderin', even if it was for the greater glory of God. More like he'd be puttin' a stop to it, and in no uncertain terms."

"Thank you, Father," said Acton, as he rose to offer his hand. "You've been most helpful."

The priest escorted them out through the nave, and as they passed by the white-stone statues of the saints, standing in their various niches, Doyle reflected, "The people who are fussin' about 'graven images' in artwork must be doubly unhappy that we've got statues in every nook and cranny."

"Another point of contention," the priest conceded. "Often raised by other Christian denominations."

Doyle paused, suddenly struck. "These statues aren't painted —they're all plain white marble."

"Alabaster, lass," the priest admitted. "Marble is very dear."

But Doyle was distracted by the prickling of her scalp. "Lizzy Mathis found a trace of paint in the basement—some sort of artwork-poxy, or somethin'. We thought it was meant to touch up the statues, but that can't be, since the statues aren't painted in the first place."

"That they're not," Father John agreed.

But Doyle paused in surprise, because she could sense a sudden, strong surge of dismay emanating from her husband. She glanced at him, but he said nothing, only thanked the priest again before they left to go outside.

On pins and needles, Doyle could hardly wait until they

were outside on the pavement before asking in a low tone, "What about the paint evidence? What is it you're thinkin'?"

But Acton was silent for a moment, as he steered her toward the Range Rover. "I don't like what I am thinking," he said, and it was true. Apparently, it was also true that he didn't want to disclose whatever-it-was to the wife of his bosom.

In some alarm, she ventured, "Should we go home and bar the door?"

"Not as yet," he replied, but she could see that he was preoccupied, as he opened her car door.

She waited until he'd come around and slid behind the driver's seat to ask, "Did you find out what you needed to know about the Santiago people?"

"Some," he replied.

"Fine," she groused, and crossed her arms in annoyance. "Keep your precious secrets, husband."

He paused to gaze down the street for a thoughtful moment. "I find it of interest that Spain seems to figure largely in these events."

"Except for Rizzo," Doyle noted. "He's Italian. Or he was, anyways. Got started in the Serie-A, when he was only fifteen."

"Interesting," said Acton, who continued preoccupied.

Watching him, she added, "And Father Ambrose wasn't Spanish—he was Polish, I think. Everyone in his family was killed by the Nazis, and that's why Father John thinks he didn't mind skirtin' the Church rules about 'just cause murders' and such."

Her husband's distracted interest returned to her. "Yes. I do remember."

As he started-up the car, Doyle watched him narrowly. Something's rocked him off his pins, she thought, and I wish I knew what it was. The paint? The less-expensive alabaster stat-ues? What?

He said, "With your permission, we will lunch at home, and then go to headquarters after."

"Lead on," she replied, and turned to gaze out her window as he pulled into traffic. It was early to have lunch—at least for Acton, who liked to keep a regular schedule for such things—and Doyle would bet her teeth that her husband wanted to research something from his home computer, rather than from his work one. He'd discovered something that made him uneasy —or not necessarily uneasy, she decided, it was more like *dismayed*. The man's dismayed, for some reason, and whatever it was that was dismaying him, he didn't want to tell his better half about it.

With a mental sigh, she resolved to possess her soul in patience. She'd find out whatever-it-was—she always did, after all—but in the meantime, she'd keep a wary eye on her knocked-off-his-pins husband; if it was enough to dismay the mighty Acton, heaven only knew what was afoot.

This thought brought to mind the other dismayed man in her life—truly, it never rained but it poured—and she pulled her mobile phone. "I should check-in on Williams, poor boyo. He was that miserable when Mathis took him home."

But Williams did not answer her call, which she found a bit alarming. "Are we worried? Should I start callin' the hospitals?"

Acton considered this. "I wouldn't. Mathis reported-in after she'd taken him home, and he appears to have recovered." Glancing her way, he added, "Perhaps you should to wait for him to make first contact. He may be embarrassed."

"Oh—good point, being as our attempt at a dinner-party turned in to a crackin' blood-bath, with no little fault to him." She sighed hugely, as she contemplated the passing scenery.

"Poor Williams; love's a rare tangle-patch, and sometimes you've just got to take your lumps, and move on."

Doyle's husband tilted his head in mild disagreement. "We are not a tangle-patch, surely?"

She had to laugh out loud. "Holy Mother, Michael; we're in the flippin' Hall of *Fame*."

He smiled slightly. "I stand corrected."

"And speakin' of tangle-patches, have you had a chance to find out anythin' about Martina's husband? Although I suppose Williams is burnin' up a keyboard as we speak, tryin' to find out the very same thing."

Thoughtfully, Acton disclosed, "I could find no indication that she'd ever married. And—perhaps in a related development —Martina wishes to pay a visit, so as to apologize for the disruption."

"Oh-oh," said Doyle, thoroughly alarmed. "What's she up to?"

"I do not know."

She eyed him sidelong. "You don't know a lot about *any* of this, Michael. It must be a strange and bewilderin' experience, for the likes of you."

"It is," he agreed.

With some trepidation, she asked, "So; when's she comin' over?"

"I suggested tea time tomorrow, if that is agreeable."

Doyle blew out a breath. "You've nerves of steel, my friend. Always on the front foot."

"Mainly, I am curious as to her motivation, given what we now know."

The words were true and were actually something of a relief; for whatever reason, Doyle herself harbored a rather uneasy feeling about Martina's motivations, but Acton did not seem overly-concerned. Which only made sense, of course; if Martina indeed belonged to an ancient Holy Order, it was unlikely that she was bent on causing trouble.

For some reason, Doyle's scalp started prickling, but before she could explore the reasons why this would be, her husband offered, "It is probably best not to mention her coming visit to Williams."

"No—I'm stayin' out of it," she declared. "I'm mighty tired of dealin' with Williams' love-life, and let this be a lesson to him."

"A lesson well-learned," Acton agreed, and Doyle had the brief impression he was amused about something.

24

They were back at the flat, and—as Doyle had predicted—Acton was not as interested in having lunch as he was interested in retreating to his newly set-up office—now located downstairs.

And so, Doyle entertained Edward at the kitchen table as Reynolds hurried around the kitchen, called into lunch-service when he wasn't quite ready for it. He was a bit agitated, was our Reynolds, being as he was the sort of person who didn't like to be caught off-guard. Acton was one who didn't like to be caught off-guard, either—and it was as rare as hen's teeth, of course—but unlike Reynolds, Acton never panicked, and simply worked to turn the situation around to his advantage. When it came to nerves of steel, he carried off the palm.

Doyle handed Edward another crayon, since the previous ten had all wound up scattered around on the floor. "So, Reynolds; have you recovered from our donnybrook-disguised-as-a-dinner party?"

"It was unfortunate, madam," the servant admitted, as he

carefully loaded his quiche into the oven. "It would have been far more appropriate for Mr. Savoie to have contacted Inspector Williams in a more discreet manner."

Doyle quirked her mouth. "Not a bundle of discreetness, is our Mr. Savoie, what with his tryin' to pass you packets of cash between courses."

"'Discretion', I believe is the word you mean, madam."

But Doyle had paused in puzzlement, because she'd realized that her accusation was actually not true—it was not true at all. Savoie was a past-master at discreetness—or whatever the word was—as well she knew. For some reason, however, he'd decided to throw a spanner into the dinner-party works, and to do so in an embarrassingly public manner so as to shake-up poor Williams–not to mention he'd been outright rude to the fair Martina. It seemed very out-of-keeping, for him.

Her thoughts were interrupted when Reynolds added, "A shame, that the honoree was cast in the shade."

Doyle eyed him. "Remind me what that means, Reynolds."

"Javid, madam," the servant explained with deep patience. "Lord Acton held the dinner party to honor the artist, but the unfortunate events overshadowed her moment."

"I don't know as that's true," Doyle disagreed thoughtfully. "I'm not sure Acton wanted to honor Javid as much as he wanted an excuse to see how they'd all react to one another, just like in one of those Agatha Christie stories."

Reynolds' doubtful silence indicated he did not necessarily agree with this assessment, which was only to be expected, since in Reynold's world, an aristocratic dinner-party far out-ranked a paltry police investigation. Not to mention that you'd never guess that Acton harbored such a motive in the first place; he seemed all cool politeness on the outside when he was actually like a hound to the point on the inside, and small blame to

Reynolds for not knowing this as well as the man's tuning-fork of a wife.

The servant ventured, "I hope the unpleasantness has not spoiled any chance of future dinner parties, madam."

"Not the smallest chance," she assured him stoutly. "We've got the ball rollin', now; this place is goin' to be brimful of dinner parties, hence, each hard on the heels of the last."

Reynolds did not deign to respond to this out-and-out falsehood, but with a tentative air, he paused at the fridge. "If I may ask, how does Inspector Williams, madam?"

Doyle shook her head slightly. "I haven't a clue. Acton thinks I should let him lick his wounds, but I've held off as long as I can." Suiting action to word, she pulled her mobile and texted, "R U alive?"

The response came back promptly. "Barely. Meet for coffee later?"

"OK. R U off-campus?"

"Crime scene Harley Street."

"Right. Text when U R free."

"He's at work," she announced to Reynolds as she rang off. "He doesn't sound too broken-up, but he's the type who's got all sorts of deep emotions, rattlin' about, so you never know when he has to be talked down from the ledge." She paused, much struck. "You know, Reynolds, *everyone* seems to have deep emotions, save me and you."

"Nonsense; if I may say so, you have hidden depths, madam," Reynolds said in the tone of someone trying to say something complimentary.

"Very deep depths," she agreed, and leaned to give Edward a great, smacking kiss. "It's a burden to be borne, it is."

"You do excellent detective-work," Reynolds added, perhaps aware that he's offered only tepid praise, thus far.

She quirked her mouth. "Not on this Rizzo case, though; there are too many mixed-signals comin' in. It's a bit like our dinner party, with everythin' all topsy-turvy and not a'tall what you'd expect."

Pausing in puzzlement, Reynolds asked, "Are you speaking of Rizzo's death, madam? Do the police not yet know why he took such a drastic step?"

Reminded that she shouldn't be speaking on a pending case, she only answered vaguely, "It's ongoin'. Reynolds. Hence."

"Very good, madam. Will you be returning to work with Lord Acton after lunch?"

"I will," she replied, "No rest for the weary. And speakin' of which, does Gemma have her Russian lessons today?" Gemma, the nanny's adopted daughter, was Russian by birth, and as part of her education the little girl was formally learning the language.

"Yes, madam," Reynolds replied as he bent to check on his quiche. "I will fetch her here from school today, so that Miss Mary may nap whilst Edward does." Their nanny was newly pregnant, and was suffering a bit from it.

Doyle turned the page of Edward's color book, and commented, "My hat's off to Gemma, Reynolds; I wouldn't be any good with learnin' Russian—I'm barely able to speak English as it is."

"Since Miss Gemma did speak Russian in her early years, it seems she remembers quite a bit. Indeed, she is often able to correct my own mistakes."

Surprised, Doyle raised her gaze to him. "You're learnin' Russian, Reynolds?"

The butler confessed, "I thought it would helpful if she'd someone to practice with. I must say it is a difficult language."

"Try Gaelic, my friend," Doyle countered, as she turned back to her coloring. "Or Welsh—no one can hold a candle to Welsh; it was invented by cross-steppin' fairies who never saw a vowel they didn't like."

The servant took another peek into the oven. "As you say, madam."

Doyle paused to eye him in amusement. "You're worryin' me, now, Reynolds; don't let Mary and Howard try to steal you from us, what with all your Russian-speakin' and your grand dinner-parties. If you left us, I'd have no one to set me straight, since Acton would rather fall on a sword than correct me."

The servant deigned to offer a small, dry smile. "Certainly not, madam. I am quite content where I am."

"And don't let Savoie steal you away, either," she added. "No matter how many buckets of cash he throws your way."

With a hint of disapproval, her companion replied, "I do not believe Mr. Savoie is one to require a servant, madam."

Bending down to retrieve yet another crayon, Doyle advised, "Oh, I don't know, Reynolds; Savoie's got those hidden depths, too. We'd all probably be very much surprised."

"If you say, madam," said Reynolds in a doubtful tone.

25

Once back at headquarters, Doyle sidled up to Munoz's cubicle. "D'you mind if I look up a 'John Doe'? It should only take a minute, and I'm too lazy to log-in just for the one task."

"We're not supposed to use someone else's log-in," Munoz reminded her, even as she slid her chair away so as to allow Doyle access.

With a serene air, Doyle noted, "We're not supposed to be marryin' a superior officer without tellin' anyone, either."

"You're one to talk," Munoz fired back.

Doyle leaned over the other girl's keyboard. "That's how I recognized the signs—it takes one to know one."

In a low voice, Munoz asked a bit anxiously, "Does anyone else know?"

"I may have mentioned it to Williams, but he'll stand bluff. How's everythin'?"

The other girl couldn't resist a slow smile. "Everything is *wonderful*."

Doyle teased, "Well, there's nothin' like a secret romance to spice up your life; a shame you can't keep it secret forever."

With a sigh, Munoz confessed, "He's not happy with the secrecy—he thinks we should make an announcement, and hold a reception."

"Well, he's a straightforward sort of fellow," Doyle conceded, and could not help but note that she was married to the exact opposite—faith, talk about a keeper-of-secrets, the only reason the fair Doyle ever managed to winkle-out Acton's secrets was because she'd an advantage, and that advantage included various ghosts who showed up to prod her in the right direction.

Thus reminded, she began tapping out a morgue-records search for a recent "John Doe" who matched the painter's description.

Munoz's smile was still in evidence as she confided, "He's a little inexperienced, in bed."

"Not your usual," Doyle teased. "Hence, it must be true love."

Reminded, the Spanish girl checked the time. "Hurry up. He's working a case out in the field, and I'm meeting-up with him for a quick lunch."

Doyle raised her brows. "Of course, you are; someone's got to show the man the ropes."

In happy anticipation, Munoz began to pack-up her ruck-sack. "My parents are going to *freak.*"

"Oh, I don't know," Doyle disagreed thoughtfully. "He's a good man, and he loves you—he's a champion, who'd slay any dragon. Surely that counts for somethin'."

For some reason, her scalp prickled, and she paused, wondering why. That Acton was the fair Doyle's champion wasn't exactly a news-flash; was she thinking of someone else? Who else was a champion? Williams? Savoie?

Her thoughts were interrupted, however, when the "John

Doe" search came up with no photo that matched her ghost. To be thorough, she also looked through the general database of recent deaths on the chance he was someone who'd been duly reported-and-processed, but this search also came up empty. This was not much of a surprise to Doyle, since she was almost certain the poor painter had been murdered and dumped anonymously; he'd seen something he wasn't supposed to see in St. Michael's Church, when he'd gone in early so as to listen to that wonderful silence.

"Nothing?" asked Munoz, who'd been watching the screen with her.

"No. The man I'm lookin' for may have been a witness on a case. A witness who's disappeared."

"A containment murder?" the girl asked, as she rather pointedly stood up, hoping to hurry Doyle along.

"Mayhap." Thoughtfully, Doyle closed down the screen. "Although I think the murderer regretted havin' to kill him."

Munoz made a derisive sound. "That's a bit fanciful, even for you, Doyle. The only regret a murderer has is when he gets caught."

Thoughtfully, Doyle closed the program. "Not this murderer. I wish I knew what his motive was."

"If you can't figure out a motive, you have to just follow the evidence," Munoz reminded her. "We can't deal in theory–we haven't the budget."

"I know, I know," Doyle agreed as she straightened up. "But Acton deals in theory all the time. Faith, I think he's always more interested in discoverin' the motive than he is in discoverin' the evidence."

"Well, Acton is Acton. Lesser beings like you and me can't go around chasing theories." The girl checked her mobile. "Let's go."

Doyle smiled as they began to make their way down the aisle-way toward the lift. "It's champin' at the bit, you are—speakin' of motives."

"Shut up, Doyle." But the words were said without their usual rancor. "Are you going up to see Acton? Can you deliver my report? It would save me the trip."

With some surprise, Doyle accepted the manila envelope. "You can't deliver it electronically?"

"He'd rather it wasn't in the system," the other girl explained. "Its witness interviews for the Rizzo case, and the press would love to hack-in to see what the witnesses are telling us."

Doyle nodded. "I will, then; after all, you've a new husband impatiently on the watch."

Munoz smiled as she pushed the button for the lift, and then smoothed her hair in the steel door's reflection.

26

Thoughtfully, Doyle made the trek up to the brass's offices, across the walkway over to the adjacent building. Whilst it was true that it was a constant race to outfox the determined hackers—who'd be paid handsomely if they could find something to leak to the press—she would bet her teeth that her husband wanted paper copies of the Rizzo witness reports because he wanted to keep a tight lid on whatever was being discovered. After all, it was far easier to manipulate the evidence if it was old-fashioned paper-and-ink, and if Savoie was being framed for murder, the case might shine an unwanted spotlight on the questionable doings of the notorious Frenchman and the illustrious Chief Inspector.

Acton had admitted that there was something here he didn't understand, and Doyle had the strong sense that her husband was stepping very carefully—he was being mighty cautious about how best to go forward.

But—on reflection—it did seem unlikely that Acton's wariness came from Savoie's role in all this; Doyle knew down to the soles of her shoes that Acton wouldn't hesitate to step in and save the Frenchman's sorry hide—faith, it would just be a normal day's work for the man, and hardly worth a moment's anxiety. Something else was afoot, and whatever it was, it was no doubt connected to the fact that Acton hadn't wanted the fair Doyle to listen-in to the Kingsmen CFO interview.

She emerged from the lift to approach her husband's office, only to be advised by Nazy that Acton was away from his desk on an undisclosed errand.

Ah—I wonder what it was, that he discovered at home, thought Doyle; and I wonder if there's trouble brewing.

Hoping to do a bit of probing, she handed over Munoz's report and affected a casual air. "So, has Sir Vikili brought any other Kingsmen personnel over to visit, hopin' to pull the wool over our eyes?"

With an air of excitement, Nazy disclosed, "No, but the Chief Inspector asked that I deliver a packet of required-disclosure documents to Sir Vikili this morning—over to his chambers, at the Inns of Court."

"Never say," Doyle teased. "And? Do his chambers have pillars of gold?"

The girl lowered her voice. "I learned something very interesting, when I was there."

"He proposed marriage," Doyle guessed.

With a smile, Nazy replied, "Not yet. But I saw a painting, there—in his chambers. It was hanging behind the door, but I noticed it because it was from the story of Ramin and Vis—it is a famous story, in our culture." Happily, the girl leaned in to say with a conspiratorial air, "It gives me information about him—about Sir Vikili."

Amused, Doyle offered, "That he has buckets of money to spend on fine art?"

"No—the story in the painting is frowned upon by the stricter people, because it is about a forbidden love."

Doyle lifted her brows in surprise. "You're right, that doesn't seem to be in keepin'. I would never have pegged him as the romantic sort."

Her eyes wide, Nazy nodded. "Yes—yes, that is it, exactly. Do you see? If he has such a painting in his chambers, it means that he is not so very strict."

The light dawned, and Doyle concluded, "Oh—and hence, he's more likely to marry a girl like you, who's not so very strict, herself."

Happily, Nazy gazed out the window. "It was very beautiful— the painting. I wondered if he painted it himself—it was signed, 'Javid'. I was too afraid to ask him, though."

Doyle stared in surprise. "Sir Vikili's last name is 'Javid'? Why, that's what my artist's name is, too. I wonder if they're related."

Almost kindly, Nazy explained, "'Javid' is not an unusual name, in my culture."

"Oh. Well, I learned something new, then. Besides, my Javid only does portraits, I think—she's famous for them."

But Nazy was more interested in dwelling on her encounter with the object of her affections, and disclosed, "Sir Vikili was very kind to me—and very respectful of the Chief Inspector."

Oh-oh, thought Doyle in alarm; Nazy was not the sort of person who would suspect a defense solicitor of pumping a DCI's smitten assistant for information, but Doyle was not so naïve—after all, Doyle had been subject to many such an attempt, herself. And more to the point, it was very unlikely that someone like Sir Vikili was truly interested in someone like Nazy—especially considering Williams' theory about the man's sexual preferences. "What sort of things did you speak of, Nazy?"

"We spoke of the Rizzo case. He was very regretful that he died; that he had such talent, and so much to live for."

"You can't speak about pendin' cases, Nazy, no matter how handsome the asker," Doyle reminded her gently.

The Persian girl immediately colored-up. "No, no—of course not, Officer Doyle. I know better."

In a teasing tone, Doyle continued, "There's a reason he has such a cock-o'-the-walk reputation, after all. He's not above winklin'-out information wherever he may, and if he's goin' to attempt some winklin', he should at least take you out to dinner."

Laughing, the girl protested, "Even then, Officer Doyle, I would not give anything away."

"Good on you," Doyle declared, and didn't have the heart to inform the girl that any and all state secrets would no doubt have been winkled-out without her even being aware.

27

D oyle was sitting at a table at the local Deli, which was a popular establishment with the Yard's rank-and-file mainly because it was close by, and not as stale and familiar as the building's canteen.

Normally, when she went to have coffee with Williams he would beat her there, but today she was the first arrival and therefore had to guess at what Williams usually ordered for himself. Nothing too sweet, she decided, what with the diabetes and all. Playing it safe, she ordered two plain coffees.

She chose a perimeter table on the presumption that he wouldn't want their conversation to be overheard—faith, he'd weathered a mighty blow, poor man—and devoutly hoped she wouldn't be called upon to pass him handkerchiefs or anything. It was another point to be toted up in Acton's favor that he never got overly-emotional—well, almost never; the circumstances surrounding Edward's birth came to mind, but if that wasn't cause for a welter of emotions, nothing was.

She watched the door and lifted a hand upon sighting

Williams. Good; he didn't look overly-miserable, and in need of handkerchief-handing. "Hey," she said.

"Hey, yourself."

As he sat down, she offered, "If you don't want to talk about the forbidden subject, mum's the word. I just wanted to check-in."

He let out a mighty sigh and sank back in his chair. "You don't know the half of it, Kath. I really messed up."

"Not your fault," she said stoutly. "You'd think a girl would mention that she was married sometime durin' your first date, at the very least. *Shame* on her."

"Well—yes, that did come as something of a shock, but then I made a bad situation worse, and decided that I should just get married, myself."

Doyle stared at him, agog. "*What*? You married Martina? Holy *Mother*, Thomas, there are laws about that."

"No," he said heavily. "I married Lizzy Mathis."

These words, put together in this particular order, made no sense to Doyle, who continued to stare at him in profound surprise. "Are you all right, Thomas? D'you need me to call you an ambulance, again?"

He ran a hand over his face. "No. It's true; I married Lizzy Mathis."

"Oh—oh, Mother a' Mercy, Thomas—I'm that gobsmacked." Tentatively, she ventured, "Is she pregnant?"

He lowered his hand to stare at her in incredulity. "Holy *Christ*, of course not. I've never even been alone with her, before."

Doyle shook her head, as though to clear it. "Then how —*how* on God's green earth did this happen?"

"I don't really remember," he said heavily.

Doyle considered him for a moment. "That's crazy talk, my

friend."

"I know; I know. I was upset about—about Martina."

"Yes," she agreed, remembering his misery. "Go on; how did you manage to leap from one to the other?" With an inward sigh, she thought, men; *honestly*.

"I must have—I must have made a mistake on my insulin, because I was feeling a little wooly. I cut my hand at home somehow—I think I broke a glass—and I was angry at Lizzy, who wanted to take me to the hospital for stitches. I didn't want to go, and so she stitched me up herself. She made me eggs, and—"

"And?"

He took a deep breath. "And I'm not sure how it happened, but—I wasn't thinking straight, of course—I decided I'd pull a Munoz, and just be done with it."

Doyle leaned back in her chair, gazing at him in wonderment. "That's crackin' impressive, Thomas."

He leaned forward to cradle his head between his hands. "I'm going to annul it, of course."

"Of course," she agreed. "Can't go about marryin' every girl who makes you eggs."

"Don't tell anyone. I only told you because I imagine you'd find out, one way or another."

"Not a word, then. Does she know not to tell anyone?"

"Yes." He took a deep breath and lifted his head. "I'm such an idiot."

With a comforting gesture, she reached to clasp a hand around his forearm. "You were 'impaired', as they say down in Booking, and not in the best shape to make rational decisions."

"I feel badly," he confessed. "Lizzy looked after me, and in return she doesn't deserve this mess."

Doyle pointed out, "Unless you tied her up and held a gun to her, she's complicit in this mess, too."

"It's different; she's always liked me, and I took advantage."

Doyle suddenly stilled, and wondered if perhaps this was a glimpse into the new Mrs. Williams' strategy; Williams was too honorable by half, and this tendency, perhaps, was being deliberately used to her advantage.

Doyle ventured, "She'll agree to an annulment?"

"Of course; she wants whatever's best for me.'"

Which was exactly what Lizzy should say to Mr. White Knight, thought Doyle, who suddenly had a strong feeling that this strategy was being put forward by someone miles more clever than Lizzy Mathis. "I should go," she announced abruptly. "I've got to track down Acton."

With some concern, he leaned forward. "Right. I hope you're not angry, Kath; I'm sorry I didn't tell you straightaway."

Because that was the plan, she thought, but aloud she teased, "Whist, Thomas; I'm not angry a'tall. I've the whip-hand, now; you'll never be able to accuse me of bein' hare-brained again."

He smiled sheepishly. "Exactly."

"Let me see your hand, please."

He proffered the bandaged hand, and she observed the dressing. "D'you think you should see a medico?" Williams hated the fact he was diabetic in the first place, and so tended to compensate for this perceived weakness by neglecting his health.

"No," he said, and ran a slow finger over the neatly-wound bandage. "I don't see any sign of infection. Lizzy wants to leave the stitches in for a week because it's my palm, and it needs to heal correctly."

Doyle conceded, "She knows her stuff."

"Lucky for me," he agreed absently, and ran an idle finger over the bandages again.

Observing this, she said, "Keep me posted," and drew her private mobile. "Where R U?" she demanded of her husband.

Acton's response came promptly. "Everything all right?"

"No," she texted. "I M coming w/joint stool to brain U with."

"Best not. The Modern Art Museum."

She glanced up at Williams. "Where's the Modern Art Museum?"

"Millbank, in Westminster," he replied. "Martina goes there all the time."

This seemed a coincidence too far, and Doyle struggled to maintain her poise. My wretched husband had better not be meeting-up with Martina on the sly, she thought, but it was an empty threat because she knew—in the way that she knew things—that such was not the case; Martina and Acton did not inspire warm feelings in one another.

In fact—now that she thought about it—it seemed a bit strange that Williams had only made a passing reference to the fair Martina up to now; you'd think he'd be all broken-hearted, and such.

Williams interrupted her thoughts, "Any chance you're free for some Rizzo-case slog work? I've some catching-up to do, since I didn't want Personnel to know that I was out."

"Who's been taking up the slack?" Doyle asked, having a very good guess at the answer.

"Acton's been covering for me," he admitted.

Of course, Acton's been covering, thought Doyle, trying to control her temper; the better to keep a firm finger on the pulse of any new Rizzo-leads that might prove inconvenient for the worthy Chief Inspector.

"I'm happy to help," she assured him. "And it's very sweet

that you pretend that you're askin' for a favor, instead of a rankin' officer who can order me to do push-ups on the Deli floor here and now, if you wish."

"I don't wish," he smiled. "Although it would be a treat to see."

She grimaced in memory. "Push-ups were the bane of trainin'."

"Ballistics, too," he teased. She'd first became friends with Williams when he'd offered to help her pass ballistics.

As they chuckled together, Doyle decided that her companion didn't seem very broken-up at all, and if she couldn't see Acton's fine hand behind all of this, then she was a no-account sorry excuse.

Hard on this thought, she decided to offer, "Here's a lead, of sorts; there's a painter who's missin'. A painter who was workin' in St. Michael's—I think he may have witnessed somethin'."

"Already got it," Williams assured her. "Tommy Dryden. He was an itinerant painter who kept close tabs on Rizzo's career. Keep it quiet, but Acton thinks he may be the prime suspect, which is why he's gone doggo. A crazed fan, apparently."

Doyle stared at him in profound silence. No, she thought; not a crazed fan. Instead, he's Acton's decoy.

28

D
oyle's husband was waiting for her in the lobby of the Modern Art Museum, and bent to kiss her cheek in greeting. "Kathleen; I am sorry I was away from my office."

In an ominous tone, she began, "Don't think I'm not aware that you wanted to meet me here in the fond hope that you'll avoid a well-deserved scoldin'."

"Surely not," he demurred, but nonetheless steered her toward the Exhibit Halls, which were sparsely populated at this time of day.

Being as she was not one to allow a hushed atmosphere to constrain her in any way, Doyle immediately began, "You set it up, Michael. There's no denyin' it, so don't bother—I was that fashed about Williams and his stupid love-life, and so now you've gone and buckled him up—nice and tight—to another one of your loyal foot-soldiers."

She paused, and then added crossly, "And a penny to a pound says she put somethin' in his drink, too. Faith, Lizzy

Mathis is like that Roman woman who was forever poisonin' everyone, and she should never be allowed within callin' distance of food-service."

Acton tilted his head toward her in a conciliatory gesture. "It is not such a terrible turn of events, surely? I believe you mentioned that the ghost at Trestles once tasked you with finding a husband for Mathis."

She eyed him sidelong. "I thought you didn't believe in my ghosts."

"I believe in you, though."

In exasperation, she chided, "For heaven's sake, Michael; you can't control love—love is *untamable*, if that's a word."

"None knows this better than I."

This gave her pause, and she managed to calm herself a bit. "That's unfair; you shouldn't be so sweet whilst I'm tryin' to give you a bear-garden jawin'."

"It is only the truth."

Her scalp started prickling, and she was distracted for a moment, wondering why it would. Not a news flash, certainly, that love was untamable, and one need look no further than her untamed husband, who'd decided he didn't want his wife to worry about Williams anymore and so had resolved all problems with a minimum of fuss. A devoted man, he was—sometimes a bit too devoted, to be making such decisions without so much as a passing nod to the consequences.

Again, her scalp prickled and she closed her eyes briefly, trying to decide what it was she was trying to understand. Who else was devoted—so devoted that nothing else mattered? Geary? No, not Geary. Mathis? No, not Mathis; someone else—

"All you all right?" he asked gently, observing her preoccupation.

She couldn't catch the elusive thought, and so she rested her head against his arm and sighed. "I'm feel as though I'm on a tinker's route, where I keep treadin' the same path, day after day, and the scenery never changes."

He put an arm around her and leaned to say into her temple. "Please trust me to do what's best for us, Kathleen—that is all I ask."

"I wish I could, but your definition of what's 'best' and my definition of what's 'best' are not even passin' acquaintances."

"Surely not," he soothed.

She decided it was past time to serve up a surprise of her own—a bit of a brush-back, just so he was aware that he didn't have full reign to drive her mad. "As an excellent case in point, Michael, it's not fair to pin Rizzo's murder on an innocent man. Just because the poor fellow's dead doesn't mean you can take advantage."

Ah; that remark made him wary, even though his outward composure did not change. "What have you heard?"

"Never you mind, my friend. What are you about? Are you framin' this poor painter-fellow to save Savoie from *his* frame-up? Make it appear to be a shadow murder, of some sort?"

She could see that he weighed what to tell her, and then admitted, "More along the lines of a murder in thrall."

She knit her brow. "Remind me what that means, Michael."

"A murder by someone who is obsessed, like a crazed fan."

She made a derisive sound. "Well, that's a fine fairy-story, my friend, because it seems clear-as-glass that Rizzo's must be a containment murder—this killer was desperate to contain the fallout from the money-launderin' rig." She glanced up at him. "I think you think so, too, else you wouldn't be settin' up this decoy for everyone to chase."

They walked for a few steps in silence, and then she decided she may as well ask, "Who's the real killer, then?"

"I do not know," he replied, and it was the truth.

She stared up at him in surprise. "Faith, Michael; you're doin' a lot of scurryin' about, for someone who doesn't know." Reminded, she asked, "Then the gentleman's documents were nothing more than another may-dance?"

"Almost certainly. Contained within them were the identifiers for several blind bank accounts, held by Philippe Savoie." He paused. "I have not followed up, as yet."

She made a wry mouth. "You must be drivin' him barkin' mad, Michael. But no one deserves it more–faith, what's his aim, with all this Savoie-baitin'?"

"I have had some ideas," he admitted. "But nothing seems to fit this particular sequence of events."

"Because you don't have a motive, as yet." As they walked along the quiet gallery, she put her hand in the crook of his arm. "It's like I told Munoz; you like to start with motive, and then work it backwards. If Rizzo was hip-deep in the money-launderin' rig, you'd think that there'd be plenty of motives out there; he may have threatened to squeak about the operation unless he got a bigger cut–or somethin'–and they decided—with deep regret, I suppose—that they'd have to eliminate such a threat, even though in the process they'd lose their cash-cow."

"But," prompted Acton, as they paused before an abstract painting.

Slowly, Doyle reasoned, "But—that theory doesn't make a lot of sense, because Rizzo is Rizzo, and his death has brought down a white-hot spotlight on all the other conspirators, so *surely* they weren't wantin' that. It would have been far better had he just been threatened with broken legs, or somethin', to pull him back into line. The last thing they'd want—one would think—would be to give Chief Inspector Acton an excuse to haul them all in for a sweatin'-out on a murder charge."

"Precisely." He added, "I believe the players in this money-laundering rig are as surprised as anyone by Rizzo's murder. Surprised, and rather panicked."

But this revelation raised no small disquiet in Doyle's breast, as she eyed him sidelong. "I'm afraid to even ask how you know what the players in this rig are sayin' to each other, Michael. Please tell me you aren't a participant."

"Of course not," he said, and it was the truth.

She made a wry mouth and turned to consider the painting before them once again. "Of course not, because you're a one-man operation, and you much prefer to work alone. But you're not above snatchin' some of the money out from under their noses, if you can arrange for the opportunity."

There was a small silence into which he made no response, which was response enough. In a grim tone, she added, "Remember that I'm not comin' in to Wexton Prison for conjugal visits, Michael, so plan accordingly."

"You are extraordinary, and I don't know why I continually underestimate you."

This was typical Acton, that rather than be alarmed that she'd twigged on to one of his murky schemes, he was all admiration for her sleuthing skills. She closed her eyes for a moment. "I despair of you, my friend—its wringin' my hands, I am."

He squeezed her into his side. "All will be well, Kathleen."

"At least tell me that someday the scenery will change, on my tinker's route."

"I understand your concerns, and I am working on it, believe me."

This wasn't much of an answer—he'd left unsaid exactly what he was working on—but she decided that she'd say no more, because it was always a tricky balance; she knew instinctively that if she hounded him about his dark doings, he'd only hide them even deeper, and put paid to the fragile trust she'd built up with him. The best course—she'd decided long ago—was to let him know she wasn't best pleased, and hope it was enough to make him re-think the risks he took.

Unfortunately, she also knew that Acton very much enjoyed the risks he took. The man truly needed to find a different hobby, and birdwatching definitely didn't seem a risky-enough substitute.

Hopefully, her wishes would prevail; Acton lived to please her—only see what he'd done to solve the Williams problem—and now that he knew she'd twigged onto his money-skimming scheme, he'd stand down—fingers crossed. Ironic, it was, that Acton's deep-seated need to build on his mighty fortune was in part to provide for his bride, but that self-same bride would be just as happy to live in a snug terrace-house, just so long as they could be together.

She frowned, because there it was again—that elusive thought that she couldn't quite catch. What? Acton lived to serve her—and protect her, of course. Faith, even before she was aware that he was in love with her, he'd arranged to leave his fortune to her, the knocker.

Pausing, she closed her eyes for a moment. This was important, for some reason. Who else was so devoted—so devoted that nothing else mattered?

"What is it?" he asked softly, watching her.

"This killer," she said aloud, as she opened her eyes. "He's miserable about it, but he's that desperate."

"You believe there is an undisclosed personal motivation," he offered. "And that may be why it is so elusive."

She nodded. "I keep thinkin' that it's—" she paused, catching herself before she said, "someone like you." Instead, she offered,

"I think it may be one of those 'thrall' things that you were talkin' about."

But Acton—being Acton—immediately found the flaw in this theory. "Perhaps; but then why would the killer set it up so that Savoie would take the blame? That's not in keeping with an obsessed murderer."

Seeing the logic in this, she could only admit, "Right you are —if the killer knows that Savoie is a likely person to take the fall, then it sounds as though Rizzo's murder was strictly business, and not personal at all. Containment would indeed be the motive." She paused. "Unless it's both, I suppose."

He tilted his head, trying to come up with a working-theory for this suggestion. "Perhaps the killer is afraid? He is desperate because the rig has been twigged, and he's worried about what Rizzo will confess? It's every man for himself?"

With acute frustration, she raised her palms to her eyes. "That can't be it, since this murder only exposed Rizzo's under-handed doin's, and the killer *must* have known it would. Saints, Michael; none of this makes a spoonful of sense."

"I will take another look at Rizzo's personal connections," he said thoughtfully, as they resumed their progress. "Perhaps someone he trusted was involved in the scheme, and that person panicked, and decided that his murder was the only way out."

She made a wry mouth. "Not much of a way out, since it only brought Scotland Yard down on his trail like a pack of brayin' hounds. You needn't humor me, Michael, if you think I'm got it by the wrong leg."

"On the contrary," he replied. "You have excellent insights, Kathleen."

"Well, I always manage to catch *you* up, dead to rights," she said with no small irony.

"You do, indeed," he agreed, and bent to kiss the top of her head.

With a smile, she glanced up at him. "Although I suppose that's not exactly true; I didn't have the first clue that you were in love with me, and busily schemin' to carry me away."

"Ordinarily, you have excellent insights," he amended, and steered her toward the next painting.

But she was distracted, as she thought over the apparently unsolvable riddle that was the motive for Rizzo's murder. "Well, here's an insight to chew on, Michael—could we have the cart before the horse, hence? Mayhap the killer *wanted* to point a big shiny arrow at the money-launderin' rig. After all, the walls weren't closin' in on them until after Rizzo was murdered; up until then there was no reason to panic."

"It was a revelation murder, to expose the rig to the police?" He ducked his head, thinking this over. "Then why go to such lengths to frame Savoie?"

"Right you are," she sighed. "Back to square one."

29

They paused before the next painting, which appeared to Doyle to be an array of random overlapping lines and circles. "I'm not one to appreciate this," she admitted. "For me, this whole 'abstract art' thing seems like a sorry excuse, so that those who can't manage to paint a real paintin' can pretend to be above it all."

He smiled. "A view shared by many, certainly."

With a knit brow, she expanded on this thought. "Portraits are the hardest, I think. It's not easy, to catch the sense of a person with a brush, like Javid does. You can see straightaway who is able, and who is not."

"I would tend to agree."

She glanced up at him. "You like landscapes best, I think."

"Mainly," he cautiously conceded.

With a shake of her head, she turned to contemplate the artwork again. "It shouldn't alarm you that I know you so well, Michael."

He squeezed her gently against him. "It alarms me less and less, perhaps."

She nodded. "I will agree that we are makin' some progress in that department, but it's slow-goin' my friend. I love you to pieces, and I'm not goin' to abandon ship, no matter what—although this shacklin' of Williams to Mathis does give me pause. That's a fine bit of brass, even for you."

He made no response, but smiled slightly—proud of it, he was, the wretched man. And—true to form—he was never going to openly admit that he'd done what he'd done. He was very wily, that way.

With a mental sigh, she decided not to embark on yet another round of the love-is-untamable subject, and so instead asked, "Why are we here, husband?"

Thoughtfully, Acton replied, "We are here because I believe the painting before us is a fake."

She stared at him in astonishment, and then brought her attention back to the abstract painting. "Mother a' mercy, how can you tell? It's a hodge-podge of foolishness, masqueradin' as somethin' worthy."

He cocked his head. "Exactly. As you just observed, it would not be as difficult to forge abstract art as it would be to forge landscapes or portraits."

The penny dropped, and Doyle breathed, "Saints and angels; it's part of the money-launderin' rig? They transfer fancy art, instead of plain old currency."

"Much harder to trace, or to prosecute," he agreed.

As she scrutinized the painting, Doyle ventured, "Someone is fakin' the artwork, so that the authentic version can be smuggled about with no one the wiser?"

"I would not be surprised. Or, black-market buyers are duped into purchasing fakes for large amounts."

She shook her head in wonder. "Holy *Mother*, Michael—talk about brass. Wouldn't someone notice?"

"I imagine someone on the inside is complicit. And, if the forgery were to be discovered, the Museum would understandably want the recovery of the original to be kept very quiet, so as to avoid embarrassment."

Doyle made a face. "Which would allow for yet another round of money-launderin'. The co-conspirators can then openly pay each other to recover an allegedly stolen artwork."

"Indeed. It is a clever scheme." This said in the tone of one who was a fine arbiter of clever schemes.

With some consternation, she continued to regard what appeared to be a jumble of geometric shapes. "How on earth did you twig it?"

"The trace of epoxy paint, in the basement at St. Michael's."

"Oh—oh, of course. Faith, my hat's off to you, Michael." It was a testament to how his mind worked; the rest of them had seen an out-of-place smudge of paint at a construction site, whilst Acton had seen an out-of-place smudge of paint at a crime scene.

Doyle blew out a breath. "So; the villains were stashin' fake art—along with ill-gotten jewelry—at my poor church, more's the shame to them. Was the jewelry fake, too?"

"No," said Acton. "The jewelry was genuine, because it was meant to frame Savoie."

"Not that we'd ever know," she observed a bit sourly. "Mathis wiped it down, quick as a cat."

"Forensics could lift no prints," he agreed in a mild tone. "Indeed, it was one of the reasons Mathis was released from Detention."

Shaking her head, Doyle couldn't help but laugh. "I almost feel sorry for this killer; not only did his scheme fall to pieces, but now your mother's got a nice new sapphire necklace that she doesn't deserve."

"You have one, rather."

"Of *course*—what was I thinkin'? Your mother's none the wiser about the whole holy-show." Again, she shook her head in wonder. You're *somethin'*, Michael; back and edge."

"The stones are very high quality," he defended himself.

"Well, I suppose I'd rather have the necklace than this stupid paintin'—even the original one," she declared. "D'you suppose the same thing is happenin' at every D'Angelo Construction site? The blacklegs are rotatin' artwork and jewelry all over greater London?"

But he shook his head slightly. "I would doubt it. The co-conspirators cannot allow too many to know too much. In fact, it is possible the construction company itself doesn't know about it."

She made a derisive sound. "That's doin' it too brown, Michael; the construction people are the ones who had the security cameras installed in the basement. Not to mention that D'Angelo got himself washed overboard under suspicious circumstances—he must have been in it, up to his neck."

"A falling-out among thieves," Acton agreed. "Very plausible."

He indicated they should move on, and as they walked away, she glanced up at him in curiosity. "So; now what? D'you have enough to roll it up, or will you set-up surveillance so as to catch them in the act?"

Thoughtfully, he replied, "I would like to see the Museum's maintenance schedule for the artwork—which paintings are scheduled to be taken down for maintenance in the near future."

She nodded as they approached the main lobby. "Because

that's likely when they substitute the fake one. Unless they just march in, after hours, and switch them out."

"Too much risk," Acton decided. "Much more likely they use maintenance as an excuse."

"Shame on them," she repeated. "If you can't trust toplofty people who pretend to love modern art, then hence, who *can* you trust?"

"It is shocking," he agreed, and held the door for her.

30

That night, the painter returned to Doyle's dreams.

"Tommy?" she ventured.

Very pleased, he nodded in affirmation. "How about that? You know my name."

"I do, and I'm that sorry he's tryin' to pin this wretched murder on you. That's not fair a'tall, with you bein' such a fan."

He shrugged. "I don't mind being the decoy, but I should probably be the assist, instead."

After a small pause, she confessed, "I never played football. Or watched it, or—or anythin', so I'm never sure what it is you're sayin' to me."

"The beautiful game," he declared in reverent tones. "You missed out."

"Not a lot ever seems to happen," she ventured doubtfully.

He smiled. "On the contrary, there's lots happening. You just have to be able to see it."

There was a significant pause whilst it occurred to Doyle that her companion wasn't necessarily just referring to the game. She admitted, "I know there's a lot happenin' in this case that I don't understand. He says he doesn't know who the killer is, but he definitely knows *somethin'*, and he's bein' very careful not to allow me a glimpse." She paused, thinking this over. "I've been here too many times before, and it makes me very uneasy."

The painter nodded in affirmation. "There—you see? You're doing just fine, ma'am, don't be discouraged. It's a set play, and he's springing a trap."

With a knit brow, Doyle regarded him. "Well—yes—that's what he does, I suppose; it's as natural as breathin', for the man. Sprung quite the trap on me, once."

"Right-o," her companion agreed in an encouraging tone. "He doesn't want to tell you, because he knows you'll try to wave him off."

Crossly, she retorted, "I don't know why he worries; I've never have much luck, in the wavin'-off department."

The painter's expression turned a bit grave, as he fingered the cap in his hands. "This one's a real dinger, though—he could come a cropper, if he's not careful."

She stared in surprise. "*Acton* could come a cropper?"

"Clattered," the ghost affirmed.

Bewildered, she stared at him. "How—how's that?"

The ghost shrugged a shoulder. "They're coming in on his flank; he needs to keep his head on a swivel, or he'll wind up gutted."

There was a small moment of silence, and then Doyle offered, "I think you may be mixed-up, Tommy. The killer's tryin' to frame Savoie, he's not tryin' to frame Acton."

"There, you see? You're making my point," the ghost declared. "The best offense is a good defense."

Doyle decided she was getting nowhere with the indecipherable sports-talk, and instead mused, "It's not like him, to be so cautious; he likes to strike quickly, because he knows it shakes everyone up and the general panic works to his advantage. But he wants to tiptoe in, this time, and take a quiet peek at the maintenance schedule."

The painter chuckled. "Oh, no, ma'am; there you're wrong. He's a bone-rattler, and he's going in hot. It's a head fake, and you're a green 'un, getting juked out of your boots."

"I do my best," she replied defensively. "I do catch him, most times, even if I'm not very good at the wavin'-off."

"You're plucky, even when you're out-gunned," he agreed. "But with this one, he's skirting disaster."

"He *always* is," she declared crossly.

"Oh—this one more than most. He's up against it." The painter seemed to consider this for a moment, before he added, "He's trying to shut it down before she gets herself caught, but he's got to be careful, or she'll get herself killed, instead."

Surprised, she asked, "Who is this 'she' you keep talkin' about? Is it Martina? All I have to say is it better not be Munoz again—I'm pig-sick of stupid Munoz bein' in danger. And anyways, Munoz has a champion, now—a slayer of dragons."

With a smile, he agreed, "Exactly. Everyone does, all around."

"Oh," said Doyle, who wasn't quite following.

"I told you there was a lot going on," he explained, almost apologetically. "Stay focused, and keep your head up. You'll get there, ma'am; you're pluck to the backbone, if I may say so."

Grateful for the vote of confidence, Doyle was moved to declare, "If nothin' else, I'm goin' to have him clear your name, Tommy."

Very pleased, the ghost lifted his brows. "Now, wouldn't that be fine? Can't say as I ever had a champion, myself."

"Don't you worry, Tommy; I only have to figure out who

Rizzo's killer is—that's top o' the list, and then everythin' else will sort itself out."

"Not exactly," the painter warned. "Keep your head on a swivel—eye on the flank."

Doyle blinked. "There are *two* killers? But—but that can't be right; the killer's a desperate man—I'm certain of it."

The ghost nodded in affirmation. "Yes; they were closing in on the net, and so it was time for a professional foul."

Very much annoyed, she looked upon him in open vexation and he hastily apologized, "Sorry. Only remember this, ma'am; I should be the assist, and not the decoy."

Her eyes flew open, and she stared at the shadows on the wall for a moment, trying to regain her bearings whilst her heart hammered in her ears.

"Everything all right?" Acton had been awakened by her startled reaction, and sleepily, he pulled her to his chest. "Did you have a dream?"

"I did," she admitted.

He ran a soothing hand down her arm. "Can you say?"

He knew that she was reluctant to speak of her dreams, and so he tended not to press her. This time, however, she was genuinely puzzled, and said aloud, "Why would *you* need a champion?" After all, Acton was not someone who needed help dragon-slaying, Acton was a world-class dragon-slayer, himself.

As could be expected, Acton was having trouble making sense of this remark. He ventured, "Did you dream about the Trestles knight?"

This was a good guess—considering the reference to a champion—and as was always the case with her dreams, Doyle had to fight a strong inclination to button-up and say nothing—with the added concern that if Acton discovered that various ghosts were ratting him out, heaven only knew to what lengths he'd go to hide his doings under even more layers of guile.

Therefore, she rubbed her eyes and tried to sort out what it was that she wanted to say, without giving away too much. "No— it wasn't the knight. Since Edward's been born, the knight's not that much interested in you."

"Now, there's a blow," he teased.

But Doyle clasped his hand with her own, as she frowned into the darkness. "I'm worried someone's in danger. Someone female."

"Are you in danger?"

This of course, would likely result in Acton locking her in the laundry closet for the foreseeable future, and so she assured him, "No—not me." Her scalp prickled and she added, "In fact, I'm perfectly safe."

"Then what's this about a champion?"

She closed her eyes, trying to remember what the ghost had said. "Everyone has a champion—a white knight—and for some reason that's important. Munoz has Geary, and Martina has Thomas—although I suppose after the fiasco-disguised-as-a-dinner-party, that may no longer be true."

He squeezed her against him. "Speaking of which, did you see the announcement about the reception?"

Making a show of rubbing her eyes again, she admitted, "Oh —oh, I didn't get a chance to look over my emails today." Or yesterday, for that matter, but best not mention this unfortunate fact to her CO.

"Mr. and Mrs. Geary are throwing a reception at St. Michael's to announce their wedding."

"Are they indeed?" She shifted her head to meet his eyes. "I don't know if that's the best idea, Michael. After what happened at your Confirmation and Sofia's Baptism, mayhap St. Michael's should just stay out of the reception business, hence."

"Nonsense," he soothed. "We will have to think of an appropriate wedding gift."

"Riot gear," she decided. "Especially if her family's comin'."

31

Doyle had been assigned to interview a witness at a dispensary near the housing projects–the usual situation of illicit drug-smuggling had come to light. Truly, it was a foregone conclusion, almost, and equally impossible to figure out how to prevent such a thing from happening, although the Met had fostered various prevention programs. The personnel who were willing to work in such an environment tended not to be of the highest quality, and often went into the job with the express intention of reselling narcotics for fun and profit. No matter how tightly the substances were controlled, it all came down to the integrity of the medical personnel and whether they'd be able to resist temptation; unfortunately, temptation tended to win.

And—as surely as night followed day—the witness had seen nothing, had heard nothing, and had nothing of interest to relate. Better to keep one's head low rather than risk the wrath of those ruthless people who were making a lucrative business reselling drugs—assuming, of course, that the witness wasn't taking a healthy cut of the action, herself.

Timothy McGonigal had even mentioned that his organization—*The Curing League*—was having difficulties keeping its doctors safe on their volunteering stints, with several of their members having been robbed at gunpoint whilst walking back to their cars in this same area. A shame, it was, that even the do-gooders had to rethink their commitment.

One benefit from having to conduct the interview, though, was that it gave Doyle a chance, in the clear light of routine process-and-procedure, to think over her dream and to acknowledge that Tommy-the-painter had the right of it, Doyle was a green-'un who'd been juked out of her boots.

Acton knows who it is—he knows who's the female in danger, she acknowledged. He *must* know, because he deftly changed the subject as soon as I brought it up, in the way he always does when he wants to distract me, and then he threw a wedding-reception-for-Munoz stick that I happily chased, and we never returned to the subject.

With a frown, she thrust her hands in her coat pockets as she walked through the lobby at headquarters, listening with half an ear to the buzz of activity that was always ongoing in the echoing room. The whole thing made little sense—why wouldn't he want her to know? Surely, the endangered-female had to do with the money-laundering rig—Tommy had been killed because he knew too much, so presumably someone was in the same danger as Tommy. And why wouldn't Acton want her to know who it was?

She lifted her head, suddenly struck. Could it be Mathis? Lizzy Mathis was the one who'd found the paint in the first place —and she knew about the jewelry, too–but surely, that was not a secret worth getting killed over, was it? And it wasn't much of a secret anyways; both she and Williams knew of it, and Acton had already twigged onto the fake-artwork scheme, even though he was being very careful to keep it under wraps, so that he could set-up surveillance. Well, not *too* careful, since they'd gone to visit the Museum yesterday—

With the force of a thunderclap, the penny dropped, and Doyle halted in her tracks, her head lowered as she roundly cursed herself for an idiot. It just went to show what a *crackin'* dim-bulb the man's wife was, that she hadn't realized it sooner.

Tommy was right; Acton was a bone-rattler, and he'd been busy rattling bones all over the Museum. After all, the moment the illustrious Chief Inspector asks the Museum for their maintenance records, the blacklegs are going to know the gig is up. Not to mention he was openly parading about with his wife in plain sight of the CCTV cameras, taking a long, cool look at the faked artwork. Faith, it was a wonder the villains hadn't run out into the Exhibit Hall and surrendered themselves on the spot.

With grim determination, she resumed her progress over toward the lobby lifts. I need to nose about, and try to find out what's going forward on the Rizzo case, she decided. For some mysterious reason, Acton was openly allowing the Museum-blacklegs to know that he'd twigged them out, even though he was holding off on arresting anyone. Did he want them to fold their tents and disappear? Was he trying to stampede them into taking some misguided action—or worse, did he want to force them to abandon their ill-gotten gains so that he could seize them for himself?

Trying to puzzle it out, she decided she wouldn't be at all surprised if her husband's uncharacteristic actions were somehow connected with the counter-measures he'd taken to prevent Savoie from being framed. After all, Acton had a personal stake in keeping Savoie away from nosy law-enforce-

ment types, and so he may be walking a fine line betwixt rolling
up the rig and making sure no one laid a glove on Savoie. Therefore, it was possible he'd decided to give fair warning to the art-
smugglers so as to save Savoie.

Another flippin' moral dilemma, she thought crossly. On the
one hand, she was sworn to uphold justice, but on the other
hand, she shouldn't be actively working to throw her own
husband in jail, and mayhap that was what the ghost was referring to, when he seemed to be saying there was a danger fast
approaching that Acton didn't see coming. The story of my sorry
life, she groused to herself, and I suppose I should at least be
grateful that I've a variety of ghosts, trying to tilt the pitch in my
favor.

With this in mind, Doyle went straight to speak with
Inspector Habib, who was ostensibly her supervisor even
though the man would always defer to Acton when it came to
her assignments, and which was no doubt the very reason that
he'd been chosen to be her supervisor.

"Hallo, sir," she offered, pausing at his cubicle with a studied
show of nonchalance. "How's that baby?" Inspector Habib had
recently married and become a father, which sounded very ordinary if you left out the various hair-raising adventures that been
part-and-parcel of the process.

The Pakistani man turned to her and smiled his dry little
smile. "Thank you for asking, DS Doyle. Her mother says she is
a little angel."

"She is, indeed," Doyle agreed. "I'm back from the witness
interview on the infirmary case, and I'll file a report straightaway. I didn't glean much, which I suppose is to be expected. We
may have to set-up surveillance."

The Inspector was seen to sigh, because surveillance was

expensive, and the game was probably not worth the candle. "No other leads, DS Doyle?"

Reminded, Doyle told him, "The volunteer doctors—you know, the ones that go about to the clinics to help-out—they keep gettin' themselves robbed, and I wonder if they'd be a better source of intel than the staff. They don't ordinarily work in that area of town, so they may be less fearful, and more willin' to cooperate."

He raised his brows in interest. "This is so? I do not remember seeing any reports of such robberies."

"I don't know the particulars—I only heard it from a friend of ours, who's a volunteer. Mayhap the doctors are unwillin' to take the trouble of filin' a report."

He thought it over. "The robberies may not be connected."

This was a good point; it did seem unlikely that infirmary personnel who were pilfering drugs on the sly would be spending their spare time accosting doctors in broad daylight. And—again, as Inspector Habib had a budget to worry about— he could ill-afford a wild goose chase.

Habib suggested, "Perhaps your friend could discover if anyone who has been robbed would be willing to come forward with a description."

Doyle nodded. "I will ask him, sir. And even if it's not connected, I suppose we should try to keep the volunteers safe, else they'll go back to their fancy Harley Street offices and pull up the ladder."

"An excellent point, DS Doyle."

Habib then turned back to his computer screen, but Doyle stayed him. "May I ask you a football question, sir?" Habib was quite the fanatic, himself, and had been very much down-pin since Rizzo had departed this mortal plane.

With a precise nod, Habib did not betray in any way that this topic was unexpected, as he turned back toward her. "Yes?"

"What's a 'professional foul'?"

"It is an intentional foul, to stop a breakaway," he replied.

Rather than ask why sporting-talk enthusiasts always assumed everyone else could understand their mysterious language, Doyle held on to her patience with both hands. "I'm not sure what that means, sir."

He explained, "The defense has been caught outnumbered, and has no chance to stop a player from scoring, so the defender intentionally trips up the player handling the ball."

Doyle stared at him in incredulity. "Faith, that doesn't sound very fair."

He shrugged. "Everyone understand it is the only option. That is why it is a 'professional' foul—a necessary evil, and there are no hard feelings. It allows the defense to re-set, and avoid being scored upon."

She frowned, thinking this over. "What's an 'assist', then?"

Habib's unreadable gaze rested on her for a moment. "They are two very different things, DS Doyle; one is defense, and one is offense."

"Oh," said Doyle. "What's it mean, then?"

"An 'assist' is when an offensive player passes the ball to someone who has a better chance to score. The player who facilitated the score earns an 'assist'."

Trying to follow, Doyle ventured, "But the 'decoy' is not the 'assist'."

Habib nodded. "No, the 'decoy' is not involved in the scoring play. He acts only to draw the defense away from the scorer."

Doyle raised her gaze to contemplate the windows for a moment, and then admitted, "He says he shouldn't be the decoy, he should be the assist. But I haven't the first clue what he's talkin' about."

"If I could have your report by noon, DS Doyle." It seemed clear that Habib had tired of the football-talk, especially since it only re-opened old Rizzo-wounds.

But Doyle was doggedly determined to garner more information, and so lingered at the cubicle wall. "How is that Rizzo case goin', sir? I've heard a whisper that it may have been a crazed fan."

Habib nodded gravely. "Indeed. A fan with mental problems, who then took his own life. We are in the process of gathering evidence, DS Doyle, so you must say nothing to the media."

Again, Doyle felt a stab of annoyance that poor Tommy was to be left the blame of murdering his idol; small wonder the ghost was poking at her to straighten it all out. It suddenly occurred to her that she'd seen no record of a death that matched Tommy's description, and so she asked, "And the suspect's suicide wasn't in the Metro area?"

Habib paused, and offered fairly, "It is not clear whether it was death by suicide or death by accident, as there was alcohol in his system. It would be an extraordinary coincidence, though, and so suicide seems likely."

"And this was where?" Doyle prompted.

"His body was found in the Channel, DS Doyle, and it is presumed he drowned himself."

This was of interest, since a body found in the English Channel would be investigated by the Admiralty and not the Met—yet another way for the blacklegs to confuse the authorities.

"Thank you, sir. And DI Williams has asked me to follow-up with witness interviews from the day-of, if that's alright with you."

"Of course," Habib agreed, rather distractedly. "As for the infirmary case, I will let you know by end-of-day. I will either post a field officer at the site, or apply for a surveillance warrant."

"Can't do both," Doyle agreed. "But even if we think surveillance wouldn't be worth it, having an officer hangin' about would make everyone think twice before breakin' the law."

"We would hope, DS Doyle," he said with a great deal of meaning. No doubt he was referring to a best-be-forgotten case where the police officers themselves were bent, and busily facilitating the drug-selling.

"I'll get right on interviewin' the doctors, sir," she lied with only a small twinge of guilt, and then took her leave.

32

Thoughtfully, Doyle began the walk back to her desk. Now she understood why Tommy had mentioned—out of the blue, it had seemed at the time—that he'd never been one for boats. So; he'd seen something he shouldn't, the killer had murdered him to contain the fallout, and then his body had been disposed of in the Channel to further muddy the waters, so to speak. She had to take her hat off to this killer; it was a good piece of work, to scramble-up Tommy's murder on the fly.

She paused in her tracks and frowned, because this didn't seem—it didn't seem *right*, to her. She was assuming that Tommy's killer was Rizzo's killer, but that didn't seem to make much sense—it wasn't in keeping, that this wily Tommy-killer had so clumsily staged Rizzo's murder, and then followed it up with the equally-clumsy Savoie frame-up.

Were there two different killers? Tommy had never answered the question, but instead he'd only cautioned Acton to put his head on a swizzle-stick, or something equally indecipherable.

Remember the basics, Doyle, she cautioned herself; something's not adding-up, and so it would probably be a good idea to shake your stumps and figure out time-of-death for Tommy— although *surely* his death occurred after Rizzo's and not before; otherwise the CID would have ruled him out as the killer long before now.

This perplexing train of thought was interrupted when her mobile pinged, and she saw that it was Lizzy Mathis. To her shame, Doyle hesitated a moment before deciding that she should see what the newly-minted Mrs. Williams wanted to talk about. Mentally scolding herself for a coward, she answered, "Ho, Lizzy."

"May I speak with you, Lady Acton? Could you spare a few minutes?"

It didn't sound like work-talk, and so Doyle concluded that Mathis must be aware that the fair Doyle had been informed of her erstwhile marriage. Mentally girding her loins, Doyle replied, "Of course, Lizzy. What's up?"

"Could you come down to the lab, perhaps? It shouldn't take more than a few minutes."

So—she wanted to speak privately, and Doyle's tumultuous day just got a whole lot more tumultuous-er, or however you said it. Stupid Mathis must want to talk about stupid Williams, and Doyle was in no mood, having come tantalizingly close to finding out what it was that Tommy was talking about. As she teetered on the edge of telling the girl she was busy, Doyle paused, and reconsidered. She mustn't forget there was a woman in danger, somewhere, and if Acton didn't want Doyle to know who it was, mayhap it was Mathis.

"On my way," Doyle replied, and tried to sound more enthusiastic than she felt.

The on-site lab was relegated to the basement near the

Evidence Locker, since in the perpetual fight for prime office-space the forensics people didn't have much pull. It was sterile and cold, and inhabited by very clever people, which meant it wasn't Doyle's natural habitat and she avoided the area as much as possible.

Mathis was watching for her and nodded a greeting as she indicated Doyle was to sit on a lab stool she'd pulled up next to her own. "Thank you for coming, Lady Acton."

Why, she's a bit nervous, thought Doyle, and wondered with a flare of alarm if the other girl had discovered that she was indeed subject to some unknown danger.

Mathis pressed her lips together for a moment, and then began, "I hope you won't think me rude, but it is—it is rather common knowledge amongst the staff at Trestles that you and Lord Acton enjoy quite a healthy sex life."

Doyle stared at the other girl, blushing to the roots of her hair, and decided that this was exactly what she deserved for swimming naked in the stupid pond.

Watching her, Mathis ventured, "I am in need of advice, and I'm not sure who else to ask."

Finding her tongue, Doyle disclaimed, "I don't know as I'm one to have a lot of advice to give, Lizzy."

Mathis nodded, her cheeks turning a bit pink.

Doyle decided that she shouldn't be so unhelpful—the other girl was obviously in a quandary, and was no more eager for this conversation than Doyle was. Therefore, she should deliver whatever pearls of wisdom she could come up with, such as they were.

Slowly, she offered, "The main thing—I think—is to let him know that you're constantly in want."

Mathis raised her brows. "Oh?"

Doyle nodded. "Men can't seem to resist a woman who's

dyin' to pull them into bed. It's as true-as-true can be, and we see it a lot, in our business."

Doubtfully, the other girl admitted, "I don't tend to see it much, here in the lab."

"Well, no; but trust me, there are a million examples, out there."

Lowering her voice even further, Mathis asked, "Won't he think it very strange?"

"No," Doyle said bluntly. "He won't. And for heaven's sake, don't be subtle."

"I see." Mathis nodded. "Thank you."

Doyle then ventured, "How is everythin', Lizzy? Have you had any—well, has anythin' happened that would be concernin'?"

But Mathis clammed up like an oyster, as she'd evidently been given strict instructions not to explain how her marriage had come about—the girl wasn't aware, of course, that Doyle had already twigged on to the fact that a certain wretched DCI had been busily pulling the strings.

Mathis is nothing if not loyal, Doyle conceded; and—all in all—Williams needs a nice dose of loyalty, just now. Mayhap her string-pulling husband wasn't as wretched as he first appeared.

The girl then proceeded to make an awkward situation even more awkward by venturing, "There are advertisements for—for various devices—"

"No need," said Doyle, ruthlessly cutting off any further talk of such. "If you think a prop would be helpful, though, you can't go wrong with spiky-heeled black boots."

"Oh?" This said in a doubtful tone, as no doubt Lizzy Mathis had never come within hailing distance of spiky-heeled black boots.

"Yes," Doyle repeated firmly. "But don't wear much else." It wasn't clear if Mathis understood this basic principle, and so it probably should be emphasized.

The girl nodded. "I see. Thank you, Lady Acton."

"Kathleen," Doyle prompted with a smile, as she slid off her stool.

"Of course."

"Good luck," said Doyle, a bit awkwardly, since she wasn't certain what one said in such a situation.

She pushed open the security door, reflecting that the interview was not a'tall what she'd been expecting, which just went to show that she shouldn't try to out-think herself all the time—thinking was overrated.

As she walked down the linoleum hallway, she pulled her private mobile and phoned Acton.

"Kathleen."

"Code Five," she announced. "New suite; twenty minutes."

She could hear the amusement in his voice. "Can you hold that thought? I'm headed into Detention for an interview."

"Twenty minutes," she repeated. "If you're not there, I'll have to solicit the doorman."

"Right, then," he said, and rang off.

With a small smile Doyle called for the lift. Taking her own advice, she was.

33

After a very satisfying round of lovemaking, Doyle had the grace to ask, "What did I pull you away from? Anythin' dire?"

"Nothing that couldn't wait. The suspicious death of a surgeon in Harley street."

Doyle made a sound of commiseration. "Now, there's a shame. The poor doctors are havin' a hard time of it, lately; mayhap they should throw it in and find some work in a nice fish market, instead."

"They'd already have the cutlery," he noted.

They were lying side by side, and Acton was idly playing with the fingers on her hand, which he tended to do when he was well-content. "Have you remembered our tea?"

"Oh—oh, Martina is *today*? Saints, what's Reynolds goin' to think, when we pop up to take a shower in the mid-afternoon?"

He smiled. "I think we can assume Reynolds will express no opinion, one way or the other."

"Good point. He's the soul of discretion, is our Reynolds."

He held up her hand, splayed against his, for a moment. "You will let me know, if Martina strays from the truth?"

"I will. Is she the woman in danger, Michael?" May as well ask; sometimes Acton felt he'd no choice but to tell the truth when Doyle took the direct approach, and thus would be willing to throw her a bone.

"Perhaps," he offered.

She blew a tendril of hair off her forehead. "Why is whoever-it-is such a secret, my friend?"

He propped himself on an elbow, and gathered his thoughts as he ran a hand along her hip. "There is something here that I do not understand, and so caution is advised."

She glanced up at him, as she interlaced her fingers through his. "When did our suspect throw himself into the Channel?"

Acton tilted his head slightly. "Unfortunately, with a water-borne death it is difficult to ascertain exact time-of-death."

She decided to take the bull by the horns, and asked, "Did you kill him, Michael?"

He was not surprised she'd asked, but answered simply, "No."

She nodded. "I did wonder, since you seem to be in an all-out battle to cover-up for Savoie. Although I suppose you aren't coverin' for Savoie as much as side-steppin' a frame-up, which is a completely different thing." She paused, and then decided she had to warn him, even if she wasn't sure what it was she was warning him about. "I'm a bit worried—I suppose I'm a bit worried that there's somethin' here you're not seein', and it's comin' in to bite you." She paused, trying to remember what she'd been warned. "On the flank."

Interestingly enough, he didn't ask why she thought this, which told her that he'd had similar thoughts, himself. "Savoie will attend Munoz's wedding reception," he said slowly. "Perhaps you could mention Rizzo's death, and sound him out."

In some surprise, she raised her brows. "Holy Mother, Michael; then you think it truly *could* be Savoie, behind all this? Why on earth would Savoie kill Rizzo?"

"I don't think he did. But he definitely knows something we do not."

She nodded, sensing his deep concern. "All right—I'll do my best. Faith, you're lucky you're married to a handy-dandy truth-detector—I should ask for a raise."

"I am sorry, Kathleen." He was sincere; Acton didn't like putting her perceptive abilities to use; indeed, if it ever came down to a choice between catching the villains or making the fair Doyle uncomfortable, the fair Doyle would win every time.

She brought his hand to her mouth so as to kiss its back. "Whist, never had a nicer time, I assure you. Except when I'm bein' paraded around the Art Museum, like so much bait on a fishin' lure."

There was a prolonged silence. "You are extraordinary."

Making a sound of exasperation, she rolled onto her stomach and eyed him through her tousled hair. "You're tryin' to get them to stampede and do somethin' stupid; even a first-year could see it. Why won't you just tell me?"

"There are times," he suggested delicately, "when you are a bit transparent."

"I'm not as guileful as some I could name," she retorted crossly. "Best to tell the truth, and shame the devil."

"Words to live by," he agreed, and it was not exactly true.

"Hence," she warned in an ominous tone.

34

Martina Betancourt brought a lovely bouquet of flowers and apologized profusely as they all sat down to tea. As usual, she was neatly dressed without a hair out of place, with her sword-necklace hidden beneath the demure neckline of her dress.

"I am so sorry to have created such an unpleasant scene, Lord and Lady Acton. I do hope you will forgive me."

In what Doyle characterized as her husband's public-school voice, Acton assured their visitor, "Please do not apologize, Ms. Betancourt. Had I known Mr. Savoie would seek to embarrass you in such a way, he would never have been invited."

With a smile, the young woman confessed, "I was a bit surprised to see Mr. Savoie in attendance."

There was a small silence. If you think you're going to plump Acton for information, Doyle thought as she sipped her coffee, you've got another think coming.

And then—speaking of plumping for information—Acton offered with all appearance of sincerity, "If you don't mind my asking, Ms. Betancourt, is the Missing Persons Unit aware of your husband's case? Perhaps I can help to turn over a few stones; it must be a very difficult time for you."

"I would appreciate it," the young woman said quietly. "It is indeed."

Doyle duly noted—almost with some surprise—that their visitor was sincerely grieved. All things considered, Doyle wouldn't have been much shocked to discover there was no husband at all; Martina was like a will o' the wisp, and not easy to pin down.

"I can't give up hope that he may yet be alive."

This was true, and again, Doyle hid her surprise. Unless the man had been knocked on the noggin and had amnesia, one would think he'd have found a way to tell his wife that he'd survived his presumed drowning. It seemed a bit naïve, for such a woman to say such a thing. Of course, they'd never found a body, and it must be hard to let go of hope.

Doyle's own husband sipped his tea, and offered with a thoughtful air, "He was in construction, I believe."

Oh-*ho*, thought Doyle, who could sense Martina's sudden wariness. Now, there's a broadside; something's up, and obviously Acton's not telling me everything he knows no matter how much I soften him up with afternoon sex.

"Yes," their visitor said calmly, as she set down her cup. "D'Angelo Construction."

"Your husband was—is—Mr. D'Angelo."

"Yes."

Doyle tried without much success to hide her extreme astonishment, and carefully set down her coffee cup so that she didn't rattle it in the saucer. Holy saints and angels; it wanted only this, and if this stupid tea party was going to devolve into another crackin' bloodbath like the stupid dinner party did, Reynolds was not going to be able to quit fast enough.

And *shame* on her husband for not telling her, not to mention that this little tidbit of information explained why he'd drawn Martina in, like a spider to a web. After all, D'Angelo was another Kingsmen investor, and knee-deep in the money-laundering rig that got Rizzo killed. And for some incredible reason, no one seemed to be aware that Martina-of-the-Art-Museums was related to the man by marriage.

She must be in on all of it—she's a co-conspirator, thought Doyle in deep surprise, which would explain why she's been dating Williams and nosing around for information about Acton. It was downright diabolical, to be so abusing her position in an Order of the Church—although to be fair, the Church had been used as an excuse for questionable behavior almost from the moment it had been founded.

Her scalp prickled, and Doyle frowned slightly because—because this thought seemed *wrong*, for some reason. Martina may be a will o' the wisp, but Doyle would be very much surprised if the young woman was not a true believer. And it was very unlikely that a true believer was going to get herself involved in all this wholesale, wall-to-wall sinning.

Unsurprisingly, Martina decided to turn the subject away from her underhanded husband, who'd gone missing for his sins. "Your portrait was beautiful, Lady Acton. Stunning."

Doyle was willing to indulge their guest in this change of topic, and replied, "Thank you. I have to say it feels very strange, to have a portrait. I feel as though I should joke about it, and draw cat's ears on my head."

With a smile, Martina turned to Acton. "And yours, Lord Acton? Will you sit for a companion piece?"

"Already underway," Doyle answered for him. "Not yet

finished, though—it's no easy task, to arrange for both Acton and Javid to be in the same room at the same time."

"Javid is very much in demand," Martina agreed. "I understand you have a fine collection of artwork yourself, Lord Acton."

"I do," Acton agreed and offered nothing further.

Good luck, Martina, thought Doyle, as she felt brave enough to lift her cup and saucer again. The man's a sphynx.

As they all paused to sip, Doyle duly noted that—beneath the young woman's calm façade—she was indeed frustrated, and it suddenly occurred to her that it wasn't necessarily Acton who was doing the spider-web-drawing-in, but Martina, who was the one who'd asked to come pay this visit. She must have come, hoping to winkle-out what law enforcement knew about the money-laundering case, and she must be very much surprised to discover that she's met her match.

They spoke of inconsequential things for a few more minutes, and then Martina stood to take her leave. "Again, I do beg your pardon, and I hope you will forgive me."

"Whist, it wasn't your fault, it was Savoie who caused the ruckus," Doyle offered, and couldn't help but note that the girl had never once mentioned poor Williams, who'd been her pawn in all this. Mayhap she wasn't such a true believer, after all.

As they moved toward the door, Acton reached into the flower bouquet, and—with a casual gesture—drew out a small net cachet, which appeared to be filled with potpourri. "Did you leave this, Ms. Betancourt?"

Hiding a flare of alarm, Martina took it from him. "Oh—oh, yes; thank you—I was wondering where it had fallen."

There was a small silence, and then Reynolds offered, "Your coat, Ms. Betancourt."

35

D oyle could hardly wait until Reynolds had closed the door and retreated into the kitchen before addressing her husband in a low voice. "Holy *Mother,* Michael—was that a listenin' device?"

"No doubt," Acton replied, unperturbed.

In wonder, she followed him back over to the sofa. "My hat's off to you, my friend. Although I suppose once you twigged onto the whole D'Angelo connection, you've been mighty wary of the fair Martina."

"Indeed."

She eyed at him sidelong. "It would have been nice to give me a bit of a warnin' husband."

With a preoccupied air, he rested a hand on her knee. "I am sorry," he said, although it didn't seem that he was very sorry at all; no doubt he hadn't told her because his bride wasn't at all sphynx-like, when it came to monumental secrets. That, and he was striving mightily to make certain that the less anyone found out about any of this, the better.

He leaned back into the sofa, deep in thought, and so Doyle stayed quiet, respecting his process and only reaching to nibble on the occasional finger-sandwich. He still doesn't understand how this mish-mash of a case falls together, she decided; the man's that distracted.

After a few minutes, he glanced over at her. "What were your impressions, Kathleen?"

"Well, I don't think she's makin' a run at you, so at least there's that. On the other hand, she must be a blackleg—if her husband was D'Angelo—and the coals should be heaped on her head, with her holy-sword-necklace, and such; there's nothin' worse than a false prophet. But I do think you sent a shot across her bow, and it shook her up a bit." She paused, and added fairly, "You're a bone-rattler, and that's your style."

Acton nodded. "I confess I would like to better understand her motivation for cultivating Williams, and for approaching us today. If she was complicit in the rig, and her husband fell afoul of his cohorts, she should instead be melting away, and covering her tracks."

Much struck, Doyle could only agree. "Aye, that. She should be afraid that she's next in line to be thrown overboard, but instead, she's over here, beardin' the lion in his den and plantin' listenin' devices, for good measure."

Thoughtfully, he agreed. "Yes. She does not appear to be in any way concerned about criminal liability."

Doyle pondered this in silence for a few moments, and then ventured, "Mayhap we should do like they teach you in the Crime Academy, and go over the 'known-knowns', to see if it helps us figure out her motivation."

"By all means," said Acton, in the tone of a senior officer indulging a junior. "A fresh look may be helpful."

Doyle began to count on her fingers. "We know that Martina

was involved in the vengeance group—the one that went after the players in the sex-slavery case."

"Yes."

"We know she was held in Detention on a jewelry charge, but we think that was trumped-up just to keep her safe from the vengeance-group."

"Yes."

"We know that she's RC, and that she belongs to a religious Order out of Spain."

He tilted his head in mild disagreement. "I'm afraid we do not know that for certain."

"You're right," Doyle had to concede. "Sorry; *not* a 'known-known'."

He continued, "It may be a cover, of some sort. I find it of immense interest that her background is untraceable."

She stared at him for a moment in silence. Trust Acton to leap to the heart of the matter; small wonder he didn't prattle-on through the known-knowns. "You're right; that's the strangest 'known' of all. We know her background's been thoroughly scrubbed, and that's no easy task."

"Yes. And we know that she has access to large sums of money."

Doyle ventured, "*Could* she be intelligence, of some sort? That would explain the infiltration into these two different international crime rings, and her scrubbed background—she's an infiltrator." She paused. "It would explain the listenin' device, too."

But it seemed clear Acton had already considered this possibility. "I doubt it. Any branch of international intelligence operating within our jurisdiction would have made contact with our own intelligence operations, so that there would be no misunderstandings."

"Right, then; I'll have to take your word for it, since I wouldn't know." She took up her count yet again. "We know she knows Savoie, and there's somethin' between them."

"Yes."

"We know she's encouragin' Williams—or was, before he got himself leg-shackled to Mathis—but she was definitely encouragin' him." She paused, thinking this over. "Although—although she sincerely misses her husband, Michael, and truly doesn't know what's happened to him."

He raised his brows. "Indeed? That is of interest."

"A new 'known'," Doyle agreed. She resumed her count. "We know she spends a lot of time hangin' about at the Art Museum, which indicates she's probably involved in the fakery that's goin' on over there. Faith, she brought up the Trestles art collection just now, which does not bode well—best make sure it's under lock and key."

"Yes," Acton agreed. "And what do all these 'known-knowns' have in common?"

Since it seemed clear he believed there was a commonality, Doyle frowned, considering it, and finally could only raise her palms. "I haven't the first clue—I'm tryin' to find even *two* things that have somethin' in common. It's all a massive hodgepodge— can't make heads nor tails of it."

But this was apparently not the correct answer, and Acton reached to take her hand in his. "Do you remember what you told me about Martina, when you went for your brunch with Williams?"

Staring at him for a moment, she remembered, "Yes—it seemed to me that she was fishin' for information about *you*. And that's still her aim, it seems." With a knit brow, she considered this. "She must be tryin' to winkle-out how much you know about the rig. After all, you're the SIO on both the sex-traffickin' case and this money-launderin' case. That would also explain why she's cultivatin' Williams, since he's the assigned CMO."

But this promising theory had a flaw, and Acton pointed it out. "We know Martina was playing a role in the sex-trafficking investigation, but D'Angelo wasn't a suspect in that case. Indeed, I can find no connection."

Stubbornly, Doyle insisted, "There *must* be a connection, Michael; why else would she be infiltratin' these groups and pretendin' to be somethin' she isn't—not to mention scrubbin' her background information? She must be tryin' to find information."

"To what purpose? Her husband is dead, and the rig has been exposed. Why was she here today?"

Doyle knit her brow. "And— since we know that D'Angelo was dead well-before Rizzo was killed—D'Angelo can't be his killer, so she's not on some sort of righteous mission to save her dead husband's reputation."

"I would have to agree," he concluded.

She looked up at him. "And another thing, Michael; when you think about how she came here today to plant the device, that seems like it should be a crackin' desperation move, but she doesn't seem panicky in the least."

"No," he agreed. He gazed out the windows, and asked thoughtfully, "What did she hope to discover?"

"She has her own 'unknowns'?" Doyle guessed. "Mayhap she's worried that she's next on the list of containment murders? But then she should be disappearin', rather than always underfoot."

They sat in silence again, and then Doyle ventured, "Could it be that *Martina* is Rizzo's killer? She's tryin' to get you involved, you're not takin' her bait, it's drivin' her mad, and that's why she's plantin' listenin' devices?"

"Perhaps," he acknowledged. "Particularly if she holds a grudge against Savoie, it would explain the attempt to frame him."

Thoughtfully, Doyle informed him, "I'm don't think they're exactly enemies, though—Martina and Savoie. At the dinner party, I didn't get the sense she was angry at him. It was more like—more like they were sharin' a private joke." Thinking about this, she added, "And besides, it seems very unlikely that she'd arrange to murder Rizzo and prod you into framin' Savoie, since that's only going to expose her dead husband's role in all this. She truly loves her husband."

Slowly, he noted, "All working-theories seem to run up against the same hurdle; Rizzo's death shined a bright light on the money-laundering rig, and now law enforcement is closing in. It is hard to imagine what would motivate one of the conspirators to wish for just such a result."

Suddenly struck, Doyle turned to him in barely-contained excitement. "Oh—oh, *faith*, Michael; that's it—Rizzo's death was a *professional foul*."

With some surprise, her husband's gaze fastened upon her own. "I beg your pardon, Kathleen?"

But Doyle knew she was on the right track, and hurriedly explained, "You know—it's from football. When things are desperate, and the only thing left is for the defense to knock someone down and accept the foul."

With lifted brows, he observed, "You astonish me, Lady Acton."

But Doyle persisted, "That's it, Michael; I'm sure as sure can be. This wasn't a containment murder, to keep Rizzo quiet; instead, his murder was a desperate attempt to put a stop to the money-launderin' rig—it was a professional foul." Thinking on this, she shook her head in wonder. "Who would do such a thing? Who would steel themselves to kill Rizzo, of all people?"

"It is a very interesting working-theory," Acton observed in an indulgent tone. "But if this was a revelation murder, to shine a light on the rig, then why set-up Savoie to take the blame?"

"Oh," said Doyle, staring at him.

He leaned forward to take her hand again. "And why was it necessary to kill Rizzo? Much simpler to offer an anonymous tip."

"Oh," said Doyle again. With a long sigh, she dropped her head to hold it in her hands. "Faith, you're right. Back to square one."

Her husband ran a thoughtful hand down her back. "No matter; there is something at work here that we do not understand. We need only the final piece."

"Nothin' makes sense," she complained. "Hence, it's a crackin' ball of snakes."

"I do think it would be helpful to discover how Savoie knows Martina. Perhaps this could be another subject you could raise at Munoz's wedding reception."

Fairly, she pointed out, "He may not cooperate, you know. He's a bit hard to pin down, too."

Acton only cocked his head, to gaze out the window. "I wonder if he should be made aware that someone is trying to frame him for Rizzo's murder."

She smiled. "Good one. There's nothin' like the prospect of life in prison to bring about a bit of cooperation."

"I cannot disagree," he replied.

36

That night, the painter came for another ghostly visit, and Doyle complained, "We're goin' 'round and 'round, Tommy, and not gettin' any closer to solvin' it. It's a rare tangle-patch, and there's somethin' here he doesn't understand."

Raising his brows, the ghost offered, "Oh, now, I have to disagree, ma'am. He understands it better than just about anybody."

Thoroughly shocked, she stared at him. "But—Acton doesn't know who the killer is; I'm sure of it."

"Oh, no, no; but he would understand, just the same."

"What is it that Acton would understand?" Hesitating, she ventured, "Was Rizzo's murder a cover-up?" Acton had been known to commit the occasional cover-up murder, whenever he thought the circumstances warranted.

"Oh, no—not a cover-up at all." The painter wrinkled his brow, thinking about this. "Quite the opposite, really."

Feeling vindicated, Doyle declared, "Because it was a professional foul, just like you said it was. The killer was desperate, and had no choice but to kill poor Rizzo so as to put a stop to the rig."

He nodded. "A shame that it had to be done, but there it is. You've got to leave everything on the pitch, or die trying."

But Doyle pointed out, "It still doesn't add up, though. Acton's right; why do somethin' so drastic? Why wouldn't the killer just tip-off the Met, instead? We get anonymous tips all the time—no need to kill poor Rizzo, and stir-up such a firestorm."

"Because Rizzo's the bell-cow," the ghost explained, as though nothing more need be said.

Summoning up some patience, Doyle replied, "I'm not sure what it is you're gettin' at, Tommy."

"He's the bell-cow. He's the reason it works—no one would dare accuse him."

Seeing the wisdom of this, Doyle mused, "Yes—that's exactly what Acton said. Rizzo's the perfect bagman, because he can waltz through security and customs—faith, when he goes through, they probably ask if they can hold his bags of illegal cash so he can pose for snaps."

Nodding his head in admiration, Tommy could only agree. "I would have. He was the greatest, after all."

"He was as crooked as a dog's hind leg," Doyle reminded him firmly.

"No reason you can't be both," the painter explained cheerfully. "Lots of the lads get into trouble–I think it can't be helped, when there's so much money, and no one to say you nay."

There was a small pause. "It's a bit like Acton," Doyle decided. "Although I suppose I can 'say nay' to him—so, at least there's that."

"You do a right good job, ma'am."

There was another significant pause, but Doyle decided that

they were wandering off-topic, and pulled her thoughts back to the puzzle at hand. "Who's the female that you said was in danger? Was Rizzo killed so as to protect Martina—is she the one? That theory would make sense if D'Angelo was Rizzo's killer, but he was already dead, so it can't be him."

Tommy lifted his brows. "He's dead?"

"Yes." Doyle thought it might be bad manners to point out that Tommy should be more up-to-speed on who was dead and who was not, and so she kept the thought to herself. Instead, she said, "Acton's right; Savoie must know somethin', and he's not tellin' us whatever-it-is."

"I think you have everything backwards, ma'am," Tommy ventured in an apologetic tone.

Doyle stared at him. "I do? How's that?"

"You're not seeing the play that's unfolding—don't be caught sleeping in the backfield."

Puzzled, Doyle could only reply, "You keep sayin' that, but Acton is well-aware there's a play afoot, and Acton's as wily as they come. Faith, he's bein' extra-careful about makin' any moves—especially because he doesn't understand the motive."

"He would understand better than most," the ghost repeated.

Again, there was a small silence, where Doyle had the feeling that the kindly ghost was waiting for her to understand whatever-it-was that she was supposed to be understanding. Slowly, she tried to make sense of it all. "Acton's muddying-up your time-of-death, because he's tryin' to save Savoie's from a murder charge. Meanwhile, the killer's that frustrated that Acton's not throwin' Savoie in the nick, even if we don't know the motive for Rizzo's murder in the first place. We know there's a woman in danger, and that Acton shouldn't make you the decoy —you should be the assist, instead."

"Very good," he said, pleased. "You're very coachable, ma'am."

She ventured, "I don't suppose you could just tell me who killed you, Tommy?"

"I'm afraid not," he answered apologetically. "It doesn't work that way."

"No," she sighed. "It never does."

37

They were at Munoz's wedding reception, a rather simple, punch-and-cake affair in the church's newly-renovated hall, and Doyle whispered to her husband, "I don't see any of her Spanish relatives, Michael, do you?"

"No; they were unable to attend on such short notice."

Her antenna quivering, Doyle glanced up at him. "And how would you be knowin' that?"

He explained, "Since we are acquainted, I contacted Munoz's grandmother to extend a personal invitation."

Agog, Doyle breathed in wonder, "The clash of the titans; tell me there was no blood spilt."

With a small smile, he disclaimed, "Not at all; she said all that was appropriate, and assured me she'd send along a substantial wedding dowry."

Doyle had to laugh. "Good one, my friend—there's nothin' like a shovelful of money to mend a few fences. Lucky I'd no fences to mend, since I'd no dowry a'tall."

"You brought me more than I could ever ask," he said sincerely, and bent to kiss her temple.

That's very sweet, Michael, but a bit o' dosh never goes amiss. Faith, mayhap my dowry could have paid for one of the saucers at Trestles."

He smiled, but further conversation was interrupted when they were greeted by another guest and forced to engage in another round of idle chit-chat about the unexpectedness of the elopement. It was to be expected, of course; because many of the attendees were CID personnel, everyone felt it necessary to make nice to the ranking brass—not to mention his wife, the famous bridge-jumper. It was one of the great ironies of life that Doyle, who'd always been rather shy and retiring, was now thrust into the spotlight, will-she or nil-she. I'm a nine-days'-wonder, she thought with stoic resignation; if only the nine days didn't seem to keep going on and on.

As a case-in-point, one of the first-years who worked with Munoz's Unit approached deferentially and asked, "Would you mind if I took a snap of you with DS Munoz, ma'am?"

"Let's not," suggested Doyle rather bluntly. It was another ironic twist of fate–that she and Munoz were now forever linked, even though both young women would rather they were not. And poor Munoz was forced to be all beholden and such to Doyle, even though she truly hated to be famous for needing to be rescued even more than Doyle hated to be famous for doing the rescuing. Although—although Tommy had said Doyle was doing a good job, rescuing Acton. Coachable, she was.

With a small frown, Doyle paused with this thought. That's not what he'd said—surely? Instead it was about how she was the only person who could pull the brake on her wayward husband, and say him nay. Although she supposed it could be deemed a rescue of sorts—and a long-running one, at that. A constant battle, it was, to try to save the man from himself—

"I'm so sorry, ma'am," the flustered DC apologized.

Recalled to the conversation, Doyle realized she'd been rude, and said, "Oh—oh, no worries a'tall; it's just that I'd rather keep the focus on the new couple, today. Instead, let's have a snap, ourselves." With a show of amiability, she pinned on a smile, and let the officer take a selfie of the two of them.

Doyle then went back to listening with half-an-ear to whoever was speaking with Acton; the CID ranks were well-represented, as well they should be, since Munoz was one of their own–not to mention that police officers were always happy to use any excuse to hold a party, and swap tales of their trade.

The Inns of Court were also well-represented; Sir Vikili was in attendance, along with many of the other defense barristers and solicitors they ran up against regularly in the course of their work. Doyle had always found it interesting that the men and women on both sides of the criminal cases—who acted the part of mortal enemies when they were representing their clients—were usually very friendly out-of-court, and happy to socialize with each other.

They're like the aristocrats, Doyle decided; they think they're a breed apart, and that there's no one else who can relate to them. I suppose it's true in a way; it takes a rare breed to hold another person's future in one's hands—whether they will go to prison or walk free. Not just anyone can handle that sort of pressure.

Her scalp began to prickle, but before she could decide why it would, Acton noted in a low aside, "Savoie has arrived."

"Right," she replied, a bit guilty because she'd been wool-gathering instead of paying attention to her assignment. "I'm on it."

It wouldn't behoove the fair Doyle—who was, after all, a member of law enforcement—to make a beeline over to speak to Philippe Savoie, and so she began to move in his general direction, necessarily being greeted by various guests as she did so.

As she made her way past the area near the double entry-doors, she was treated to the sight of Williams, arriving with Lizzy Mathis in tow. They'd come together, which seemed to indicate that the annulment was taking the slow boat. On the other hand, it also seemed clear they were in the midst of an ongoing argument.

Her color high, Mathis asked in a level tone, "Perhaps we could solicit Lady Acton's opinion."

"No," said Williams. "Leave off, Lizzy."

Never one to pour oil on troubled waters, Doyle asked with interest, "My opinion about what?"

Mathis explained, "I think he should look into an artificial pancreas—at least find out whether he's a candidate for it."

"What's that?" Doyle asked, having no idea.

"Not an option," Williams said with finality.

Ignoring him, Mathis continued, "It is a regulating device you wear at your waist. It maintains your blood sugar levels, so there is no need for blood tests, or monitoring."

"That sounds good to me," said Doyle. "I hate needles."

"I don't need it," Williams said in the tone of one who will not be persuaded.

"You should at least explore the option," Mathis insisted. "You're being childish."

In a vehement undertone, he pronounced, "It is *none* of your business, Lizzy."

But the girl only retorted, "Of course it is, and I'm not going to let you stubborn yourself into an early grave."

"Why not; I'd *welcome* the silence."

Williams stalked off in one direction and Mathis stalked off in another, and with a thoughtful expression, Doyle watched them go.

She wasn't left alone for long, however, because Savoie sauntered over, which was much-appreciated as it saved her the awkwardness of having to approach him.

"*Bon jour*," he said, and rested his gaze on the newly-wedded Gearys, who were making their way around the hall to greet everyone. "This is the big surprise, yes?"

"Indeed it is. Who would have guessed that our Munoz would be one to jump over the traces? It just goes to show that you never know."

"*C'est vrai*," he agreed. "You never know the jumper."

She teased, "Are you sorry that you missed your chance, and it isn't you, bucklin' her up?"

"*Non*," he disclaimed. "Me, I do not do the buckling."

"I suppose not. Well, please try to behave yourself, and don't start another fist-fight like the last time you were here; Father John will never allow any of us to darken his door again."

The Frenchman offered his thin smile. "I am already in the trouble. Your husband, he tells me not to speak the saucy with you."

She made an apologetic face. "My fault—I knew he'd misunderstand the whole 'sword' thing. Sorry."

Savoie tilted his head and gave her a meaningful glance. "I do not wish to be in the trouble with your husband."

"No, I imagine not." This seemed like the perfect opening, and so she continued, "Although he's doin' you a favor, Philippe; I'm not sure you even realize."

He lifted his brows. "Yes?"

Nothin' for it. She lowered her voice and said, "He thinks

someone's tryin' to pull you into the Rizzo case. Someone's tryin' to suggest that you killed him."

Surprised, he brought his gaze to hers. "Ah—this is so?"

"It seems so." Doyle duly noted that the man was genuinely surprised, and continued in a mock-joking tone, "Please tell me you didn't murder Rizzo, Philippe."

He made a sound of annoyance. "*Non*—instead, it is the very bad thing, for me. There is much money lost."

This may have been a reference to the money-laundering rig, and so Doyle decided she probably shouldn't dwell on that particular aspect—or at least not just now, whilst they were all making merry at Munoz's wedding reception. "Who would want to frame you up?"

Being Savoie, he didn't seem much shaken-up by the idea— no doubt he was constantly rubbing elbows with back-stabbers of the first order. "I know not. But me, I am very careful."

Doyle made a wry mouth. "And you have a top-o'-the-trees solicitor, to pull your coals from the fire." Of course, the Frenchman also had a Chief Inspector who needed an under-world partner, but this pertinent fact should probably not be spoken aloud.

Trying to sound diffident, she ventured, "After that disaster of a dinner party, I'm a bit suspicious about Martina Betancourt. There's no love lost, between you; could she be the one who's tryin' to frame you up?"

In response, she noted he seemed genuinely amused, and shook his head slightly. "*Non*, she does not do the frame-up."

This was true, and so she prompted, "Well, best watch your step, is all; she's a bit too mysterious, for my taste. I'm curious as to how you met her."

With a gleam, he bowed his head. "Me, I pulled the coals."

Blinking, Doyle tried to decide what he meant. "You *rescued* her?"

He seemed very much amused. "Yes. *Après tout*, I am the St. Bernard."

"That you are," she agreed. "Don't tell anyone, or it will ruin your reputation as an out-and-out blackleg."

He tilted his head to her. "What does this mean?"

"A no-account chouser." Then, realizing this may not have been helpful, she simply offered, "A bad 'un."

Thoughtfully, he nodded. "No more, though; I must not be the chouser–yes?"

She wasn't certain what he meant, but replied, "Good luck in turnin' over that particular new leaf; you've a charge sheet as long as my arm."

"*C'est vrai*," he agreed, with all due modesty.

Doyle pulled her attention back to her assignment, since she truly couldn't remain in conversation with Savoie-of-the-impressive-charge-sheet much longer. "If you rescued her, why would Martina pretend she doesn't know you?"

He shrugged, slightly. "There are many secrets."

"Yes, so it would seem." He wasn't going to tell her, apparently, but she consoled herself with the fact she'd managed to find out what Acton needed to know. A good afternoon's work, and besides, Munoz and Geary were now circulating over to them, and so—with a wary glance at her companion–she smiled to greet the new couple.

38

To his credit, Inspector Geary did not bat an eye when Munoz's former beau offered his hand to congratulate him. "*Beaucoup de félicitations, Monsieur.*"

"Thank you, Mr. Savoie. I am a lucky man."

The Frenchman then bestowed a lingering kiss on Munoz's cheek, which her new husband tolerated with the air of the victor. "My congratulations, Isabel."

"Thank you, Philippe. How is Emile?"

"Emile is a good boy; he will come here for school, and so I must come to stay, *aussi*."

"Oh?" asked Geary, with a slight edge to his tone. "Now, there's some good news."

But Savoie assured him, "Do not worry; I will not be the chouser."

"Now, there's a faint hope."

In a cautionary gesture, Munoz twined her arm around her new husband's and asked, "Where will you live, Philippe?"

The Frenchman raised his brows. "I will live at my flat, Isabel. Do you not remember it?"

Hastily, Doyle changed the subject, "Lucky for you, St. Margaret's School is right around the corner."

With grim irony, Geary added, "You can offer to volunteer."

"Oh, look; there's the Assistant DCS," Munoz noted brightly. "We should probably go say hallo."

The new couple moved on, and Doyle warned her companion in a low aside, "Don't be upsettin' the apple cart, Philippe."

"*Non*," he agreed, thoughtfully watching Geary's back as the other man walked away.

"Not that you can, anyways," she observed fairly. "Love is a mighty, mighty, thing, and not somethin' you can control."

"*De vrai*," he said briefly, and she wondered if perhaps he was thinking of his son Emile—a prime example of the power of love, that hits you from out of the blue and takes no prisoners.

She decided that she should report what she'd discovered to her husband—not that it helped move the case, but at least they could rule-out Savoie as a murderer-with-a-side-helping-of-double-crosser. Doyle had to admit that—even though Acton's wariness seemed justified–she'd never truly felt that Savoie was the culprit, here. Savoie did have his own code of honor, and he and the fair Doyle were friends-of-sorts; she'd have been very surprised to discover that he'd turned coat. Not to mention there was that comment he made—something about turning over a new leaf, or such.

Maneuvering to take her leave, Doyle offered, "Well, it was nice to see you again, my friend. Sir Vikili's here, somewhere; you should give him your regards."

Savoie's mouth twisted. "*Non*; that one, I see him too much."

"I suppose that's true," she ventured diplomatically. "You must keep him knee-deep in clover."

He tilted his head. "What is this 'clover'?"

"Riches," she explained. "Bucketfuls of money."

"Ah. Yes—he needs this clover."

He slid her a meaningful gaze, rife with amusement, and so she said in some surprise, "What? Never say he's pockets-to-let?"

"The pockets," her companion confirmed with a nod, "they are of let."

Agog, Doyle could only stare. "*Truly?* He always seems so— so *fancy,* and well-turned out. Mayhap he's got a bad habit, or somethin'."

Her companion shrugged. "I do not ask the questions."

"Then how do you know that he's under-water?" Doyle asked, still trying to come to terms with such an unexpected disclosure. "Did he leave you to pay the shot at a pub, or somethin'?"

"He looked to sell the jewels—jewels from his family." He rubbed his fingers together in demonstration. "Very nice jewels, but I tell him *non*, I have no need for the jewels." With a gleam, he added, "Isabel, she would want them, but she is with me no more."

But Doyle wasn't listening, over the roaring in her ears and the almost overwhelming need to clutch at his arm to steady herself. Her mouth dry, she managed, "What—what sort of jewelry, Philippe? Was it emeralds—green stones?"

"*Non*," he replied. The blue stones—what are they called? In French it is *saphirs*."

"*Holy* Mother," she breathed.

Puzzled by her reaction, he bent his head to hers. "You wish these jewels, little bird? I will buy them, then."

But Doyle couldn't answer, because she'd fixed her gaze on

the floor, and was taking a deep breath to steady herself. Don't look up, she frantically scolded herself; and for heaven's sake, don't look at Sir Vikili.

But Doyle's husband—who tended to keep an eagle-eye on his bride—suddenly materialized at her side, and asked in an ominous tone, "Is everything all right?'

"I did not speak the saucy," Savoie immediately defended himself.

With a mighty effort, Doyle mustered up a smile for her husband. "No—no, Michael. I just misunderstood somethin', is all."

Taking her husband's arm, she managed to flash a friendly smile at Savoie. "I'm due for some punch, I think. So nice to see you, Philippe."

"*Au revoir*," the other man replied, eying her thoughtfully.

39

"What did he say to you?" Acton asked, in the tone of someone who was not averse to slaying a dragon or two.

"No—for *heaven's* sake, Michael, don't start a ruckus. Savoie didn't realize it, but—but he gave me a huge clue, just now. He—he told me that Sir Vikili is pockets-to-let, and when I asked him how he knew this, he told me that Sir Vikili had tried to sell him a sapphire necklace." In wonder, she looked up at him. "He must have had Savoie handle it, so as to leave his prints behind."

Her husband met her eyes, and she could feel his immense surprise, which was rather reassuring in an odd way, since it meant he'd no idea that Sir Vikili was behind all this, either.

In astonishment, she shook her head. "Mother a' *mercy*, Michael, no wonder we can't come up with a decent motive; Sir Vikili is tryin' to frame one of his own *clients* for murder." Still reeling from this extraordinary discovery, she continued in a low voice, "Does it mean that he's the one who's killed *Rizzo*? Or that he's protectin' whoever did? Faith, Rizzo's *another* one of his clients—for the love o' Mike, what's he about?"

"I do not know," her husband replied slowly, and it was true.

Her scalp prickled, and she knit her brow, trying to summon up the elusive thought. "You're supposed to know better than most," she said slowly, "but I don't understand why."

With an air of puzzlement, Acton bent his head to hers. "*I* am supposed to know the motive? How so, Kathleen?"

But their conversation was interrupted when Father John approached, and the two detectives were forced to engage in wedding reception polite-talk—no easy task when they'd just experienced a break-through on a knotted-up case.

"A fine couple," Father John observed in a genial tone. "I understand they were married at St. Brigid's, Kathleen; your own home parish."

"It's ground-central, for comin's and goin's," she agreed. "They should install a turnstile, or such."

"I would recommend against any renovations," Father John joked in mock-dismay. He then turned to Acton and said, "Thank you for your help, Michael; the new company will be on premises Monday next, and they assure me the work will be completed within two weeks."

"Don't know as I believe it," Doyle offered. "I think 'two weeks' is code for 'maybe never'."

"Aye, that, Kathleen; truer words were never spoken. But at least this hall is completed, and a fine job they did, at that." Father John rocked back on his heels as he cast a pleased eye around the newly-refurbished room. "And—thanks to the new Mrs. Geary—we've even got ourselves some artwork, so that we can hold up our heads just like the fancy churches."

This, in reference to a painting Munoz had presented to the church for the occasion; a street view of St. Michael's in its original state, before the renovation work. It was hung on the wall nearest them, and Doyle dutifully admired it alongside the very pleased priest. "You've got to give the devil her due—Munoz does good work."

"I don't know as I'd call her a devil," Father John chided in a mild rebuke.

"Sorry, Father. She's been learnin' at Javid's knee—d'you know Javid, the famous artist? Although I suppose we can't say there was any influence on this one, since Javid only does portraits."

She paused, aware that this was not exactly true; Nazy had said there was a Javid landscape in Sir Vikili's chambers. No—no, that wasn't right, it wasn't the same Javid; Javid was a common name, Nazy had said. Doyle stilled, her scalp prickling to beat the band.

"Has there been any progress on the project we spoke of?" Acton asked Father John with a great deal of meaning.

"Indeed," the priest replied with a gleam. "Shall we tell her?"

"Not as yet," said Acton, rather playfully.

"Plottin', you two are," Doyle chided, but she spoke absently, because there was something here—something important. Her husband was in the process of throwing another stick; despite his fancy-polite joking-about with Father John, he was striving mightily to turn the subject, like he always did when he didn't want her to figure something out. He'd smoothly turned the subject away from Javid, giving lessons to Munoz.

The penny dropped, and Doyle closed her eyes briefly, castigating herself for an idiot not to have figured it out sooner. As Father John moved on, she took her husband's arm and drew him over toward the wall, ostensibly to admire Munoz's painting, but in truth, to render a righteous brow-beating.

"Come clean, my friend," she began in a low tone. "It's Javid, who's doing the fake art for the money-launderin' isn't it? For her, copyin' modern art would be easy as walkin' the dog."

"I'd suspected," he equivocated.

In exasperation, she blew a tendril of hair off her forehead. "That's why you're fiddlin' around in the backfield rather than movin' in toward the box, Michael. You're tryin' to get your stupid portrait finished before she goes to prison, and shame on you for not arrestin' the woman outright. You mustn't try to bend things to suit your likin', Michael—I've told you a *million* times."

He was silent, and she decided she'd get nowhere treading this particular tinker's route, and instead wondered aloud, "Why would someone like her be mixed-up in such a despicable rig?"

He'd a ready answer. "Her husband is mixed up in it."

Again, Doyle decided she wouldn't inquire as to why Acton knew so much about the players in the rig—one crisis at a time. "Well, *shame* on her—she shouldn't aid and abet her wretched husband, and now a man's dead, as a result. Two men," she added, thinking of Tommy. "Shame on her," she repeated.

"Theirs is a different culture," he reminded her. "She may have felt she'd no choice but to obey her husband."

This was a fair point, and even though such a knuckling-under wasn't in Doyle's nature, she'd seen plenty of women of all cultures who were unable or unwilling to mount a protest, when their menfolk threatened them. "She must be under tremendous pressure," Doyle agreed, thinking this over. "Because she's another bell-cow."

Puzzled, he bent his head to hers. "How's that?"

Doyle explained, "The rig wouldn't work without a high-quality artist. For it to work, they needed an untouchable athlete to breeze through security, and a high-quality artist to copy the fakes. If either one of them drops out, the rig collapses."

"Very good," he agreed. "You have done extraordinary work, Kathleen."

Unable to hide her alarm, she glanced up at him. "The rig *has* collapsed, Michael, because Rizzo is dead. And—and that leaves Javid as the weak link in all this—if she's only cooperatin' under duress. Mother a' mercy, Michael—I'm that worried; I think she's the woman in danger. Let's go arrest Sir Vikili, and sort it out from there."

"Arrest Sir Vikili on a murder charge?" he asked in a practical tone. "On Savoie's word?"

She stared at him in frustration, as this was a good point; it would be no easy thing to connect Sir Vikili to the rig—not to mention the unholy hue and cry that would be raised if such a famous defense solicitor were to be thrown into Detention on a scandalous charge.

She brought her fingers to her temples for a moment, fighting a sense of panic. "We have to do *somethin'*, Michael. Should we have a quick word with Sir Vikili, and see what there is to see?"

Acton informed her, "He left, about fifteen minutes ago. Rather in a hurry, actually."

Trust Acton to have noticed; he tended to keep a sharp eye on whatever was happening around them whilst his dim bride tended to wander off the nearest cliff.

"We have to stop him, Michael—I'm that worried Javid's in danger," she urged. "I know it's hard to believe it of him, but I suppose if you lie down with dogs, you get up with fleas."

She could sense Acton's extreme reluctance, as he took her arm and they turned to leave. "I suppose it is possible, but I would be very much surprised if Sir Vikili is a player. Allow me to take a careful look, first; if he is indeed involved, it must be handled very circumspectly."

But Doyle was in no mood to slow down when it came to throwin' over the money-lenders' tables—it was important, for some reason, that they move on it, and move quickly. "It's an emergency," she insisted, "and we've got to clear the ball away. We can think up a strategy after."

But he only repeated in a practical tone, "What would you have me do?"

This gave her pause, because even Doyle—who tended to see things in black and white—had to admit that he'd nothing on which to base a twenty-four hour hold. Faith, even if they did have grounds, it would be a major blow to the Inns of Court to expose Sir Vikili's role in the money-laundering rig, not to mention Rizzo's murder. After all, if Sir Vikili went to prison, who would all the blacklegs hire, to get them off scot-free? No one else came close, which was why the man had the most luxurious chambers in all the Inns of Court—

Suddenly, Doyle halted in her tracks and lifted her head. "Where's Nazy? I have to ask her somethin'."

"Just now?" Her husband was understandably surprised by this request.

"Now," she informed him firmly. "It's important."

40

They found Nazy socializing with some of the younger attendees, and after Doyle waited through everyone's respectful greetings, she drew the girl aside. "Ho, Nazy; I was tryin' to tell Acton what it was you told me about the paintin' on Sir Vikili's wall—remember the one? I can't remember the story's name."

Nazy readily explained, "It is the story of Vis and Ramin, Officer Doyle."

Doyle prompted, "You said it was unexpected, because a lot of people think the story's scandalous, or somethin'."

There was a small pause, and then–in the manner of someone having to speak of an embarrassing subject whilst her boss was listening in–the girl's cheeks flushed slightly. "Yes. It is a story of forbidden love."

"Fancy that. What's the story about?"

Nazy lowered her voice. "It is an old story, Officer Doyle, and quite long, but mainly it is about Ramin, who fell in love with his sister-in law, Vis."

Doyle glanced up at her husband in surprise, because she could feel a strong jolt of awareness, emanating from him. "What?" she asked him.

"It is a famous story, in my culture," Nazy continued, "But many of the stricter people do not approve, because such a love is forbidden, outside marriage."

Acton nodded understandingly. "Then we will say no more about it. Thank you, Ms. Chaudhry."

"Yes, sir," Nazy replied, a bit chastened. "Perhaps I shouldn't have mentioned it; I am truly sorry."

"My fault," Doyle soothed the girl with a smile. "I'm always lookin' out for a snippet of good gossip, and let this be a lesson."

As they drew away, Doyle squeezed her husband's arm, and demanded in a low voice, "Tell me."

"Wait until we are home," he suggested.

But Doyle knew—in the way that she knew things—that time was of the essence, for some reason. "Tell me immediately, or I'll push you down the basement stairs, husband."

"Javid is Sir Vikili's sister-in-law. Her husband is his older brother."

Doyle stared up at him in surprise. "He *is*?"

"I thought you knew."

"No."

As he steered her toward the church's doors, she mused, "So —Sir Vikili's in love with his sister-in-law, which is as forbidden as forbidden can be, and meanwhile she's a player in this money-launderin' rig, which must keep him up a' nights, frettin' over her fate."

"Remember," Acton offered, "that she is probably more a cat's-paw, than a player."

"Which means?" she prompted, impatient.

"It means she has little choice but to do what her husband tells her to."

Doyle nodded, seeing the truth of this. They emerged out the door and into the sunlight, where she paused, blinking. "But if she's paintin' such a paintin' for Sir Vikili, she must be in love with him, too. Hence, it's recip—recrip-"

"Reciprocated," he supplied. "An unfortunate situation."

In some confusion, she began moving forward again. "I was told that you'd understand more than most, but that can't be right; he's not like you—not a'tall. If I'd been married when we'd first met, my poor husband wouldn't have lasted a fortnight."

But he disagreed, as they began to descend the steps. "It would depend on whether you loved him or not."

Much struck, she paused yet again, on the step above his, and considered him thoughtfully at eye level. "Yes. *Yes*—that's exactly right. Because you'd only want what's best for me. And Sir Vikili is Javid's champion, and he only wants what's best for her. So why does he think that exposin' the rig—and in such a desperate way–was a good move? They weren't under any sort of threat from law enforcement—why would he take down Rizzo, and leave her exposed?"

"He was trying to frame-up Savoie," Acton reminded her. "Perhaps his intention was to draw law enforcement's attention away from her."

In wonder, Doyle shook her head. "There's another thing that doesn't add up—he's tryin' to frame-up his own client." Slowly, she offered, "Although I suppose that actually falls-in with my theory–if he doesn't want Javid to be arrested, he's got to find a scapegoat."

Thoughtfully, he lifted a hand to smooth a stray tendril of hair back behind her ear. "A scapegoat that he knows he can get off."

She stared at him. "Mother a' mercy—of *course*. That's why there were holes in the case against Savoie—why you thought the frame-up seemed so clumsy. It was done like that on purpose. No one would know how wiggle a blackleg off the hook like Sir Vikili."

She could see that her husband was beginning to buy into her working-theory, but he lifted his chin to gaze out over the street. "Why do it, though? Law enforcement was not yet moving in. Why would he do something so desperate?"

They stood for a moment, thinking this over, and Doyle added thoughtfully, "And why wouldn't he just throw himself on your mercy, when all was said and done? You'd be happy to roll-up the rig, and if the price paid was to soft-pedal Javid's part in it all, you'd be more than willin'. Everyone knows there's a different justice system when it comes to pretty women; she'd probably get probation at the worst."

But her husband shook his head. "You must see that he could not come to me. Not only would he be betraying his clients, he'd be betraying his own brother."

"Oh—oh, that's right, I'd forgot about the wretched brother. What a dilemma; you can almost feel sorry for him."

They began their descent down the steps again, and she hooked her hand in his elbow. "It *still* doesn't make much sense, does it? The rig's been rollin' along with no one to say them nay, and then Sir Vikili suddenly throws a mighty spanner in the works, risking utter disaster unless he can throw enough dust in your eyes to frame-up Savoie-as-murderer, so that he can get him off and everyone can go home. What was the trigger—why would he panic?"

But apparently her husband had developed his own theory. "I would not be surprised if the trigger had to do with D'Angelo's death. There were suspicious circumstances, and it may be that the players were starting to turn on each other."

"No honor amongst thieves," she agreed, as he opened the car door for her. "And meanwhile, you were rattlin' bones at the Art Museum, and throwin' them all into a panic. Mayhap Sir Vikili realized that the blacklegs might be panicked enough to silence Javid, since she's most likely to twig them all out. That may be why he was so desperate to bring it all down; he'd rather she was in prison than dead."

"Do you think her own husband would sign-off on her murder?" He asked in the tone of one who was genuinely curious.

She shook her head, slightly. "I didn't gain much of an impression either way, Michael, so's I can't say. But I do think Mr. Javid's a bit of a worm, so mayhap we could go bluster at him a bit—make him aware that we're on to them." She paused, and then looked up at him. "I'm worried that we've got to do *somethin'* and do it fast."

Acton started the car. "D'Angelo's yacht is docked at St. Katharine's Marina. It is the means by which they smuggle the goods to the Continent, and I believe they have a run scheduled for today."

She pressed her lips together briefly, because the fact that he knew this interesting little tidbit only confirmed her suspicions that he was merrily skimming-off proceeds whilst he was also dragging his feet about closing in on the blacklegs.

Striving to maintain an even tone, she said quietly, "I think it's past time to start makin' arrests, Michael; we don't need any more money–especially blood-money—and you'd think you'd have learned this lesson, by now. And Javid will just have to finish-up your portrait in prison, where at least she'd be safe."

His response was to phone-in to Dispatch, asking for two

field units to meet him at the marina. When he listened to the response, she could sense his surprise as he rang off. "The units were already on their way. They'd received an anonymous tip."

"Sir Vikili called it in," she concluded. "In the end, she was more important to him than his life's work, or even his own brother."

"Yes," he agreed quietly, and there was a full weight of meaning in the single syllable.

41

Despite the fact she was dying to be in on the take-down, Doyle's husband left her with strict instructions to remain in the Range Rover whilst the confrontation took place, and to not stir an inch.

She could see the wisdom of this—much was at stake, and these people were dangerous—and so as a compromise, he'd parked the car in the adjacent lot so that she could watch events as they unfolded down below on the docks.

The marina was quiet, with the various power and sailboats secured in their respective slots on the dock—yacht space was scarce, in London, and so each vessel seemed impressive and luxurious as would befit the ridiculous cost of the upkeep. D'Angelo's yacht was tied next to the egress opening and plainly visible; a large, sleek sailboat with teak decks and shiny brass fixtures.

The field units had arrived before them, and the uniformed officers were standing on the dock alongside the yacht, questioning the two crew members. Doyle duly noted that two of the

PCs were asking the questions whilst the other two PCs stood slightly back, their torsos slanted at an angle.

 So; she thought, watching the interaction; the coppers don't like this, for some reason, and are standing ready for trouble. And for their part, the two crewmen are trying to convince the coppers that nothing's amiss, and there's nothing to see, here. But it's all for naught, because here comes DCI Acton, and hell is comin' with him.

Acton strode up and showed his warrant card, clearly directing the PCs to search the vessel. The two crewmen eyed each other in panicked alarm, and Doyle was relieved to see two more patrol units pull up to the dock, their lights flashing. The fair Doyle would have been hard-pressed to sit in the car rather than head off any fleeing suspects, and so it was just as well that she wasn't going to be faced with the choice.

One of the PCs who'd descended into the yacht's hold now came back up on the stairway to report something in an excited tone to Acton, who then lifted his mobile.

Calling for SOCOs, she guessed. They've found the goods, and will sequester the yacht. Thank God fastin'; hopefully they've found all the evidence they'll need to unravel this rig.

The PC rather roughly pulled a third crewman up from the hold, and Doyle gasped to see that a distraught Javid stumbled up after him, her hands bound before her.

The poor woman was sobbing and disheveled—no doubt she'd been pleading for her life with little hope for it. Doyle had seen more than her share of human brutality in her job, but there was something about the callousness of this that made her wince—hard to imagine how ice-cold you'd have to be, to just toss a bound person into the sea, knowing they'd hopelessly struggle. She offered up a prayer for poor Tommy, who'd no doubt suffered the same fate.

When her hands were cut loose, Javid immediately collapsed against Acton, clutching his coat and weeping into his chest.

He's not your champion, thought Doyle. Your champion is no doubt watching, somewhere, and shedding some tears of his own.

Suddenly, there was a quiet tapping on the driver's side window, and Doyle glanced over in alarm only to see that it was Martina Betancourt, smiling in reassurance, and pantomiming her desire to speak with Doyle.

Here's a winkle, she thought, and nodded her consent as she lowered the far window. Despite the girl's mysterious ways, Doyle's formidable instinct had always told her that Martina was not a danger to her, and never had been. Still and all, here she was in the thick of it, and the fair Doyle had best be wary.

The girl leaned in to begin, "I hope I didn't startle you, Kathleen, but I was wondering if I could beg a ride home."

Doyle blinked at the unexpected request, which was completely true. With a gesture toward the docks, Doyle explained, "Acton's got to oversee the processing of the crime scene; it may take a couple of hours, I'm afraid. I'd drive you home, but I'm not a very good driver, and this is not the area to test it out."

Nodding, the young woman offered, "May I drive you home, then? You see, I was hoping to speak with you privately, and without interruption." She paused. "It really can't wait."

This was true, and again, Doyle didn't have the sense that the girl was concealing a worrisome purpose. Nevertheless, she decided that she may as well ask, "Shall I read you the caution? I imagine the yacht belongs to you, now, and it does seem that it's a floatin' hotbed of crime."

Unperturbed, Martina replied, "You may read me the caution if you like, but we haven't much time." She paused, raising her head to watch the action around the yacht for a moment, and then ducking to return to her position at the window. "I need to speak with you about your husband."

For the first time, Doyle felt a twinge of unease. On the one hand, she didn't feel the girl was a danger to her, but on the other hand, Martina's involvement in these events remained unclear, and she hadn't offered any explanation for her presence here at the dock. It would surely be nice to finally find out exactly how Martina Betancourt fit in to these strange events.

Coming to a decision, she nodded. "Right, then; let me text Acton."

She pulled her private mobile and texted, "Martina here wants to drive me home OK?"

"HIE?" The reply came promptly, and Doyle knew he was asking whether her hair was in her eyes—whether she was alarmed about the situation.

"1," she texted in reply, which was police code for a non-urgent situation. This would no doubt prompt him to put a tail on them—Acton may be busy with this take-down, but he'd take no chances when it came to Martina-of-the-scrubbed-background. Neither would Doyle for that matter; her gun was snug in her ankle holster, if needful, even though Doyle didn't have the sense it would be. Of course, she'd been wrong on that subject before, on a best-be-forgotten occasion, and had the body-count to show for it.

With one hand casually resting on her leg above the ankle holster, Doyle smiled at Martina as the girl started up the Range Rover.

42

As they navigated out of the parking lot and onto the access road, Doyle decided she may as well ask, "What's up, then?"

Martina glanced over at her. "Now that the police are taking an interest in this matter, I have a conundrum."

"Oh," said Doyle.

Martina smiled slightly as she turned the steering wheel. "It means a dilemma—there are two paths to take, and I am not certain which is the best."

Confused, Doyle ventured, "Oh. Wait, is this about your husband, or mine?"

"Yours."

Doubtfully, Doyle eyed her. "What's the cond—com—what's the dilemma?"

"I represent a private interest that fulfills security duties for a client."

"The Order of Santiago," Doyle agreed. "Defendin' the Church."

With some surprise, the girl glanced her way. "Who told you this?"

Doyle wondered if Martina was worried about Savoie's having loose lips, and so assured her, "No one. We figured it out, between Acton and me."

Doyle could see that this was unwelcome news. "Will you tell me how you did?"

"No," said Doyle bluntly. "I won't." Although she'd have liked to give herself a pat on the back for drawing the sword-cross; mayhap this artist business wasn't so very hard, after all.

Martina nodded, and then continued, "As I said, I am a private security contractor, and my organization operates outside of law enforcement. Oftentimes the secular justice system does not have the same goals that the Church does."

"Don't I know it," Doyle heartily agreed. "I have to keep remindin' myself that the only perfect justice will be served-up in heaven."

The girl smiled in acknowledgment. "'A joy to the righteous'. But in the meantime, I work to protect the Church, which is besieged by enemies on all sides." She paused for a moment. "These people were involved in an elaborate scheme to siphon money away from the Vatican. It was disguised as a world-wide charitable fund."

Doyle stared at her in surprise. "The *Vatican* is involved in this money-launderin' rig?"

"Not knowingly, of course," her companion assured her, and Doyle noted that this was not exactly true, and not exactly false. "My husband was working to infiltrate the scheme, but his role was discovered, and so he was killed."

Much shocked, Doyle could only stare at her. So—another despicable drowning, and it appeared that D'Angelo was not the blackleg that he'd seemed. She offered, "I'm that sorry—he wears a martyr's crown in heaven."

"Thank you," the girl said quietly. "I can only hope that is the case." After a small pause, she continued, "Unfortunately—or fortunately, depending on how you look at it—the discovery of his true identity created a panic amongst the perpetrators."

The last piece of the puzzle suddenly fell into place, and Doyle offered slowly, "Yes; your—your vengeance operation was twigged-out, so the blacklegs started coverin' their tracks like a house a'fire." And Sir Vikili had must caught wind of the fact that the panicked players were planning to ruthlessly extinguish the Javid weak-link, so he decided to wave a red flag in front of DCI Acton so as to expose the scheme, and save her life; in an ironic twist, it was law enforcement who was going to come to the rescue, by throwing her in prison.

And give him credit, Acton was right; he'd guessed that D'Angelo's death was some sort of trigger, even though he didn't understand why. Small blame to him; the villains weren't panicking about the possibility of law enforcement's closing in —instead they'd discovered that a powerful Holy Order was hell-bent on destroying them, with the emphasis on hell.

Thinking on this, Doyle asked, "Does your Order go about killin' people?"

Instead of answering directly, her companion replied, "The Church will absolve 'just cause' murders, so long as there was no choice, and innocent lives were at stake."

"It's all very Old Testament," Doyle agreed politely, and carefully kept to herself her opinion of roving vigilantes who felt they had the authority to make decisions as to what was a just cause, and what was not. It was the self-same problem that she was forever bangin' on Acton about, and come to think of it, in a just-cause world it would be Martina who was married to

Acton–although there'd probably be scorched-earth for miles, so mayhap it was just as well the man was married to the wife who was always trying to wave him off.

In an even tone, Martina continued, "It appears that one of the persons involved in siphoning money from the Church is your husband."

Oh-oh, Doyle thought, struggling to hide her acute dismay; Holy Mother of God—Acton's sins were coming home to roost with a vengeance.

Feigning astonishment, she faced the other girl and exclaimed, "*What*? Mother a' mercy, Martina—that makes no sense a'tall. He's a DCI, after all; you must be mistaken."

In response, the other girl only met her eyes for a moment.

Hurriedly changing her tactics, Doyle offered, "Well—be that as it may—I'm certain that even if he were involved, somehow, he didn't know about the Church's involvement—that the Church was one of the victims. After all, he's recently converted, and donates very generously."

"Hence, my dilemma," her companion agreed.

"Hence, he's a good man," Doyle insisted.

"Yes. And he is obviously devoted to you." Again, her expressionless gaze held Doyle's for a moment. "A word to the wise, is all."

They'd come to Doyle's street, but rather than turn into the parking garage, Martina pulled over to the kerb, and set the gear. "Thank you for allowing me to speak with you, Kathleen. I should go, now."

In her cool manner, the young woman slid out of the car and walked around to the pavement, where Doyle lowered the passenger side window to say with all sincerity, "Thank you. I do appreciate the warnin'."

Martina paused, and addressed her thoughtfully. "I hope we meet again, under happier circumstances."

"Me, too," Doyle replied. She then duly noted that Trenton —Acton's personal security man—walked by on the pavement behind Martina, casually glancing into the car. They'd a signal they used if an intervention was needful, but Doyle ignored him, and kept her hands still.

The other girl hoisted her shoulder-purse and turned to walk away. She suddenly faltered in mid-step, however, and Doyle could feel the full force of her profound shock as she stumbled and nearly fell.

Scrambling out of the car, Doyle hurried over to grasp Martina by the elbows so as to steady her. "Are you all right? Here, sit down for a moment."

As she steered the shaken woman backwards to sit in the car seat, Doyle glanced around to be certain that whatever had upset Martina did not still threaten. With some surprise, she noted that the newsstand man who operated the kiosk on the corner—usually so cheerful and friendly—was staring at them in profound alarm, and upon seeing Doyle's scrutiny, he thrust his hands into his pockets and strode away, abandoning his post.

"Antonio," whispered Martina through pale lips, watching him.

Doyle turned to stare at the white-faced girl. "Holy *Mother*; that's your husband?"

Taking deep breaths, Martina lowered her face and said in a low voice, "Please—please; say nothing."

"Not crackin' likely," Doyle retorted. "For the love o' Mike, but there's some brass for you—let's track him down and see what he has to say for himself."

"No—no; please. He must be in deep cover." With her head still bent, she took a long, shuddering breath.

Doyle eyed the top of the other girl's head. "Didn't serve you very well, for all his deep cover. A nasty trick."

But Martina did not respond, and appeared to be making a mighty effort to pull herself together.

Doyle urged, "At least come upstairs and let Reynolds make you tea. You can have a lie-down."

"No—no, thank you. I—I just need to sit for a moment." She lifted her face to Doyle's, and repeated, "I'd appreciate it if you didn't mention this to anyone."

"Not a word," Doyle lied. "Although I could ask the same of you, I suppose."

The other offered a wan smile at this irony, but replied steadily, "I must put my mission before all other considerations."

"It's a champion, you are," Doyle noted fairly. "They're thick on the ground, around here."

43

W hilst Doyle waited with Martina so as to allow the girl time to recover, she was completely unsurprised to be interrupted by her husband, who was another champion, and not about to fuss with international money-laundering take-downs when he'd been given word that his wife was behaving strangely on a Kensington street. Laying a hand on Doyle's back, he bent to address Martina. "Everything all right? Shall I call for an ambulance?"

"Thank you, Lord Acton, but I am quite recovered. I'm afraid I felt a bit faint."

"Allow me to have my driving service drop you home, then."

"No—no, thank you. A bracing walk is just what I need."

With a pang of pity, Doyle knew that Martina was going to walk past the kiosk and hope her husband would make contact with her. Faith—talk about mixed emotions; if Acton had pulled such a trick, Doyle would be half-inclined to hug him so hard that she accidentally strangled him.

Acton met Doyle's eyes briefly, and she silently communicated that all was well, and that the other girl should be allowed to leave. However, as Martina walked away, Doyle stood to give her husband an unexpected embrace. "Check the car for a listenin' device," she murmured into his ear.

Acton leaned in to run his hand under both seats, and then he pulled his mobile to engage the scanning application that sought out interference from unknown electrical devices. "Looks clear," he said. "What happened?"

Doyle thought it over. "It's a long story, so it can wait," she offered. "But believe you me, it's a doozy."

He glanced over to where Martina could be seen blending into the passersby on the pavement. "Shall I put her in Detention, on a twenty-four hour hold?"

"I wouldn't," she replied. "She'd only turn around and do the same to you."

He lifted his brows. "She's law enforcement, then?"

"After a fashion," Doyle equivocated. "Like I said, if you're busy, it can keep."

His mobile was constantly pinging even as they spoke, and he signaled to Trenton to come over. "Save it until this evening, then. I should head over to the Art Museum."

"Rattle their bones," she advised as she climbed into the car beside Trenton. "Flood the zone."

"We'll see," he equivocated, and then closed the car door behind her.

Doesn't want the fair Javid to go to prison, he thought, eying him as they pulled away. The man wants his matching portrait, he does.

After Trenton had escorted her up to the flat, Reynolds expressed his well-bred dismay that she'd caught him cleaning the kitchen. Hurriedly peeling off his rubber gloves, he asked, "How was the wedding reception, madam?"

"Grand, it was. Savoie was there, and sends his regards."

Reynolds pressed his lips together in disapproval. "I hope Mr. Savoie did not distress the bride, madam."

Doyle smiled as she unwound her scarf and handed it to him. "There's a faint hope, my friend; Savoie's a ruckus-raiser, born and bred. May as well bark at the moon." She paused, and then added fairly, "Save for those times when he's savin' the day."

The butler raised his brows as he hung up her coat. "I cannot imagine Mr. Savoie in such a role, madam."

"You'd be surprised," Doyle replied absently, as she wandered over to listen at the nursery door. "I think Edward's awake."

Reynolds indicated the monitor that sat on the kitchen counter. "I believe he is still asleep, madam."

Doyle opened the door, and said loudly, "Ho, Edward. Are you still asleep?"

In response, the baby gamely rose to clutch the crib rails, and bestow a sleepy smile upon his mother.

"I will prepare a sipping-cup for master Edward, then. Will you have coffee, madam?"

"No thanks," Doyle said, gathering up her son and squeezing him fondly—he was always so docile and sweet, when he first woke. "Instead I'll have whatever he's havin'."

"Very good, madam. I've baked some biscuits."

"Acton's goin' to be late," she advised, "so we'll eat without him. Finger food on the floor, mayhap."

"Very good, madam. "

With a sigh, Doyle stretched out on the rug before the fire, and allowed Edward to happily grab fistfuls of her hair, crowing with delight.

As Reynolds moved about the kitchen, he offered, "I took the liberty of purchasing a pamphlet for you, madam. A simple explanation of the rules of football."

"You're a trump, Reynolds. An end-to-end player."

Thus encouraged, the butler suggested, "When Edward is older, perhaps you will take him to see the Kingsmen play."

Not the smallest chance, thought Doyle, but said, "I should; Timothy's bought him a Rizzo jersey, so I may as well put it to use."

This gave the servant pause, and he stilled for a moment. "Such a shame. A life brought short."

Glancing his way, Doyle raised her brows. "So; you think he was murdered, then?"

The servant disclosed, "Lord Acton mentioned as much; he said that the suspect was a crazed fan."

"Gettin' his story straight," she agreed.

"I beg your pardon, madam?"

She sighed. "We'll probably never find out exactly what happened," she offered truthfully. "But you're right, it's a crackin' shame, all around."

"Devotion gone wrong, madam. It is very hard to imagine."

"Not for me," she said thoughtfully. "Love takes all forms and shapes, and sometimes it does go a bit off-kilter."

Interestingly enough, she caught a flare of emotion from the emotionless butler, as he set down the plate of biscuits on the rug. Watching him, she thought; now, that last bit hit a nerve, for some reason.

Her thoughts were interrupted when Edward decided he'd like nothing better than to stand up, steadying himself against her legs, and slap his hands on the top of her hip.

Watching her son with a half-smile, Doyle said absently, "I'm that tempted not to tell him anythin' about it, because I know exactly how this song goes."

Reynolds paused. "I beg your pardon, madam?"

Hugely, she sighed, and laid down her head on the rug. "It's nothin', Reynolds. There's a set play comin', is all, and even though I've seen it a million times, I've never been able to figure out a defense for it."

44

T hat evening, Doyle recited her tale to Acton as they sat on the sofa, watching the fire.

"Extraordinary," he said, at its conclusion.

"So, we had it wrong—it turns out that D'Angelo was on the side of the angels, all along. And ironic, it is, that you've been spared some terrible fate due to your good RC charitable works. Best double your contributions, to stay on the Santiago people's good side."

"Indeed," he replied absently, rubbing her shoulder and gazing into the flames.

She followed his gaze, and quirked her mouth. "You'd have been very proud of me, Michael; for once I was careful not to argue that it's a pint-full of ridiculous, to think you can pay your way into heaven."

He turned to kiss her temple. "I suppose I must be grateful to you, then."

"Our Martina's a zealot," Doyle affirmed, "And there's no arguin' with a zealot. My mother always said you can't find a hair's breadth o' difference 'twixt a zealot and the devil; each will twist Scripture toward their own ends."

"Wise words, I think."

His mild tone made her antenna quiver, and she decided it was time to cut to the crux of the matter. "Listen, husband; I know you like the back o' my hand. I know you, and you're goin' to be bent on gettin' the upper hand over these people, because you don't like bein' bested."

He tilted his head in mild exception to this blunt characterization. "I would not be so petty, surely?"

"No," she agreed. "But you wouldn't be bothered in the first place if this was a just a petty thing. It's the fact that it's–" she paused. "What's the opposite of petty?"

"Consequential? Weighty?"

"Thank you; it's the fact that it's so weighty that draws you to the challenge." She lifted her face to his. "These people are a different breed—not your ordinary vigilante group by any means. Let's stay in our respective corners, and avoid crossin' swords with them."

"Well-said," he replied, which was exactly what he'd say if he didn't want her to know what he was thinking.

"A word to the wise," she warned, imitating Martina. "Let's not bring on the apocalypse."

"A worthy goal," he agreed.

She decided to give up; hopefully he'd not risk his bride's ire, and besides, it truly did seem as though it was out of his hands, anyway—small chance that a Scotland Yard DCI would have the wherewithal to take down some rogue Spanish church-enforcers with a thousand years at their backs.

Thinking about her husband's own tendency to go rogue, she asked, "So, what happened at the Museum? I've the sneakin' suspicion that you're movin' heaven and earth to save Javid from her well-deserved fate."

Carefully, he offered, "I do believe she'd little choice. Therefore, it may be possible to downplay her role in all this."

She eyed him, unsurprised. "As a favor to Sir Vikili, I suppose."

He nodded. "And to the Art Museum. They rely in large part on the public's good will, and this sort of scandal would have lasting effects."

With her usual exasperation, she blew out a breath. "You shouldn't be decidin' who wins and who loses, Michael. Someone once told me we're supposed to let justice be done, though the heavens fall."

"I would suppose," he offered, "it all depends on one's definition of justice."

Annoyed, she retorted, "You sound like Martina's vengeance-group, and that's not a good thing, my friend. That's why the laws have been hammered out over such a long time and by so many people; not everyone's going to wind up happy with the outcome, but it's the fairest way to do it."

"Speaking of which, Mr. Javid has been arrested for his participation in the rig."

Doyle decided she'd let him turn the subject, since she was tired of treading on her tinker's route, anyway. "Well, I have to say I'm sorry I wasn't there to see it, even though it would have been unprofessional to gloat. D'you think he knew they were set to murder his poor wife?"

"I cannot see any indication, although it may well be that he was keeping himself carefully unaware."

"Not much of a champion," Doyle said with some scorn. "Poor woman. And what a conundrum for Sir Vikili; if he doesn't do a good job and his brother does go to prison, he gets to spend more quality time with his sister-in-law."

But Acton tilted his head in disagreement. "I imagine nothing would change. The reason they are at this impasse is because none of them will break from traditional mores."

Doyle took a guess at what was meant by "traditional mores" and could only agree. "Aye; I think you've the right of it. So instead, they'll just continue longin' from afar."

"As I did," he teased.

"Not for long," she observed, leaning back into his chest. "You decided to take the bull by the horns, one fine stakeout at Grantham Street."

He rested his head against hers. "I'd no choice. I was going mad."

"Well, we can't have *that*," she said, daring to tease him.

They sat in quiet contentment for a few minutes, until Doyle observed, "He's beholden to you now—Sir Vikili is. You've got a murder-secret to hold over his head. How can he continue to oppose you in court?"

"Nothing need be said; it was a personal favor, only, and will be accepted as such. He would do the same for me."

She thought this over. "Hence, I'll never understand you nobs, Michael."

"Perhaps that is just as well," he replied, and kissed her head.

EPILOGUE

Doyle and Acton were taking a tour of the newly-renovated church, and paused before a new statue—marble, instead of alabaster—depicting the Holy Mother, smiling as she held the Infant in her arms. A small, discreet plaque dedicated this new addition in honor of Mary Doyle, Doyle's mother.

"Such a nice surprise, Michael," she said, squeezing him fondly. "And it's perfect–nothin' too fancy, just as she'd want it."

"Doubly fitting," he agreed, "now that our own Mary is on her way."

There was a small pause, and then she smiled and shook her head. "Wishful thinkin' my friend. Its goin' to be another boy—a brace of boys, we'll have." She glanced up at him. "I hope you're not too disappointed."

"Not at all."

"I'd like to call him Tommy, if I may."

"Certainly. Williams will be very pleased."

"Oh—oh, right; Williams is a Thomas."

Hiding a smile, Doyle's gaze rested on another saint's statue that *had been added at her own insistence—that of St. Luke, the patron saint of painters. Over Father John's mild objection, she'd insisted that the statue not be stone but instead be painted, so as to add a bit of dash.*

Reminded, Doyle ventured, "You shouldn't pin Rizzo's murder on that poor painter-fellow, Michael. He shouldn't be the decoy."

Acton tilted his head. "Rizzo's death will remain unresolved, officially, since there is no way to prove the theory, either way."

"I know. But it just seems so unfair."

They turned to continue their tour, and Doyle had to admit that she understood why Acton had done what he'd done. Her husband truly couldn't be blamed for wanting to throw a suffocating rug over this whole mess, what with Sir Vikili determined to pin Savoie as Rizzo's killer but Acton just as determined to thwart him, not to mention bloody-minded Holy Orders and forbidden love affairs playing a starring role.

Raising her gaze to the newly-painted arches overhead, Doyle was suddenly struck by the inconsistencies. She'd assumed whoever killed Tommy had also killed Rizzo, but Sir Vikili was not a take-'em-out-on-the-yacht-and-callously-throw-'em-overboard killer; Sir Vikili was a desperately-stage-a-murder-to-frame-Savoie-and-then-get-him-off-so-as-to-save-the-love-of-his-life killer. Not the same, at all.

So; who killed Tommy? Javid's husband? She wouldn't put it past him—a bigger creep never put an arm through a coat—but he didn't seem the type to be lurking about in an RC church, early in the morning. Perhaps Doyle would have to nose about a bit, in her spare time; something here was not adding up, and she wondered what Tommy had seen that got him killed.

Her husband's voice interrupted her thoughts, as he said lightly, "My own portrait has now been completed. I thought we'd hold another dinner party, so as to celebrate the event."

She laughed aloud. "Well, that's a lie."

Made in the USA
Las Vegas, NV
23 March 2021